Adv

The Lev
by Sharon Wagner

"A buoyant story of contact and connection, filled with levity and adventure."

—Emily Jane, bestselling author of *On Earth as It Is on Television*

"Engaging, unique, and playful. From the start, there's the question of how everything connects, and the pieces don't completely slot together until the dazzling conclusion."

—Independent Book Review

"Wagner's novel is one-of-a-kind. It holds its own admirably in the drama and science fiction genres."

—Essien Asian for Readers' Favorite

"From the streets of New York City to the jungles of Guatemala, *The Levitation Game* is filled with decadent descriptions of mouthwatering dishes, lush scenery, and an out-of-this-world story sure to entertain readers."

—Joie Lesin, author of *The Passenger*

"Brilliantly told, captivatingly mysterious, and with lovable characters that pulled me into the story, *The Levitation Game* is a one-of-a-kind novel that was hard to put down. I loved it!"

—Dawn Colclasure, author of *Imprint*

"Brace yourself for an unforgettable adventure of mystery and intrigue with Sharon Wagner's latest book. From the first page, dive into an exciting world of suspense and drama. Each scene will keep you on the edge of your seat, eagerly guessing what will happen next. Wagner's masterful storytelling will leave you breathless and yearning for more."

—Suzie Housley, *Midwest Book Review*

The Levitation Game

A Novel

Defy Gravity! Sharon Wagner

Sharon Wagner

Ten|16
PRESS

www.ten16press.com - Waukesha, WI

The Levitation Game
Copyrighted © 2023 Sharon Wagner
ISBN 9781645385356
First Edition

The Levitation Game
by Sharon Wagner

For information, please contact:

www.ten16press.com
Waukesha, WI

Cover Designer: Josh McFarlane
Cover Illustrator: Sharon Wagner

Sound can be as enchanting as a mockingbird's mixtape or as dreadful as the drone of an air conditioner. I dedicate this book to those who suffer from misophonia. You are not alone.

"It was a long night, perhaps the longest in my life.
I spent it sitting next to Rosa's tomb, speaking with her,
accompanying her on the first part of her journey to the
Hereafter, which is when it's hardest to detach yourself from
earth and you need the love of those who have remained
behind, so you can leave with at least the consolation of
having planted something in someone else's heart."
—Isabel Allende, *The House of the Spirits*

Commence Cerebral Streaming—

Session One

I have a name, and it is Dob-Dec. Listeners, if you could see into the distant realm of space, approximately one-hundred and twenty-two light-years from the Pleiades, you would find my ship HaYax—a vessel built to soar efficiently, like an Andean condor of the tiny Blue Earth.

To some, the ship is nothing more than a glorified bus. I, however, marvel at its beauty and intricate design, a model that *almost* defies description. Other *Beings* think the inner workings are simple.

They are not simple to me.

Geometry and quantitative problems bewilder me. However, I love to learn. Space travel is the best way to increase my brain's neuroplasticity. My mind expands at least ten percent on each mission, like the hippocampus of a pigeon navigating the tiny Blue Earth.

All avifauna is fascinating to me. Do you know that the Arctic tern flies the equivalent of three trips to the earthly moon and back in its lifetime? The bird's journey is overwhelming. How does it navigate so far? My mind would atrophy if I had strong wings like an Arctic tern because I wouldn't need brainpower for levitation.

My position as an accumulator brings joy to me: discovering new and mysterious specimens, cataloging flora, and fauna, harvesting DNA, and over-seeing the insect drones that provide *Beings* with an infinite amount of earthly information. We—the *Beings* of planet Pleione— have studied creatures from many galaxies, but none are as curious as the meat-eaters that roam the tiny Blue Earth. *Beings* know everything about meat-eaters, as we have studied them since their primitive beginning—along the way, acquiring expectations and hopes for their advancement that date back centuries.

I have decided to record my musings. You may not understand my language, but I am fluent in yours. I know universal languages from inhabited planets, strange other-worldly customs, the names of billions of magnificent beasts, and the terms of an infinite number of trivial samples. However, many samples are of grave importance to our terraformers.

Additionally, I have assimilated knowledge that, for some, is forbidden. I should not dwell upon this data for fear that others will understand. Neural processing is one of the reasons why I cannot sleep. I should not be juggling so much data before I close my eyes. Often, it is problematic to tune out the day's infestation of ideas.

But there are other reasons. Here, in the realm of infinite black, the undisturbed stillness of space, it is always night; that is another reason why sleep eludes me like a slippery eel. I've already mentioned the overuse of beta waves. But there is a final reason, and it breaks my heart—yes, I have a heart—to admit it. The cause is loneliness: a pervasive feeling like a parasite eating my organs from the inside out.

Sula is also lonely. However, she has a family. I do not. The other *Beings* aboard HaYax may be lonely too. But I do not linger long enough on their neural surface to discover how they feel about the isolation, the almost surreal emotion of feeling lost. Sometimes, during the cruel silence of the night, I imagine the possibility of never reaching our destination, just floating alone, with time stretching in front of me for all eternity.

I pray the others feel only peace.

But with Sula, it is different. Her mind is in perfect balance, like the perpetual and regular course of the universe. I wish I could pass through her vast and beautiful brain like a neutrino particle, residing with her thoughts until the end of time. I need to be careful when I communicate with Sula. She has a mate. If she read my thoughts as I read hers, she would know that I love her more than our planet—more than the suns. Her mind is the most beautiful place I have ever experienced, and I have visited many flexible minds during my travels.

Tonight, I wandered the ship for hours. I go everywhere, even to the locations where I am not supposed to go. The crew tolerates my nocturnal safaris. At first, they reprimanded me. But now, they oblige my curiosity. Often, they say, "Dob-Dec, you have a curious mind."

Being curious is positive. However, I would not need to be curious if I were smart enough. I would know the things that elude my understanding.

Listeners, our ship has no straight corridors; it resembles a serene—yet industrious—beehive. Tonight, I levitated into the mechanical heart of the vessel, observing the liquid nitrogen chamber and the mercury swirling like a mythical dragon's breath. I floated to the viewing glass—the large domed eye of the ship— and watched the trajectory of a distant asteroid, curious about its unknown path.

Before returning to my chamber, I wandered past Sula's door. Knowing that Sula—our ship's healer—deserves undisturbed rest kept me from entering her mind. Last week, her thoughts were inquisitive, 'How could Dob-Dec get a sliver so deep, made of wood, when there is no wood aboard HaYax? —not even a slip of paper.'

Sula thought this with patience and curiosity. That is Sula's way. I wish I could have answered her. But then, she would know I was listening.

We do have wood on our ship; I brought my collection. Sometimes, after my preparations for the new mission are complete, I inspect my wood fragments, seeds, shells, various metals, dried insects, and living ants. I also love all matter of rocks, even the ones with weak magnetic properties. Quartz and natural, compressed carbon are the most prized, but all stones are fascinating.

Since it is my job to collect, decontaminate, and catalog samples of every size, shape, color, and form (the perfect job for a curious mind!), it is not a stretch that I might acquire a sliver. I told Sula it happened while examining the bark of an earthly redwood tree.

In truth, I injected the bark into my hand. I should feel ashamed, but I do not. I have ingested unfamiliar nutrition samples and exposed myself to countless questionable microorganisms to see Sula. But everything heals with time.

Dob-Dec activates the temperature neutralizer on his sleeping platform, and there are friction sounds while he slips into bed.

I should not have accepted this mission. The *Chooser* didn't fully understand my state of mind. I don't bury my thoughts; they remain audible, resting on my neural surface like loose grains of sand. *Beings* do not invade another's privacy; lingering is only allowed during games and educational proclivities. We can think like a murmuration of starlings, as a unified group—a single, undulating organism—but only when permitted.

I should have stayed home and made myself available to a potential mate. I have never had a family of my own. My education comprises a complicated, one-thousand-piece puzzle of beautiful minds: my parents' elders and community members, some of whom are very sage and old! But the puzzle could never be whole, even if it contained one million perfect pieces. There are two missing parts, and I still feel their absence keenly.

As you may have guessed, I accepted this mission to be close to Sula.

Now, alone in my quarters, I am tormented. The parasites are eating me. Ironically, sometimes, they are genuine. I find them in my collections. But, of course, I speak figuratively.

The loneliness grows. I fear I wear it like a stain. And it is not suitable for my health to yearn so deep, as bottomless as the oceans of the tiny Blue Earth, for something I cannot have.

Sleep eludes me, and there is much to prepare for tomorrow.

I wish Sula could mend my heart.

Universal Translation Mode—End of Session.

Esme

Esme's stomach dissolved into gelatinous goop when the cameraman held up two fingers; her final two life-changing minutes had begun. She inhaled deep into her diaphragm, pumping her icy fingers while surveying the quiet chaos surrounding her.

In the back of the room, computers and flatscreens flickered an eerie blue, and encircling her, three cameras on wheels loomed like one-eyed robots. Above her head, an oppressive maze of cables and lights dangled. Sitting directly across from Esme were Sidney Stone and Brooklyn Struthers, the hosts of *The Morning Show: Live!*

"You know, I used to do magic tricks as a kid," said Brooklyn, taking a delicate sip from her coffee mug and peeking at the camera through false eyelashes.

Sidney flashed his brilliant white teeth and swiveled on his stool, grabbing the glass table with his hand. "Viewers, prepare to be blown away as our marvelous magician completes her final trick," he said, smoothing his tie.

Half smiling, Esme thought about all the eyes watching her face and body—thousands? Millions? No matter. It was time to defy gravity.

Esme stood, adjusted her skirt, and picked up her prop: a plastic glitter ball the size of a cantaloupe. She glared into the nether regions of the studio, wishing her agent were there with a wagging thumb or a smile of encouragement. Instead, there was only a black void and a man scarfing a doughnut.

Esme signaled for the hosts to move into position and nervously glanced at the cameras. *Don't fall off the platform. Smile and suck in your stomach.*

Descending the stairs, she hit her mark: blue tape forming an "x" on the shiny, black floor. Sidney and Brooklyn dispersed to the far corners of the studio while Esme focused on the ball. A clock ticked inside her head.

She extended her arms, cradling the ball between open palms, envisioning its path around the studio. "Viewers, this ball has a mind of its own. Let's see where it flies today, shall we?" said Esme, closing her eyes and humming, concentrating on the ball like it would be the last thing she'd levitate on planet Earth.

In her mind's eye, she could see the ball flying, zigzagging through the rows of LED gaff lights above her head. She directed the ball around Sidney's legs, then sent it underneath desks and tables before hovering the ball over the camera crew. She squeezed her eyes tighter and focused on her humming, the sound vibrating loudly in her throat.

Finally, she imagined the ball settling onto Brooklyn's outstretched hands. Esme inhaled and opened her eyes; confident she had left the viewers and crew awestruck.

The ball still hovered above her fingers. It had barely moved an inch. Across the room, the cameraman twirled his hand again; he flashed ten fingers—ten seconds, nine, eight—Esme gulped, silently imploring the glitter ball. *Move. Go. Fly!*

Seven, six, five fingers. *Fly. Fly. Go!*

"Folks, we're going to take a quick commercial break. We'll be right back with the cast from *The Real Housewives of Fargo*," said Sidney in his best anchor voice.

The cameraman in front of Esme flashed three fingers, then two. She stared at the ball with laser focus while sweat trickled over her lips and down her chin.

The studio erupted into movement and sound. Sidney tossed Esme a sympathetic look and held up his arms in mock defeat.

Simultaneously, Esme's glitter ball escaped her fingers, flying, hitting Sidney smack-dab in the face. The ball bounced and rolled out of sight.

Sidney reached for his glasses, blood dripping from his nose. The man looked helplessly at the crew. Esme covered her mouth; she couldn't feel her feet. What was she supposed to do? If she stood there long enough, would she turn into a pillar of salt or stone?

After an awkward beat, a young woman vigorously chewing gum approached and ushered her offstage. Esme's feet wobbled like she was recovering from surgery; she imagined her bare butt peeking from an open hospital gown. She was naked, wasn't she?

Esme shuffled along, spying her glitter ball wedged in a corner. She cradled her hands, and the ball lifted, flying directly into her grip.

She emitted a long sigh.

Joseph

Joseph exited the subway, climbed the stairs into daylight, bright and hot, and pulled his sunglasses from the V-neck of his shirt; his stomach growled. The aroma from the bag of churros he'd purchased at his favorite bodega in Queens made his mouth water.

The brown bag swung at his side as he crossed Church Street. He lingered on the sidewalk for a moment, staring at the building before him. Joseph climbed the steps with noodle legs, stopping near the large, golden doors and laying a palm on the rough surface as if he might dissolve through it. His hand moved to the handle, hanging in mid-air, unworthy to grip it.

Joseph didn't open the door.

Instead, he bit his lip and returned to the steps, sitting beside a gray concrete column. He slipped his backpack from his shoulders, positioning it between his sneakers. Dipping his nose into the sack, he pulled a gritty churro to his lips, taking a big bite. The cinnamon sugar melted over his tongue. For several minutes he ate slowly, savoring every morsel, licking his fingertips. Joseph rubbed his hands together, turning to stare at the golden doors.

Mass started in approximately thirty minutes, but he wouldn't attend today. Rubbing his knees, he stared across Barclay Street, thinking dark thoughts. Joseph didn't deserve communion. Whatever possessed him had no business attending mass with the good people of St. Peter.

A senior couple with clasped hands climbed the stairs beside him. The man winked at him. Joseph smiled back. Ultimately, he sat for thirty more minutes, watching miscellaneous souls file in through the golden doors. After the last straggler slipped inside the church, Joseph stood, slinging his backpack over his shoulder, and left.

Joseph circled the building, walking the short distance to Mitzi's apartment, pausing at the double doors. "Good afternoon, Joseph," said the doorman, swinging the door aside.

"Hi, Howie. How are you today?"

"Hungry," said Howard.

Joseph laughed, passing through. "Have a good lunch, Howie," he said, his voice trailing behind him.

When he reached the front desk, Joseph placed his hands flat on the cold marble counter. "Hi, Ruthie. Are there any packages for Mrs. Ferndale?"

They exchanged knowing looks. Ruthie retrieved a small box from a stack near the mailboxes and handed it to Joseph. "Thanks. I wonder what it is today?"

"Purple hair dye," said Ruthie with a playful look.

"Hmmm. I bet it's a pet rock," said Joseph.

Ruthie giggled. "No, candy, I think. Save me a piece, okay?"

"No way!" said Joseph, smiling with all his teeth and slapping the counter with his hand.

Joseph left, heading for the elevator. He took it to the nineteenth floor, then veered towards Mitzi's door. Using his key, Joseph entered her apartment. "It's me, Mitzi!" he shouted, wiping his feet. He walked through the hallway lined with original Georgia O'Keeffe paintings, arriving in the living room. The room smelled like burnt toast.

"Shhh. I taped *The Morning Show*. Aren't you early?" asked Mitzi without turning her head.

She pushed the lever of her electric wheelchair, moving closer to the giant flat screen; voices filled the room like helium. Joseph rolled his eyes.

"A little," he said, walking through the dining room and into the kitchen. Joseph set down the box and pulled a large plastic container of partially frozen soup from his backpack.

After extracting two white ceramic bowls from the cupboard, he opened the soup, poured it into a saucepan on the stove, and ignited the burner. Joseph prepared the dining table and checked on Mitzi.

Joseph watched the television over her shoulder with furrowed brows and returned to the kitchen, started the coffee pot, and retrieved the orange juice from the fridge. Joseph poured himself a tall glass, smiling and nodding when she muted the television. Several minutes later, Mitzi rolled to the dining table. He met her there.

"We can't eat until you open the box," said Mitzi.

Pinning a cloth napkin to the collar of her dress, Joseph winked at her.

"Stop that flirting. You're too young for me."

"Maybe, you're too young for me," he replied.

"Poppycock!" shouted Mitzi, laughing.

"What's inside the box?"

"Open it!"

Joseph retrieved the box from the kitchen and opened it. He pulled out a skinny jar and held it towards the light; a gooey liquid sloshed.

"Make some toast. We can have the new honey with our lunch. Boy, your soup sure smells good."

"It's my mother's famous pozole," Joseph stated solemnly, looking up.

"She must have been quite the lady to raise such a great kid," Mitzi said, looking at Joseph with expectant eyes.

Joseph nodded imperceptibly. "I loved being in the kitchen with my mother. The smell of cilantro—we always had bunches of it. She used fresh chipotle and ancho peppers, and everything had onion. I've never been able to make a chocolate mole as good as hers. I didn't get her recipe; it was all in her head," he said, pointing at his skull.

Thinking about his childhood, Joseph smiled and rubbed his lips as if tasting every forgotten crumb. "Me and my mother, we *really* connected in the kitchen. When I cook, her spirit warns me not to burn the garlic!"

Joseph returned to the kitchen, making toast, dicing onions, and shredding cheese. He rummaged through the cupboards for tortilla chips but abandoned the effort, carrying everything they needed for lunch to the dining table. Joseph sat and buttered their toast, placing the slices on two small plates. Finally, he opened the amber-colored honey that Mitzi had received from Savannah.

"You know, you can't get good honey in New York. Oh, they try. They have rooftop hives. They even have hives in cemeteries. Can you believe that? I don't trust it. One time, they discovered a honeycomb that was lime green. What do you suppose the bees got into to turn it that color? Ack! Don't trust it!" she cackled.

"Mitzi, have you seen the bronze bee sculpture at 9th Avenue Station? It's called *Bees for Sunset Park.*"

"No," she said, shaking her head.

"I'll take you to see it."

They started eating, slurping soup. The room grew quiet, except for the drone of the refrigerator and a ticking clock.

"This is chicken in the soup, isn't it? I thought you were giving up meat."

"I don't deserve meat," Joseph muttered, crushing his napkin.

"What did you say?" Mitzi asked, her spoon paused and ready by her lips.

"It's weird; some days, I can't stand the sight or smell of meat. On other days, I wonder what I was thinking and make a big batch of carnitas. I guess I'm a little loco."

"Well, I hope you don't give up meat because your carnitas are heaven on a plate," said Mitzi.

Joseph smiled.

"Hey, you always talk about your mother, but what about the rest of your family? What about your dad? You've hardly mentioned him."

"No siblings. My father is working in Guatemala. He's an archaeologist on a team researching an ancient site called El Mirador."

"Joseph! Why haven't you mentioned this before? That is so interesting. Is he like Indiana Jones?

"No, not really. Archaeology is boring," said Joseph, pushing his plate away and fumbling with his placemat. "My father and I don't get along. I wanted to be a chef when I was a kid, but my dad discouraged me. I still want to cook, but now, I also want to take care of people—well, here I am in your living room. Growing up, my father would come home and shoo me out of the kitchen. Cooking is an art—it feeds the body and soul. He didn't understand that. Plus, he's been gone so much of my life. Sometimes, I feel like I don't really know my dad. But I *do* know he's disappointed in me."

Mitzi stared at Joseph, chewing, a look of disbelief lining her forehead. "Well, I think you're right about the not knowing you part because if he did, he'd be goddamned proud."

Joseph grabbed Mitzi's boney hand and squeezed it. "That reminds me, we have work to do this afternoon. We need to do your stretches, and exercises. Mitzi, you need to get fit!"

"Poppycock! I hate the stretches. Let's wait until tomorrow."

Joseph laughed morbidly. "No, we *must* do them. You don't want to get so tight that you can't surf the internet for honey and motorcycles, do you, Mrs. Ferndale?"

Mitzi giggled like a schoolgirl. "Okay, but I want to watch Brooklyn Struthers and Sidney Stone while we do it."

"It's a deal, Mitzi."

"Okay, now do five to ten repetitions of the breaststroke. You're a great chair swimmer. I know you can do it."

Mitzi eyeballed Joseph and started swimming, poking the air in front of her chest like a pool of water. She did nine repetitions and collapsed backward. "Let's take a break, huh?"

"Can I turn the television down a bit?"

Joseph didn't wait for an answer; he grabbed the remote and lowered the volume. "You did great. Tomorrow we'll try jumping jacks."

"I can't do jumping jacks, you fool."

"They're chair jacks. You sit, open, and close your arms and legs like you're doing the real thing. We'll try it tomorrow.

"I can do the sitting part, easy."

"Mitzi, you know you have HBO, Showtime, Netflix, everything. Why do you tape *The Morning Show?* You can watch anything."

"I watch movies at night. You know that. Days are long when you're housebound. Besides, Brooklyn and Sidney are like my friends. The others too."

"I know what you mean. I like to think that Giada is my girlfriend. She's such a good cook that I wouldn't have to do all the cooking anymore. My dream girl. Kind of the same thing, right?"

"A handsome kid like you could get someone his age, even better than Giada. Why don't you have a girlfriend, anyway?"

Joseph rubbed his knees, knitting his brows. Mitzi cleared her throat. "Heck, kid. I don't care which way you go. I mean, who cares? You deserve somebody."

He longed to change the subject but didn't. "I just haven't met the right girl. But sometimes, I feel like I'm cheating on some imaginary person—or ideal of a person—when I go out on a date. But that's so ridiculous."

"Oh, for Heaven's sake. That's crazy talk. Wait, hold on, turn up the volume. They have a guest, a magician, something about levitation," said Mitzi, pointing at the television.

Joseph froze, his stomach turning to acid.

"What's wrong? You look like you've seen a ghost."

Joseph grabbed the remote, inflating the volume with his eyes fixed on the screen like a zombie apocalypse. "I'm okay," he said, swallowing.

The duo watched a cute and slightly chubby, red-haired girl dressed in an off-the-shoulder, white knit top and green suede skirt complete a series of magic tricks. The first trick utilized a fashionable red scarf tied around her neck; the scarf seemingly dissolved through her neck when she tugged it. The second trick involved cutting and knotting a string repeatedly and rejoining it. The girl's fingers slipped magically through a red rubber band in another stunt. Eventually, everyone in front of the camera emerged from their chairs. The girl held a clear, plastic ball filled with glitter.

"Pretty routine stuff if you ask me," said Mitzi.

Joseph nodded. They watched Brooklyn Struthers and Sidney Stone cross to the other side of the studio and wait by one of the camera people with outstretched hands. Joseph held his breath, but nothing happened. The camera panned to the girl; she appeared to be whispering silently or humming.

"She must be praying for that darn trick to work!" exclaimed Mitzi.

Joseph heard Sidney Stone tell the audience to stay tuned; more would come after the commercial break. The camera zeroed in on the girl's face. A tear slipped down her cheek before a commercial blared.

Joseph gasped. "Mitzi! Mitzi!" he shouted.

"What? I'm right here. No fast getaways for me."

"That girl. I know that girl! That's Esme."

"Esme *who?*"

"My friend Esme. My old friend Esme!" Joseph shouted, sucking saliva back into his mouth. "We played together in Guatemala. Her dad knows my dad—no kidding, Mitzi. We were friends in Guatemala when I was a kid," said Joseph, his words fast and furious.

Mitzi eyeballed the television, then Joseph, and back again. "That was a long time ago. Are you sure it was her? I thought her name was something else—Jane or Jade."

"Absolutely. One hundred percent."

Joseph returned to the television; a commercial blared. He stared in contemplation.

"Joseph. Wake up. The universe was listening. You know what this means, don't you?" asked Mitzi, excitement polishing her words.

"She's here. That girl is here in New York. She'll need a handsome shoulder to cry on after that fiasco. Take that smile and get her. The universe just handed you the girlfriend you've been too block-headed to find on your own. And for God's sake, get a haircut."

Esme

Esme entered the hotel room, throwing her purse on the fluffy white bedspread and whirling her wheel bag against the wall. She immediately stripped, extracting the constrictive body-shaper from her waist, and kicking it towards the bathroom like a discarded snakeskin. Esme rummaged through her suitcase, donning sweatpants, and a soft summer hoodie. "Worst. Day. Ever," she grumbled under her breath.

The phone rang inside her purse. She scrabbled for it, thinking that if it were her mother, she wouldn't answer. She swiped the screen, tears gnawing at the back of her eyes. "Dad! Dad," she said, her voice cracking, receding.

"What? What happened?" asked Oliver.

"I screwed up. My levitation trick didn't work—at all. I mean, what now? How can I face everyone? It was freaking live television!"

"*Nooooo,*" said Oliver, his voice sounding like an owl.

"Mom never even called."

Silence prevailed for several seconds. "Figures. Honey, you practiced for so long. I'm *so* sorry. I know things seem bleak. I can't imagine what you're going through. But stay the course, keep

practicing, and training. I don't know anything about magic...
illusions, or, however, you pull off a trick like you were trying to
do, but it must be goddamn hard. Keep at it. Don't give up. You're
young; there will be other chances— breaks. I wish I were there
with you, not here in Guatemala."

The duo fell silent. Esme sniffed and swallowed air-like
hiccups, collapsing onto the bed. She placed the phone beside her
face, hitting the speaker button. "Dad, do you know how hard it is
to find an agent? He's gone, dumped me like a bag of rats. I'll never
be able to show my face in public again. There won't be any other
big breaks. I screwed up. I suck at magic."

Oliver snickered. "Rats? Honey, people have short memories.
Nowadays, there are so many distractions—with social media,
everything. I've seen what you can do. It boggles my mind. I can't
believe you learned to do that from a YouTube video. Frankly,
I've never seen anything like it. Someday soon, that idiot will
regret dumping you. I never trusted him anyway—too slick,"
Oliver paused, then added, "Eventually, when you perfect your
act, someone else will come along. Someone better. Is your room
nice, at least? Can you see Central Park? The apple trees might
still be in bloom."

Esme scanned the small hotel room, surveying the white linen,
the crazy pink pattern over the headboard, and the flat screen.
"There's a view...of buildings. It's not even close to Central Park.
But it's alright," she managed. "Dad, I didn't learn magic from a
YouTube video; I took online classes for years. You *know* that. I'm
the one that did a YouTube video. It went viral, remember? That's
how I got the agent."

"I'm sorry. I remember," said Oliver.

Esme heard suitcases rumble down the hotel hallway.

"I hate to say this, but I've got to go. Listen, we only have cell service at the lodge. God, I hate to leave you feeling rotten. You're going to be okay, right? Because I won't be able to concentrate in the field if you don't tell me you're okay."

"I feel like shit, but I won't hurt myself. I'll drink myself into oblivion and order room service, sleep, and fly home," Esme said, sitting up. She entered the bathroom, grabbed the box of tissues, and returned to the bed.

"Well, don't drink too much, okay? I've got to go. I probably won't be able to call you again until you get back to Orlando, and after that, I won't be able to call at all when I start the trek into El Mirador."

Esme heard her dad rub around his whiskers and a weird bird mewling in the distance. Oliver inhaled. "Well, take care, honey. I'll talk to you soon. Hang in there. Love you," he said.

"Love you, bye," she said, ending the call.

Esme blew her nose like a honking goose; she was alone in New York. Again, she collapsed onto the bed, laying quietly for several minutes; her palms caressed the bedspread.

She stared at the blank flatscreen above her feet for a long beat. Eventually, she curled into a sitting position, grabbed the tissues, and headed into the bathroom to wash her hands and face. *Fuck you, loser in the mirror.* Stalking back to the bed, she flipped the white bedspread onto the floor and flopped down again.

This time, she stared at the ceiling, wondering why she couldn't move that stupid ball. An overwhelming impulse to throw all her magic-related crap out the hotel window washed over her—if only she could open the window. After today, no one would know how special she was. It was frustrating, living a lie and feeling overlooked. Magic was her cover story, a story she had cultivated for years. She'd never told anyone what she could *really* do, not even her dad. Telling her mother was out of the question; Ethelene would assume that Esme's power had something to do with Cosmostheology.

Life wasn't like a movie, and she didn't feel like a superhero. Was she a superhero? Not today. Esme sniffed, stretching her hand towards her suitcase. She concentrated, humming softly, feeling the vibration rattling in her throat. She pictured her makeup bag. On the other side of the room, nowhere near her suitcase, something shifted, and the room service menu lifted from the table by the window, floating to her outstretched hand. She'd been trying to move something—anything—inside her suitcase.

Her power was so unpredictable. She needed to control it. But who could teach her? No one could. Esme stroked her stomach, wondering if the ache she felt was from hopelessness or hunger. She opened the menu, scanning the pages; a craving for meat tickled her tongue.

Again, Esme turned her attention to the salads but was distracted by thoughts of meat. She could barely remember how a hamburger tasted. An internal tug-of-war ensued until, finally, she decided.

She ordered a double cheeseburger and propped herself against the pink headboard, organizing her tiny bottles of vodka and gin and turning on the television.

Tonight, was going to be a long night.

Esme woke with an urgent, bubbling spasm in her throat; puking seemed inevitable. She smacked her lips, scouring her velvety teeth with her tongue. *Holy cow, I shouldn't have eaten that disgusting burger. Oh God, it did taste good, though.*

Rubbing her eyes with the tips of her fingers, she escaped the bed, pulling her nightgown over her underwear. Esme stopped short of the bathroom and stretched her arm, beckoning the water bottle near her purse. It vibrated like a cat on the hunt, landing perfectly inside her outstretched hand.

Esme yelped, then buttoned her mouth, eyeing the wall to the next room. How could it work so perfectly? Now that it didn't matter at all. She wanted to scream at the top of her lungs but stifled the need and drank.

After draining the bottle, she brushed her teeth and eyed the clock. She felt restless, and sleep seemed unreachable. There was something else, too, another needling thought, an overwhelming impulse. She wanted to meet someone. But who? Feeling sociable after wishing to hide from the world under a blanket of shame and embarrassment seemed strange.

Esme dressed, slipped the key card into the back pocket of her yoga pants, and grabbed her hoodie. At the last moment, Esme snatched her purse and left, padding down the hall in her flip-flops. She entered the elevator and pushed the button for the lobby. The elevator bell pinged, and Esme stepped out, pausing to survey her surroundings. She wandered to the bar off the lobby—the Library of Distilled Spirits—hearing voices mingling, enchanting from within.

But liquor was the last thing she needed; she still felt boozy. Esme wasn't hungry either; her stomach was still raging. There was an all-night fitness center, but she hated working out. Esme could almost hear her mother urging her toward the Stairmaster; her eyes narrowed. Entering the bar, she slipped into a seat at a large communal table. She didn't know what she was doing there, but at least she wasn't alone.

Esme looked around, suddenly aware that she was underdressed and, quite possibly, disheveled. She preened her hair and scanned the room. On one wall, backlit liquor bottles sat in cubicles like tiny contestants on *Hollywood Squares*. The air popped with voices and glasses clinking. Laughter.

Esme straightened, zipping her hoodie. A man before the bar swiveled on his stool while nibbling on a skewer of olives. He gave her the once over. She wondered if he recognized her and felt her cheeks flush.

A pretty waitress with a long ponytail and dark purple lipstick approached, handing her a paper menu. Esme scanned it, looking up at the waitress through her eyelashes. "Do you have anything non-alcoholic? I'm not sure what to order," said Esme, flipping the menu while rubbing her stomach with her other hand.

"How about a ginger beer? We mix it with rum, but it's good by itself and helps with an upset stomach. It's non-alcoholic," she said with a helpful smile.

"Perfect," Esme replied, smiling back. She waited for the waitress to leave so she could scratch an itch on her tiny, freckled nose.

Esme's eyes followed the waitress in her retreat. She drummed her fingertips, bracing as an icy trickle of déjà vu crept down her spine.

After a few minutes, the waitress returned with the ginger beer, setting it in front of Esme with a hopeful expression. "Can I ask you a question?"

"Sure."

"The bartender said you look like a magician he saw on *The Morning Show* today. Was that you?"

Esme's heart fell into her intestines and jiggled there like Jell-O. She figured she would have to get used to this. She took a sip from her straw, eyes peeking up. "Yep, that was me."

"That bad? I'm sorry. He *did* say the drink was on the house. Have a nice night, miss."

Across the room, the bartender gave her a thumbs up; Esme's shoulders drooped. She drained her drink, burping at the nose-tingling carbonation. Even though she felt glued to her seat, she couldn't stay. Esme grabbed her purse and threw a tip on the table. She left the bar.

After punching the elevator button, she felt the same watchful presence. She craned her neck and rushed into the elevator, narrowly missing a couple walking out. "Sorry," she squeaked, pushing the button for the seventh floor.

The elevator doors closed like the curtains of a horrible off-Broadway play, and Esme folded her hands over her face. Now, she couldn't wait to return to her room—back to her bed. When she reached her floor, she stalked down the hall and entered her room. The unwanted smell of French fries smacked her in the face.

Esme flipped every light switch, turning on the television and the vent on her air conditioner. She kicked off her flip-flops, unzipped her hoodie, and threw it on the bed. A loud knock stopped her fingers. Curious, she veered across the room and investigated the peephole. A fish-eyed version of a man peered back. He was wearing a V-neck, heather-colored T-shirt, jeans, and sneakers. He looked familiar and quite possibly, handsome. Esme switched to the other eye, pressing both hands on the door's surface.

She smiled.

Joseph

The last place Joseph expected to end up at midnight was Union Square. After he left Mitzi's, he stopped at St. Peter's for at least an hour, praying on the steps, steepling his fingers and closing his eyes, whispering a prayer so heartfelt and eager, it could have persuaded a cheetah to spill its spots. Still, when it came to the mysterious power that afflicted him, there were no answers. Maybe he didn't deserve one.

All night, his mind flip-flopped over the prospect of finding Esme. Mitzi had urged him to call Rockefeller Center to inquire about her location. But the studio wouldn't give him any information when he called.

With clenched teeth, he called his dad. That, too, was a dead end. Joseph figured there was no cell service in Guatemala at Oliver and Emil's remote location.

Joseph continued his sabbatical at St. Peter's, chewing his fingernails as he watched late-night pedestrians ply the sidewalk before him. At midnight, a peculiar thing happened: a feeling washed over him, like something lassoed his mid-section, yanking him toward an unknown destination. At first, Joseph resisted, not knowing who or what was at work. All his life, he felt marked, stained by Diablo. What would he become now? The possession felt even stronger—weirder.

His fingers traced the well-worn path across his head and chest as he completed the sign of the cross. "Mother Mary, keep me safe. Give me the wisdom to see the devil for who he *is*. Don't let me follow the whispers of deceivers."

Joseph stood, following the unseen force.

He wandered the path that unfurled magically before him, taking a short ride on the subway, following the whispers until he emerged at Union Square. He turned left.

At midnight, Joseph found himself dazzled by the city lights towering all around him. Instead of stinky streets, there was a faint hint of crab-apple blossoms floating on the breeze. He stared across the street at the Hyatt at Union Square, grimacing at the sudden chaos inside his head. The thoughts that weren't his own—the erratic whispers—suddenly grew loud and confusing. He was frightened that he might be listening to the devil himself. Even so, he couldn't turn back.

Joseph crossed the street, entered the hotel, and lingered briefly in the lobby. That's when he saw a woman resembling Esme walking toward the elevators. He watched the girl turn his way, then collide with another couple. But the elevator doors closed before he could decipher either way.

He followed anyway. Hitting the elevator button, he shook his head as if jiggling a stubborn vending machine into dispelling displaced snacks. All the while, he hoped his own thoughts would simmer to the forefront.

If the girl he saw was indeed Esme, she'd still be awake. But what if he knocked on the door of a random stranger? He'd feel like a fool. What would he say to them? They would think he was a weirdo or a thief. Joseph's cheeks felt like warm dough.

The elevator opened, and he hit the button for the seventh floor. When the elevator stopped, he exited, turned left, and stopped at room 707.

He knocked and waited.

Joseph heard rustling inside the room. Seconds ticked by, and the door opened. He stood, fidgeting with an earlobe, staring at Esme. She was wearing soft blue sweatpants and an olive-colored T-shirt. Her auburn hair was sexy and disheveled. She pulled her shirt down over her stomach, tilting her head in contemplation. She rubbed her freckled nose, a grand smile sweeping across her face. "Joseph? Is that really you?"

"Hello, Esme. Yes, it's really me! I saw you on television," said Joseph, splaying his arms, while his eyes followed something behind Esme's back. She turned. Joseph watched; his breath caught in his throat.

Beyond Esme, an empty plastic water bottle lifted and circled the room. The television remote, the restaurant menu, loose clothes, underwear, and flip-flops followed. After a few frantic seconds, Esme's purse heaved up, entering a growing whirlpool over the bed. Joseph's eyes wandered to the left, watching a hairbrush, a toothbrush, and toothpaste fly into the stream. Soon, jars of face cream, plastic eye makeup discs, and Q-tips flew from the bathroom. The ice bucket entered next. A breaking tug followed, and the alarm clock entered the fray with its cord flailing wildly. Esme's dinner plates with leftover French fries soon flew around the room like little twigs caught in a tornado. Toilet paper unraveled, circling in the stream like a long-tailed bird. The duo watched, feet planted wide, hips swiveling, eyes wide and glassy.

Suddenly, the television shuddered in its stand, causing a mutual gasp.

Joseph grabbed Esme's arm, then her hand. There was a humming vibration inside his ears as more items flew from the bathroom: towels, soap, shampoos, and cotton balls floating like little clouds.

He stood rooted to the doorway, not knowing if he should step deeper into the room or step out and run. Esme pulled him inside. The door shut behind them with a loud slam. They stood side by side, watching, breathing audibly in unison, mouths open.

They looked at each other.

Esme shook her head, giggling nervously—wildly. "It's amazing, isn't it?" she muttered. "I can't believe I'm doing this."

"Jesus, Mary, and Joseph," said Joseph.

Abruptly, everything fell as if unplugged. Now, the room resembled a landfill. Esme stepped towards him, grabbing, and holding him tight. Joseph hugged her back.

The room derecho was over.

Commence Cerebral Streaming—

Session Two

Listeners, the cosmos is as beautiful as Sula's glowing black eyes. What an unusual view!

My telescopic lens spectacles capture light my eyes cannot see, isolating different wavelengths on the ultraviolet spectrum. Now, when I stare into infinity, I understand the actual color of the cosmos. It is mind-boggling to imagine that in every fingertip-sized area of the night sky are an untold number of galaxies, stars, planets, and potential life, like the meat-eaters of the tiny planet Earth.

At this exact moment, I can see 444 light-years away, witnessing the birth of solar systems around Jupiter. Even the tiny details on Jupiter's massive surface area are more significant in scale than the entire realm of meat-eaters.

Jupiter's hazy clouds resemble a solar storm on my home planet Pleione. I do not miss Pleione. I would rather be here with Sula and the crew. However, I do miss sleep.

Again, I am wandering the ship, levitating with my eyes closed to exercise my brain and alternately walking on my own two feet to exercise my muscles. Time is at a standstill. I have already placed my hand on Sula's door and meditated in my chamber for two hours. After which, I foraged for meera and packa nuts in the ship's nourishment center until my gastronomic pouch was the size of a ruta melon. Much later, after running in concentric circles, I played knowledge wars until my mind was a jumble of ideas. Of course, you already know that my nocturnal activity culminated with a comprehensive survey of the cosmos. Still, I am not sleepy. Listeners, what am I to do?

Work. I must work.

I will proceed to the laboratory.

Universal Translation Mode—End of Session.

Esme

Esme awakened from a deep sleep, curled beside Joseph's sleeping body. At some point during the night, they both drifted to sleep fully clothed, with bright city lights streaming through the large picture window.

After the whirlwind subsided, they talked until the wee hours of the morning like there had been no years of separation. As they reminisced, hours vanished. Eventually, Joseph's eyes drooped, and he flopped down on the crumpled bedding, pushing debris off his side of the bed and falling asleep.

As Joseph slept fitfully, adjusting his position, he bumped the remaining clothes and sundries, sliding them off Esme's side of the bed. As each item shifted and fell, Esme used her powers, humming like a busy bee, stopping them mid-fall, flying them on invisible wings into the bathroom or wherever their previous position happened to be.

Esme had never felt more powerful. Rebirthed. Now, she felt high on adrenaline, dreaming about what this newfound ability would do for her career. There was something else, too. She felt utterly gob-smacked, off-kilter, head-over-heels in love with

Joseph. It was like she had been struck by lightning or impaled with Cupid's arrow.

Joseph had been shocked by the tornado of toiletries in the room. But Esme felt a profound relief to come clean with someone at last. He had listened to her with fresh ears as she documented her abilities from the first time she levitated a stuffed toucan to the big things, like basketballs and books.

Esme refocused, curling a hand under her face, staring at Joseph. She caressed his arm as he slept, anticipating another flurry of questions, like how he had found her. There were still so many things to discuss. Before they parted ways as kids, she had never been happier. Guatemala was her Garden of Eden, and Joseph was her best friend. The last memory she shared with him was of them running through the trees, laughing. He'd constantly warned her about snakes and spiders, but she wasn't afraid of the jungle or its critters. Kids at home played on monkey bars and swings. They had played on Mayan ruins.

Of course, they still had summer school. Oliver liked to teach outdoors, and his education had nothing to do with science or math. Her dad had taught them about birds, animals, and nature. They would go on long jungle hikes, learning everything about the flora and fauna of Guatemala. Before the trek to El Mirador, Oliver and Joseph's dad, Emil, took them on walks to the towering pyramids of Tikal and Yaxha. The other, more excavated ruins differed from El Mirador; the pyramids were already hacked loose from the jungle. Reassembled. Scrubbed clean.

El Mirador was still hidden, still mysterious. Following her dad into the wild was the most exciting thing she had ever done. It was an adventure from the beginning: hiking in and camping halfway there. The howler monkeys had never seemed closer or louder. Her mother would have been shocked at the conditions, at everything. Esme surmised that she would have had a better chance than her mother of making it on the television show *Survivor*. At least she knew what it was like to live with the bugs and beasts.

Esme shifted, groping for her phone. She could get two or three hours of sleep if she fell asleep now. A yawn escaped her mouth. Slipping from the bed, she closed the curtains and softly stepped into the bathroom to drink water. There was no glass in sight. She snickered, wondering where the glass had landed. After using her hand to slurp water from the sink, she crawled back into bed with Joseph, slowing her breath. She fell asleep.

The Uber driver pulled over at 79th street, near Central Park in Manhattan. Esme exited the car, pulling her wheel bag from the trunk. Joseph lingered, completing his conversation with the young driver. Esme stood on the cobbled sidewalk, head cocked, watching Joseph inside the car. She gripped the handle of her bag. Already, she felt riveted with melancholy at the thought of their parting.

Yesterday, her only thought was the disaster on *The Morning Show*—it seemed like the absolute end of the world. Now, leaving Joseph behind in New York felt even worse. She bit her lip, following the irregular path of a man on an electric scooter with her eyes. A honk blared, then a car door slammed, and Joseph joined her on the sidewalk. "We don't have much time before your flight this afternoon. This walk is short, one of my favorite strolls in Central Park," Joseph stated, all smiles and teeth.

Joseph grabbed Esme's roller bag, leading the way around an old stone fence into Central Park. Immediately, green, and lush trees enveloped them, flowering and scented—a soft swath in a seemingly endless architectural jungle. The sounds of birds chirping and rustling swept through the branches above. Below, conversations mingled with the sound of Esme's bag rolling over the sidewalk. Esme grabbed Joseph's other hand. "I don't want to leave," she said, bitterness souring her words.

"Then don't. Stay longer," Joseph said, squeezing her hand.

Esme glanced at him, smiling with one side of her mouth. "I have a part-time job at *Orlando I-Park*. I have to go to work on Monday," she said.

"Do you only work part-time?" asked Joseph.

"Well, yes. But I also do magic for tips in Orlando, sometimes on International Drive, by the restaurants. I thought all that was over. You know, before I screwed up on *The Morning Show*."

Joseph stopped with his hand still gripping the wheel bag, his face serious. "Esme, you didn't screw up. You're amazing. Your tricks were great, even without the addition of levitation. You don't need your power to be a great magician. Be careful. The levitation scares me. It's unnatural."

"Oh, but I *do* need it!" Esme blurted. "I'm a terrible magician. Without it, I wouldn't have a career—or the hope of a career. Levitation is what makes me special. No one else can do what I can do. It's so exciting! After what happened in the room, I feel a new power sizzling through me." She talked fast, her face glowing with excitement, counting future agents like sheep.

Joseph winced, looking away. He dropped her hand, pointing towards a seat. "Let's sit," he said.

Esme followed him to a bench with a view: a hilltop castle built with gray stone, adorned with turrets and square windows, just like the real thing. The castle melted into large granite boulders, overlooking a small, brackish pond. "This is my favorite place to sit. I love the view," said Joseph, sitting down and twirling the wheel bag into position beside the bench.

Esme sat with a queer look of concentration connecting her brows. Ahead of them, a plastic water bottle lifted from the ground, flying into a nearby recycling bin. Esme smiled brightly. "Don't do that. Someone might see," said Joseph, the words squeaking through closed lips.

"I know. I can't help it. There's so much I want to do. My power has never been this big before. I can feel the strength of it surging through me."

Again, Esme grabbed Joseph's hand. "Joseph, I've never told anyone about what I can do—not even my parents. They think it's a magic trick. I am careful. That's why it's so fun to do magic. I can use my power, show people what I can do, and they don't know it's real. You know, right now, I feel capable of anything. Watch. I'm going to move that rock into the lake."

Esme pointed at the rock. It was the size of a coffee can, sitting near the shore, surrounded by haphazard reeds. She focused on the rock. "There! See? It lifted. I've never moved anything that heavy."

Sitting up straighter, she hummed like a hummingbird investigating a flower. The rock lifted and swayed over the ground. Joseph pulled his hand from Esme's grip. "No!" he shouted.

The rock slammed to the ground. People in the distance turned and stared, wondering what had just happened.

Esme looked at Joseph sheepishly. "No one saw. Besides, they wouldn't know it was me. Why are you so upset? It's fun."

Joseph looked at his sneakers, then at her freckled face. "I'm sorry. I've always felt protective of you. Can you wait…just wait until you are home? You know, to practice."

"I didn't mean to scare you. I suppose you're right. It *is* unnatural. But I think it would be crazier *not* to perform levitation if you can. It would be like an eye doctor that doesn't like eyes or a sheepdog that prefers cows—you know what I mean. Okay, I won't do it anymore, but I don't know why you're so uptight."

A hint of a smile graced Joseph's lips. Esme could see the wheels turning inside his head. She hoped that she hadn't displeased him because she already knew she didn't want their relationship to end here. Suddenly, she sensed what he was thinking: *Sister.*

Joseph physically recoiled, shifting on the bench, as if he had sensed the intrusion. He stood, offering his hand while grabbing her bag with the other. "Should we keep walking? It's a thirty-minute loop. Very pretty, past a meadow and a balanced boulder."

Esme pulled her phone from her purse, scowling. "Oh, I wish I had more time!"

Oliver

Oliver closed the door to his cabana and entered the jungle, stopping short when something plopped on his head. Branches jostled above, and water droplets dampened his shirt. "Oh, hell. Howler monkeys," he said, removing his wide-brimmed hat.

A runny, brown substance oozed over the brim. Oliver shook his head and leaned into the trees for a banana leaf, then rubbed the nasty goop off as best he could. "Damn monkeys," he grumbled, returning the hat to his head.

Oliver entered the restaurant palapa and placed his backpack on a chair. He wandered to the buffet, pausing to stir the scrambled eggs congealing in a sad little pot. He was sick of eggs, along with bananas and papaya and cold toast with no jam. Breakfast was the same every day at the lodge near Tikal. Oliver knew he shouldn't complain. It would be worse when they hiked to El Mirador. He returned to the table with a full plate.

Between bites, he reviewed yesterday's field analysis in the dim light. Above the thatched cabana, another howler monkey gargled, low and deep, the guttural sound reverberating through the trees like an engine sputtering out of gas. A small chorus of monkeys growling in some faraway tree followed.

Turning a page in his notebook, he nibbled his toast, ever distracted by the jungle. The familiar chorus of birds waking up and tuning their lungs like a practicing orchestra was one of life's great pleasures in Guatemala. At home, the mourning doves, chickadees, and wrens filled his mornings with joy.

He poked at his plate, stabbing the fruit and scooping eggs. After a few minutes of quiet masticating, Oliver dropped his fork. He scribbled several lines onto his field analysis, never forgetting that he still needed to create a new budget for El Mirador. "Glamorous, my ass," he mused aloud, removing his reading glasses.

The saying still rang true: for every day in the field, every day of proverbial holes, there were five days of paperwork and emails with donors and clients. He didn't want to think about all the new proposals. No wonder his mind kept stretching, wondering how Esme was doing after the debacle in New York. Lately, he pictured Esme drunk or high, wandering the streets of New York alone, with a dark figure trailing in the distance. There was always a dark figure with your only daughter, wasn't there?

Oliver pinched the bridge of his nose, squinting as the morning sun filtered through the trees around the palapa. A warm glow settled on the wood table in front of him. Concentration proved futile; he shoved his plate away and closed his notebook, watching the glorious happenings framed by the low-hanging thatch. In the distance, a blue morpho butterfly flickered its iridescent wings, stopping on a feeder full of rotting fruit. Farther away, a gray fox lingered by the thicket of jungle plants, patiently waiting for stale scraps of bread. On the outskirts of palmettos, a bright orange iguana rested in a sliver of sun.

He grabbed his binoculars, watching an azure-crowned hummingbird pluck breakfast from a hibiscus bush. All around the cabana, birds of every color plied the foliage and trees. He could watch birds for hours. *Did I pick the wrong career? Maybe I would have made a better ornithologist than an archaeologist.* At least here in Guatemala, he could get his fill of both. There was never an end to Mayan ruins, and always, there were birds.

It was time to deal with his daily correspondence. Electricity was inconsistent at Tikal; morning hours ceased at nine a.m.

Soon, song and solitude would be interrupted by the rest of the crew arriving from El Remate, bringing energy, noise, and distraction. But then again, he was already preoccupied; he couldn't stop thinking about Esme.

Oliver discarded his binoculars and pulled his laptop from his pack.

Oliver didn't listen to Ethelene's message until the following afternoon while checking emails in the hotel lobby. He listened to her voice with a frown, then impulsively deleted the message. What he heard left him slightly off-kilter. Could it be true? He had no intention of calling her back or arranging a meeting. But this was Ethelene; she usually got her way.

Ethelene was a volunteer for the Disaster Response Team of the Church of Cosmostheology, and she was currently near the scene of the Mount Fuego eruption in Guatemala.

He was in Guatemala.

His ex-wife had already been at the scene for a week, distributing water—with a sprinkling of spiritual guidance—near San Miguel Los Lotes. Now, she wanted to fly to Flores and arrange a meeting with him. Ethelene was the woman he stayed married to for twenty-one years, after all. His brain told him to tell her no. But his heart told him otherwise.

Oliver knew that meeting with Ethelene would delay the trek into El Mirador for a day, maybe two, and the rainy season was just around the corner. Heck, he didn't know if he could even stay at the hotel past his reservation. But he did need to drive to Santa Elena anyway to pick up supplies for the mission. So, if he wanted to—and that was a big *if*—he could pick Ethelene up at the airport while he was there.

Oliver closed his laptop, focusing instead on a pair of ocellated turkeys picking their way across the large, open-air window. "Turkeys are like feathered dinosaurs, genetically closer to their scaly-winged ancestors than most other birds," Oliver mumbled to himself. "But these turkeys look like peacocks with luminous, rainbow-colored feathers."

Stretching his long legs before him, he leaned back in his chair. As the turkeys moved farther away, Oliver's eyes shifted toward his phone. He picked up his device; an image of Tikal's Temple Five flashed across the screen.

Oliver heard footsteps and turned towards the sound. "Señor Wright?"

"Sí,"

"Señor, it is 2:45 in the afternoon. We will shut off the electricity in fifteen minutes," said Miguel, smiling and nodding.

"I know. Gracias, Miguel," said Oliver.

He needed to decide. "Wait, Miguel?" shouted Oliver. "Do you know if my room is available for one or two more nights?"

"I will check Señor Wright. Un momento."

"Oliver shook his head, hoping to empty Ethelene from his brain like pulling the stopper from a bathtub. He pulled his laptop close and went to work. He didn't have much time.

Oliver shifted into first gear and rode the speed bump as slowly as he could muster. He hoped that, at this point, he had acquired a solid visual map in his brain of their many locations—the diabolical speed bumps designed to wreak havoc on a transmission planted randomly between El Remate and the town of Santa Elena.

But sometimes, one got him anyways. On those occasions, he'd swear as Ethelene had sworn during her seven-hour labor with Esme.

Right after bump number six, Oliver pulled over at a rustic roadside palapa laden with papayas, bananas and plantains, and mounds of other curiosities. He stepped from the vehicle, entered the hut, and ordered two coconuts. The ladies there called Oliver Mr. Gringo-nut. Always, he would laugh and shrug, accepting whatever attention they threw his way. "Por qué dos cocos?" the ladies asked in their usual provocative and suggestive manner.

"Uno es para una chica bonita," Oliver replied.

The ladies giggled with delight, chattering amongst themselves until Oliver blushed.

He retrieved his wallet and paid, then juggled the large, heavy coconuts into his jeep. Oliver secured one between his legs and took a long pull of the sweet coconut water through a big, fat straw. The other coconut, he secured on the passenger seat. That one was for Ethelene.

Fifteen minutes later, Oliver veered sideways, pulling in and parking on a small lot adjacent to the Mundo Maya International Airport. Ethelene was flying from Guatemala City on a small prop plane that held around fifty passengers. He knew she'd be uptight. She hated flying. The first thing she would say to him would most likely be, "Why did you bring me a coconut when you know I prefer gin?"

He didn't have any gin. But if Ethelene wanted rum, he had plenty. Oliver always bought Flor de Cana rum—Nicaragua's finest—whenever he was in Central America. It was as smooth as a baby's butt, but it smelled a heck of a lot better.

Oliver chuckled, sprang from the vehicle, and crossed to the other side of his jeep. He opened the door and grabbed the coconut. He knew it would be okay if he didn't go through security. Plus, it would give the locals a good laugh at his expense.

Several minutes later, Oliver stopped by a rope partition, waiting, and holding his coconut. He knew her plane had landed, and he figured that with an airport as small as this, she'd be there any second. Oliver couldn't help but smile. He realized he was happy to see the woman who had brought him unlimited grief for years. It didn't make any sense. Although, if he was honest with himself—and he usually was—he had never stopped loving Ethelene. She was the most annoying woman in the world, but there was always a connection—especially a physical one. Heck, the last time they were together, she was still as hot as hell.

Oliver watched and waited, taking a few deep breaths to calm his percolating nerves. She should be here by now, and after that boulder-sized coconut, he was starting to have to take a piss.

After a time, out of nowhere, she was in front of him, pulling her wheel bag and smiling with dimples. Her hair was shorter and blonder; her eyes were as blue as Lake Peten Itza. Her nose was freckled and tan. "Ollie!" she screamed.

"Ethelene!" Oliver said, opening one of his arms.

"I'm so happy to see you! I was scared shitless on that plane. Oh,

Ollie, you're going gray!" she stated, looking him over. She tugged at his ponytail. "I like it. Distinguished. Smart. Is that for me?"

"Yes, I'm sorry it's not something stronger, like gin. But these are refreshing, almost addictive. You'll love it."

Ethelene accepted the coconut and took a sip. "I don't drink gin anymore. Well, I don't drink at all—too much work to do at church. Besides, I want to stay *bright*. I can't get audited if I've had a drink. I thought you knew that. You should read *Cosmos Code*. I'm a consultant for the church now, analyzing CTC tests."

"Let's not talk about your church," Oliver said, resisting the urge to roll his eyes. He grabbed her bag but let go and pointed toward the *baños*. "Wait here," he stated, glad for a diversion from certain subjects.

After a few minutes, Oliver returned, and grabbed her bag. They exited the airport into moist air and headed towards his jeep.

"Ollie," said Ethelene, looking at him sideways. "It's a lot hotter here than it was in Guatemala City. Palpable, even. God, how do you manage?" asked Ethelene, fumbling to retrieve her sunglasses while holding her coconut.

Oliver thought about all the times he told Ethelene about the heat on his trips, the hardships, and the insects. It was never glamorous. He took her coconut. "It was always work, not play. I know it was hard on our marriage—being gone."

Ethelene's smile tightened and she nodded faintly, then looked in the opposite direction, returning to him with a fresh expression. "Well, now I'll get to see Tikal through your eyes. I had to see it while I was in Guatemala. I mean, it was this big, amazing place that I always thought you loved more than me. No, no, let's not go there. I'll behave."

"Ethelene, let's not behave."

Ethelene started to snicker, popping her eyes.

"No, I don't mean *that*. Well, not right now, anyway. We should get the bad stuff out of the way first," Oliver said, looking serious.

They kept walking. Oliver stopped before his dusty jeep, turned towards her, and returned her coconut. He grabbed his hat and folded his arms. Ethelene stiffened, seemingly hugging her coconut for reassurance. She shaded her eyes with her other hand.

"I'm concerned about Esme. She still needs you. Everything else is always more important. Now, it's the church. Next week, who knows? She failed miserably, and you haven't even called her."

"I did call! She didn't answer, won't talk to me. Oh, God. What happened? Wait. Hold on—" Ethelene lowered her hand and pointed it at Oliver. "I've been a Cosmostheologist for seven years. The church is important to me. It's not some flash in the pan. It's my life now. I've grown up. You know, we did good here. We helped people. You haven't always been around for your daughter either—or me. You left me at home, alone, like an old suitcase, while you were doing something important. Well, now *I'm* doing something important. Esme needs to get rid of her reactive mind. I've told her that," said Ethelene, blinking repeatedly and thrusting a defiant hip.

Oliver held up his hands in defeat. "Okay. For two days, there will be no talk of your church. And we won't talk about Esme either. But just know that you need to step up. She still needs a mother."

"I told you, before we got pregnant, that I'd suck at being a mother. Kids were your dream. Besides, we can't stop talking about Esme until you tell me what happened in New York."

"Kid. One kid," said Oliver in a guttural tone while thrusting her bag into the back seat of his jeep. "I'll fill you in on all the gory details on the drive back to Tikal. But first, we need to make a stop at the Maxi Pali. Are you sure you don't want any gin?"

Ethelene growled at Oliver and rolled her eyes before her demeanor softened.

"Well, you know how often I change my mind," she said, walking to the passenger side, getting in.

Oliver nodded and grinned, raising his eyebrows seductively. He bounced into his seat and started the engine, giving his ex-wife a thorough once over. She was wearing a pink sundress with alligators, and her blond hair was curling from the humidity. *She's still as hot as hell,* he thought. "Well, I think we better get some gin then, babe, just in case you change your pretty crazy little old mind."

Ethelene smiled and took a sip from her coconut.

A low sun glowed over Lake Peten Itza when they entered the tiny town of El Remate. The duo drove slowly, watching skinny dogs run through the ditch while chickens and pigs ran wild everywhere else. There were only a few businesses in town: little snack markets, a tourist museum, and a handful of restaurants. Everywhere along the street, locals sat against weathered buildings, chatting. Oliver slowed to a crawl when a giant, hairy tarantula darted ahead of them.

Oliver crested another speed bump, continuing down the dusty road. "Was that a tarantula? Holy cow! They sure like their speed bumps in Guatemala, don't they?"

"Yes, they do. And yes, that was a monster spider. Sometimes, tourists will blow a tire, or worse. It can be a real hazard."

"It's beautiful here, though, prettier than I expected. I mean, I knew Antigua was a beautiful city and, of course, Lake Atitlan. But the lake and misty hills—" Ethelene paused mid-sentence, looking to her left, watching a fiery ball melt into the lake. "The sun sets so early here. It was so red tonight. Is it always like that?"

"The locals cook with wood, and the smoke makes fiery sunsets. It is beautiful. I've always loved Guatemala, and I'm glad you could see it," said Oliver, stopping at a stop sign—the only one in town. "It's not far now. But, when we get to Tikal, we'll need to drive crazy-slow through the park because of the wildlife. It will take a while. Do you want to eat here, or do you want to wait?"

"I'm starving. Is there a good restaurant here?"

Oliver nodded and turned towards the lake, driving parallel to the shoreline on a narrow dirt road. They passed weathered, floating docks and thatched roof palapas. In the distance, the sky glowed a hazy orange. Closer, on the lake's edge, shorebirds walked on lily pads the size of manhole covers. Flowers bloomed in the reeds. "Two nights isn't enough," Ethelene said solemnly.

"You say that now, but there's something I failed to mention."

"What?"

"They turn the electricity off at ten p.m. at Tikal, and there's no air conditioning. The howler monkeys will probably keep you up at night," Oliver said, a smirk hanging on his mouth.

"It will be so hot! How are we going to sleep?"

"We probably won't get much sleep."

Ethelene looked at him and laughed. Oliver knew she understood his innuendo. They always had sex when they saw each other. And it was good, even better than when they were married.

"Game on," she replied.

Ethelene and Oliver sat alone at Posada del Cerro, high on a hill overlooking Lake Peten Itza. Alone, except for the occasional bat zipping below the palapa's thatch and one orange cat curled on a cushion, sleeping. The only sound was the whirl of the ceiling fans and the surrounding chorus of bugs. The light was dim, and the humidity intense.

The hotel and restaurant manager—who, as it turns out, was also one heck of a chef—had served them a fantastic meal of steak, salad, and au gratin potatoes. The chef prepared it all by himself, clanging pots, and pans, and in the end, he cleaned every dish. After serving them two final Gallo beers and conversing briefly with Oliver in Spanish, the man disappeared into the night.

Ethelene took a sip of her beer, condensation dripping onto her sundress. "Is anyone staying here? Where's Emil?" She looked around. "It's so quiet, almost deserted. How did you even find this place?"

"The crew stays here—Emil stays at Tikal, same as me. This place is nice. The crew loves it. It's quiet because it's next door to a nature preserve. Do you know what *El Remate* means in Spanish?" asked Oliver.

Ethelene shook her head. "It means *the end*. It is, too. There's not much past this place. Besides, the guys went into Flores to party since our trip to El Mirador is postponed." Oliver winked at Ethelene. "They'll be back, eventually. How do you like your beer?" He asked, poking her in the arm.

"Shut up. I'm someone else tonight," said Ethelene, her words slightly slurred.

Oliver picked up one of their empty, mismatched glasses sitting in a cluster on the thick wooden table. "Well, by the look of all these glasses, you're not very *bright* anymore. What does that mean anyway, 'being bright'?"

"I thought you didn't want to talk about Cosmostheology. It means exuding a positively charged and productive aura. If everyone were *bright*, we'd live in peace and harmony because people would continue exchanging or circulating positive energy. That's our mission—to make people glow like stars. I mean, not literally, but figuratively."

"I like being dim," said Oliver. Looking at Ethelene sideways, he took a sip of beer. "You know, we're close to where they filmed the television show, *Survivor*. I thought you might like to see it—Yaxha. That's where they filmed the season in Guatemala. I still can't see you roughing it like that. Or maybe you just had a thing for Jeff Probst?"

"Oliver! That would be amazing. I remember that season. Oh, God. I'm too old for that now. They never wanted my sorry ass anyway," snorted Ethelene. She giggled and took another sip of beer. "I was so physically fit back then, you know, from all those damn Pilates."

They both laughed, staring at each other with glassy eyes, remembering. Oliver threaded a hand through his ponytail and lifted his beer with the other, draining it. He set the bottle down and stood, stretching his hand towards Ethelene. "Babe, I have a challenge for you—a water challenge. Why don't we take a little swim?"

Ethelene accepted his hand with a coy smile, then stood. Oliver enveloped her with his sweaty arms and grabbed her left hand, swinging her away like they were dancing. He pulled her back in a swift, fluid motion. "I know you're drunk when we start dancing," she said.

"I'm not drunk, my dear, just hot. Shall we go cool off?"

Ethelene nodded, clenching his buttocks with her hands, and kissing him.

They swayed for a long beat, finally parting.

Descending the rocky staircase, they passed dimly lit outdoor lanterns. The jungle surrounded them. When they reached the bottom of the stairs, they paused beside the silhouette of Oliver's jeep. After their eyes adjusted, they crossed the dirt road to the shore. Moonlight hovered around mysterious shapes. The dock came into view.

They ditched their shoes, feet whispering over the uneven planks until they stopped at the end of the dock; gentle waves slapped the sides, and boat masts rattled and clanked in the distance. Oliver reached behind her back and unzipped her dress, pushing it off her shoulders. The dress puddled on the dock. Ethelene looked up at the sky and gasped.

"The stars!" she hissed. "This is so amazing!"

Oliver pulled off his T-shirt and unbuttoned his shorts. Ethelene shimmied from her bra and panties. When Oliver disentangled himself from his underwear, Ethelene giggled. "I hope no one can see us," she whispered.

They sat on the edge of the dock for a few minutes, naked, legs dangling in the water. "How deep is it?"

"Three feet or so."

"You better not be lying," Ethelene said, jumping in.

Oliver followed, splashing Ethelene in the face. She flailed and laughed, wiped the hair from her eyes, and grabbed him. "We always got the sex thing right," she said, her voice low and husky.

Oliver broke from her embrace, dunking himself into the water. He shot up, pushing stray hairs over his head while dislodging his ponytail. Now, his hair hung scraggly over his shoulders. "Are you seeing anyone?" he asked.

"Does it matter?"

Oliver shrugged his shoulders.

They stood facing each other, warm water caressing their waists. Oliver pulled her against his chest and kissed her, his lips nibbling a trail down her slender neck. She grabbed him around the ears, massaging his earlobes. Her hands trailed down his arms like water droplets, landing on his buttocks, grasping. "You're in good shape, Ollie," she whispered.

"Not as good as you," he croaked.

They climbed back on the dock. Ethelene pushed him into position and straddled him, deftly inserting him between her legs. Their stomachs slapped as they rocked. She looked toward the stars just as one flashed across the sky. Ethelene sighed. "Nibble my neck again. You know how much I like that."

Oliver nibbled, and Ethelene rocked. "We're so goddamn good at this," he muttered between exerted breaths.

"Ollie?"

"Yeh."

"We better speed this up. The dock is scraping my knees!" Ethelene hissed, breaking into nervous laughter.

"Some things are better in theory, I guess. Let's go finish this challenge on shore."

"Game on," she replied.

Commence Cerebral Streaming—

Session Three

Rigel confined me to my quarters for two sleeping cycles. My knowledge games are in limbo and redirected. To alleviate boredom, I have invented a new game.

I'm playing it right now.

I suspect the microorganisms on my flesh have crawled into my nose and entered my brain, inflicting havoc. They tickle my cortex with their restless pili. The creatures distract me.

I *do* understand the complex beauty of slumber. Slow, synchronized brain waves sweep distant memories into safekeeping, and cerebrospinal fluid removes toxins. It is simple.

Sleep helps our brain cells recover energy. Its importance is undisputed. Still, it evades me.

I am ashamed that Rigel had to read my mind to discover my failing. Cerebral searching is allowed if a commander suspects a mistake or action that could endanger the ship. Rigel has a beautiful, flexible mind, like all females. I should have known better.

Rigel was curious about my frequent administrations from Sula, apprehensive that I was not taking proper precautions while completing my work. I reminded Rigel that we are inoculated and genetically edited. Still, she fears contamination. Now, after scouring my diminutive cortex, she knows the truth. I am diligent.

Even so, in the future, I cannot invent reasons to see Sula. Although ironically, Rigel advised Sula to address my sleep disorder at once. This outcome is very humorous!

I can no longer make myself sick and, in turn, endanger the crew. (Even though that wouldn't have happened. I am meticulous, as I said.)

However, Rigel is also benevolent, as are all females. She has assigned Sula to the micro crew for our mission to the tiny Blue Earth. Listeners, have you ever levitated over a sea of sunflowers as they gravitate toward the sun? Neither have I. But envisioning such majesty is a fitting example of the undisputed beauty of the tiny Blue Earth. Now, Sula and I will witness the realm of meat-eaters together.

My prior desperation became happiness swirling around my heart like a healthy plytumber vine grown amidst the heat and humidity of our living domes. I'm unsure how to classify these new feelings.

Now, I fear sleep will not come because I am too excited to sleep!

The sound of tinkling and scattering erupts as objects fall to the glass floor.

In my excitement, I lost track of the objects I was juggling with my mind: my dried majoon-mir wafers and kapa seeds; my moonrocks, crystals, seashells, lava rocks, and mysterious fossils; my puzzle pieces and precious metals, pinecones, and bark—there! They are swirling again. This time, I am forming a new pattern, a helix. Yes, yes, exceptionally good. Wait—no!

There is a short pause as more objects fall to the floor.

Listeners, I will discontinue recording my musings and concentrate solely on juggling. I must keep my mind fresh while I wait for new games. After this, I will take nourishment and proceed to the laboratory. There is much work to do. Yes. Good. Now there is perfect arrangement...

Delete Forbidden Content—Continue Universal Translation Mode—End of Session.

Joseph

Joseph entered a swarm of smelly bodies and stopped. Slowly, the group dispersed to the parallel seats of the subway car, some sitting, others standing, and one fellow crouched low in the center and practically sitting on the dirty, tracked floor. Joseph grasped a greasy railing with a look of trepidation while noting the weightlessness behind his back.

He'd left his backpack at Mitzi's in his haste to find Esme. Joseph patted his breast pocket, checking for his wallet. It was there. Pulling his phone from his pants pocket, he swiped to peek at the selfie he'd taken with Esme before her flight. A faint smile graced his lips, and a brief respite from serious thoughts floated through his brain. He put his phone away.

The car lurched forward, moving down the track. Usually, he people-watched, pondering the mystery of people's lives and mining their appearance on his way to work. Now, all he could think about was the whirlwind of memory in the hotel room; he was scared for Esme and confused about himself.

Somehow, he had read Esme's thoughts in Central Park. This telepathy scared him, too. Already, he felt touched by Diablo.

Now, he could feel the fire at his feet, toasting his toes. He was an anomaly, unnatural. So was Esme.

Joseph blushed, thinking about Esme's amorous attentions: her thoughts about sex and love directed at him. He didn't want to violate her mind; it was a horrible intrusion but staying disconnected from her thoughts had been difficult.

After one night together, Esme was in love with him. He also felt a strong, renewed connection to her. It was intense, like lovers, except he didn't romantically think of her—not yet anyway.

But what troubled him most was Esme's desire for fame and attention. She should hide her strange and sinister power from the world. What if the government found out about it? What would they do? Joseph realized he was grinding his teeth and tried to relax, shifting his shoulders, brushing a pile of newspapers aside, and sitting down. When he thought about other things, his mind returned to Esme.

All he could do was pray that she would be safe. He hoped her power would diminish. Maybe it would return to a peculiar irregularity. Perhaps she would call him, crying that it no longer worked. He wanted it to go away.

Joseph took a deep breath and appraised the subway car. He noticed a woman with a sparkly gold cross around her neck. *Confession.* That's what he needed. But how could he confess when he felt too tainted to enter the church? The things he could do made him too unnatural to mingle with a holy priest. Even now, he had a sixth sense as to Esme's whereabouts. It was hazy, but he could see her moving around *Orlando I-Park*—past a lake, a fountain, passing through a brick structure. His visions seemed more than a vivid imagination; they seemed real, just like before Esme left New York.

As soon as she was in the air, heading to Orlando, he could feel the distance growing between them, like a radio frequency slowly fizzling out. There was one bright spot, however. Mitzi would be glad to hear about his intense thoughts about a girl and he couldn't wait to tell her about his time with Esme—not everything, though.

Joseph felt a vibration in his pants. He retrieved his phone, shaking his head. It was a text from Esme: *Joseph, thinking about you. Are you at Mitzi's? Here's a photo from work. Pretty cool, huh? Not everyone can say they have a dragon for a coworker. Ha!*

Joseph smiled at the photo of a dragon looming over a rooftop. He realized that his life and Esme's were stranger than a book or a movie. Joseph looked up, realizing something else too—he'd just missed his stop.

Joseph stared at the walls outside the subway car absentmindedly; he would go to Central Park. It was early, and there was time. There would be no dragons or fire, but he'd be immersed in nature, which might clear his mind. His stomach growled. Luckily, there were other things: hotdogs with grilled onions and peppers, celery salt, and a slather of spicy mustard. Glorious food made everything better.

Oliver

Oliver shifted the jeep into first gear, swerving around a pothole, then maneuvering over a bump. Ethelene wiped at her shirt and tightened the cap of her water bottle. "Oh, my God. " When will we get there?" she asked with a sigh.

"If it were easy, they wouldn't have filmed *Survivor* here. We're almost there."

They passed flat, treeless pastures and grazing cows with saggy, white skin and huge, floppy ears—this went on for miles. Every field was surrounded by living, sprouting fences resembling gnarled bonsai trees inside a net. Eventually, a thick, black jungle enshrouded them; they started climbing. Whimsical yellow signs warned of jaguars, crocodiles, and tapirs. The road curved and swooped like a roller coaster until they eventually pulled into an empty lot. "Thank God," said Ethelene.

"We're not there yet. This is where you pay. I'll be right back."

Oliver sprang from the jeep, followed a trail, and entered a small museum. After paying their admission, he strolled back to the jeep, watching Ethelene hang her arms from the vehicle. She appeared to be listening to the laughing whoop of a faraway bird, seemingly enchanted by the *otherness* of the place.

Ethelene stepped from the jeep and removed her sunglasses, looking all around herself. "That was an oropendola," said Oliver, pausing by the driver's side door. "You heard a mating call. The male sits on a branch, dips, and swings like a kid on the monkey bars. It's hilarious. They are a relative of the oriole—but huge. They build long drooping nests, like teardrops. Maybe we'll see one."

"I'm so excited! Well, for Yaxha, not the oriole. I mean, I hope we see one. But you're the birder, not me. I can't believe I'm finally here. *Survivor,* Guatemala."

They climbed into the jeep, slamming their doors. Oliver maneuvered from the lot and looked at Ethelene. "I hope, once you see the ruins, that you'll forget all about *Survivor.* It's not a Hollywood set; it's a National Park, Guatemala's third largest ancient Mayan city. I've never worked here. Still, it's my favorite site."

They climbed hills and dipped into valleys, the jungle surrounding them like a covered bridge. After another fifteen minutes of rough and tumble terrain, finally, they entered another parking lot. There was only one other vehicle. "It looks like we'll have the city to ourselves. Tikal gets all the tourism. That's what I love about Yaxha. It's just the howler monkeys and us," said Oliver, parking in the shade of a gumbo-limbo tree.

They exited the jeep. Oliver grabbed his backpack from the back seat. Ethelene looped the straps around his broad shoulders and turning to stand before him, she tweaked his wide-brimmed hat. "You look just like a birder in that outfit. All you need is binoculars," she teased.

Oliver slapped his chest. "I've got a pocket for everything. Oh, right." Oliver turned his back, hunching. "Babe, can you grab my binoculars? They're in the main pouch."

"I knew it!" she exclaimed.

Ethelene rummaged inside the pack and handed the binoculars to Oliver. She paused to inspect the glass bead hanging around his neck. "Is that the necklace Esme gave you?"

"Yup. Esme picked it out in Flores. I was so proud of her, paying with quetzals all by herself. I've worn it for so long; it's my calling card. Good luck or something. The guys don't even tease me about it anymore."

"That's sweet. Have you talked with Esme?"

"No, but I checked my phone at the lodge this morning, and there was a text. Esme's home now. She said something weird— about Joseph, Emil's kid. Well, that's all I know."

"I wish she'd talk to me," said Ethelene, grabbing her water bottle.

Oliver noticed the sincerity of her expression and softened his voice. "I know, babe." He paused, shuffling his feet. "Well, let's get to it. We have ground to cover," said Oliver with an apologetic look. He swept his arm toward the jungle.

Ethelene squeezed his bicep, grabbed his hand, and walked beside him. Together, they entered the site, walking past a small stone structure encompassed by a dusty palapa, with uneven fringe covering the roof like a mouth with missing teeth. Inside the palapa stood two ancient carved stelae towers, rising from the earth, crumbling, and cracking, almost to the point of oblivion. "Are those real?" she asked.

"The unreadable ones are often ancient, but some are reproductions. Not much is known about Yaxha. There are relatively few inscribed monuments."

They kept walking, passing a narrow ball court, flat stone plazas with dank cubbyholes, looming pyramids, and mysterious mounds still claimed, buried beneath trees and jungle. The elevated causeways were long and covered by decaying leaves and below, there were tunnels with spiderwebs and mossy walls. The duo headed in many directions inside the park, going north, south, west, and finally, east. There were birds and unusual sounds around them: toucans, vultures, and spider monkeys scrabbling through the trees. The heavy air smelled exotic, like cedar or jasmine. The ground was alive with leafcutter ants, zigzagging in every direction.

Two hours later, Ethelene stopped on the Galindo Causeway, their final trek, to watch a pair of toucans high above their heads. "Maybe if I bring home a toucan for Esme, she'll forgive me."

"She loves them. I know. They're bullies, though. Beautiful bullies. Here, temple 216. This pyramid is the tallest," Oliver stated, excitement seasoning his voice.

They climbed a narrow, wooden stairway attached to the East Plaza. Ethelene stopped several times, peering at the receding ground through rickety steps. Oliver smiled. "I know what you're thinking. It's safe, though. I think."

Ethelene turned, giving him a menacing look. She gripped the railing with white knuckles and kept climbing.

"The Mayans built the structure like a layer cake," Oliver huffed.

She glanced at him and kept climbing.

Halfway up, they entered a grand plaza. Oliver and Ethelene explored every fragile and decaying corner, silently pausing to admire weedy, cracked stones—their true purpose a mystery—and sunken, ceremonial circles. Ethelene bent to touch a final lichen-covered stone before they returned to the stairs, climbing until they reached the top. Now, they could see miles of the jungle below, and a crisp, blue sky hovered above them. "That's Lake Yaxha in the distance. It means blue-green water," stated Oliver, his breathing heavy.

He dropped his backpack, pulled out their lunch, and placed it at their feet. Then he stood, scanned the horizon, and hugged Ethelene with one arm. "Well, babe? What do you think?"

Ethelene spread her arms. "Wow! It's amazing. The whole place. Oh my God. Now I know why you're so in love with Guatemala."

Howler monkeys erupted below them, barking and huffing. The loudest yet. Ethelene grabbed her hair. "God, they are so loud! It sounds exotic now. Last night, though, around four a.m...well, not so much."

Ethelene walked the perimeter, the top of the pyramid, looking all around and squinting. She took photos with her phone and stared into the distance. Touching random, deteriorating stones, she closed her eyes. Oliver met her where she stood. "What are you thinking about?" he asked.

She swiveled, wiping sweat from her forehead with the back of her arm. "I was thinking, it must be nice to know who you are. You've always had Guatemala—being an archaeologist. You were always doing your job and succeeding. I'm like a particle floating on the wind, always searching, never finding. Esme is just like you, you know. She's always known she wanted to be a magician and is so good at it. Her tricks, like floating objects? Well, I don't know how she does it. Do you?"

"Not a clue. But that's why it's called magic."

"I'm jealous of Esme."

"Tell her that! She's feeling low right now after her act didn't pan out as she'd hoped. She lost her agent—scoundrel. Dammit! Why then? Why on live television? I feel so freaking bad for her."

Ethelene nodded solemnly. "She's determined. She'll make it. The great, powerful Jade of Orlando."

"What do you mean? Jade?"

"You haven't forgotten her middle name, have you? You're the one who wanted to name her Jade."

"Jade is a beautiful name. I still love it."

"So, I know something you don't? She's going by Jade. That's her screen name. Well, you know what I mean—her stage name. She told me, probably to rub it in. She's always hated her name. She even stopped using the romantic accent to spite me," said Ethelene with a look of exasperation.

"They found skulls here, too, ones with jade embedded in their teeth," said Oliver. He clacked his front teeth ominously.

"That's why I didn't want to name her Jade. You were always talking about the skulls, the skulls with jade teeth. I didn't want to think of skulls when I said my daughter's name! Besides, I wanted an *E* name, like mine."

Oliver started laughing.

"Oh, Ollie. Let's eat. I'm starving."

He rubbed his stomach. "I'm glad you're trying to make up with Esme. Don't stop. She'll come around. I have a feeling you'll find what you're looking for soon. Don't stop following your dreams, either."

Ethelene stared at Oliver for a moment, then smiled and nodded. She took a small bite from her sandwich. Oliver lifted his sandwich to his mouth, then paused, raising his eyebrows. Again, he clacked his teeth like a ghoul. He took an enormous bite from his sandwich and chewed with gusto.

Ethelene laughed so hard she almost spit food from her mouth.

Below them, the howler monkeys erupted into a demented chorus.

"This is the weirdest picnic I've ever had," said Ethelene.

Commence Cerebral Streaming—

Session Four

Octopuses of the Blue Earth have eight brains, one in each tentacle. I wish I had a brain in each finger. I would understand how *Beings* create H2O on planet Pleione or how wormholes propel us through time and space. I could easily grasp the intricate workings and the mechanics of HaYax. I would understand why meat-eaters hurt each other so mercilessly. Maybe, I would reprogram the brains of furry beavers to redirect them from their relentless chewing. This is humorous!

Listeners, meat-eaters study kindness at university, like a benevolent virus for spreading cooperation. For *Beings*, it is innate. This fact is sad. If I had a brain in each finger like an octopus, I might understand what happened to my mother and father.

As I speak, my quiet footsteps circle the mechanical core of the ship. Again, I am wandering.

I wish you, the listener, could see the blood red mercury surge through the reactor in the brain of HaYax. The labyrinth of gold and crystal communicating above my head is ceaseless and electrifying. I feel like I am living inside a jellyfish, floating in the ocean of the tiny Blue Earth, when I gaze at the ship's core. There is so much eerie silence and solitude amidst the many chambers. HaYax sails with the quiet grace of an earthly owl on the hunt. The calculations of the ship never sleep. In this way, we are one.

Sleep was a malevolent trickster tonight. I slept for a mere seven hours before I awoke, embarrassed. I dreamt that my inner testicles exploded like a male bee of the Blue Earth during sex. I am ashamed to admit that thoughts of mating have infiltrated my neural pathways. Tonight, I will not visit Sula's door. I must calm my mind and find balance first.

I will visit our solar gardens and food storage facilities. My digestive sac is ravenous. I will cross my legs and levitate down the glass corridor to the gastronomic chamber.

There are no cerebral transmissions for several minutes.

"Dulfim!"

Laughter. Telepathic greetings. More laughter.

Dulfim and I have agreed not to report each other. We will feast together, relaxed in the knowledge that we have lowered our blood pressure with our mirth.

Pause. Rummaging sounds. Crunching.

I will only eat one dried ori-fruit wafer and one calpac nut, as they are relegated for the Antarctic crew. However, I will eat as many kapa seeds as I want. I will cease recording and concentrate on eating.

Pop. Pop. Crunch...

Universal Translation Mode—End of Session.

Oliver

"The Mirador basin contains five kinds of tropical forest," Oliver said, looking up at Emil.

"Yeah, so? Tell me something I don't know," Emil grunted, looking down from his perch, high in the branches of a *ramón* tree.

Emil kept hacking with his machete, adjusting, clambering higher. "Well, doesn't it seem like there's only one kind? The brutal kind," said Oliver with a sigh. Wiping his sweaty brow, he dipped to collect the leaves Emil was throwing at him.

"I hear you. I think we're just getting old."

They heard laughter from the crew. "Sí. Viejos," said Diego with a snicker.

"This is as high as I can go, Diego. You're next," proclaimed Emil.

They all laughed when a group of chachalacas erupted in the trees around them, cackling as if they had their own ideas on the matter.

"The only problem with that statement is that Diego won't have a problem climbing higher. He's a pro, and he's right, too. We are old," said Oliver.

Oliver carried the *ramón* leaves, dumping them beside the mules. The beasts were rolling in the dirt, hooves flailing like they were treading water. Oliver wished it was that simple. He wished a little dust could erase the exhaustion and ease the pain in his cramped and tired feet.

They had started their day at the trailhead in Lechugal, a swampy berg known for lilies that look like fluffy supermarket lettuce (hence the name). Oliver had nothing against the boggy town except that the drive there left him depressed after seeing the endless fields of slash-and-burn agriculture. At least the park rangers did their best to prevent illegal logging in the rainforest, poachers, looters, and drug trafficking. "Life is always a rope-pull in Guatemala, between the forces that work for good and the darker, more disturbing kind," he mused aloud.

After a twisty, ankle-bruising hike through miles of rutted and baked scrubland, they had made camp on the hard-packed, leaf-strewn plaza at Nakbe. Oliver had breezed through Nakbe many times in his career. Once, he had stayed on, researching over the summer with students from UCLA. They'd studied Nakbe's ancient limestone quarry and chert tool remnants used to carve limestone into white plaster. The Maya, Oliver observed, loved to whitewash their grand cities of old. Every time Oliver stepped foot on a Mayan site, wherever he happened to be—Mexico, Belize, Guatemala—he wished he could turn back time and see the grandeur. He'd sell his soul for one accurate glimpse of the past.

However, Nakbe was only a layover this time, preceding a side trip to La Muralla and, finally, El Mirador. Oliver wasn't sure if he even had the strength to climb Structure One tonight—and he always climbed Structure One. He loved to see the great La Dante complex—the largest pyramid this side of Egypt—towering over the jungle, only eight miles away at El Mirador.

Emil thumped to the ground. "You look like a damn fool in those green Crocs," Emil said, walking up to Oliver with his machete swinging at his side. "Did Ethelene leave those behind?"

"Man, you don't know what you're missing. We'll see who's laughing after the tics get you. How are you supposed to see tics wearing a dark color like that? I think you're getting forgetful in your old age."

Emil drove his machete into a stump and looked himself over. "You might be right. But at least a fer-de-lance can't get me through my work boots. Is it true we're supervising the completion of polycarbonate roofing at El Mirador?"

"Glorified roofing experts? Yeah, that's us. A simplification, perhaps, but that's the drift, protecting the carvings from ultraviolet light. Afterward, Esteban is sending us to the suburbs to dig around outlying areas discovered during one of the Lidar flights. Getting the big picture without hacking through the jungle for years is amazing. Sixty thousand housing structures. Ten million people. Can you believe it?"

Emil shook his head and kicked at some dirt. "I'd love to investigate the outlying infrastructure—to get a feel for how they lived, fed themselves, traveled, fought. Cool stuff. You know what I really want to do? Soon, I hope. I want to investigate La Ciudad Bianca in Honduras. God, to have been the one sitting on the floor of that wreck of an aircraft, flying around with one million dollars' worth of equipment..." Emil paused, waving his arms for emphasis. "...Pitching, rolling, and yawing in that tin can while the Lidar did its magic. Imagine witnessing what turned up in those valleys—an entire untouched civilization. Someday, I hope we can see it," Emil stated, wiping his brow.

"I'm working on it. Are you going to climb Structure One at sunset?"

"Oliver, I brought Flor de Cana rum. The only thing I care about right now is a bucket shower, rice and beans, and rum—lots of rum."

Oliver couldn't help but think—as the cold water drizzled down his face—about his old college roommate, Jeff. Jeff was a peculiar fellow. He wasn't rich. Still, the odd-duck would wear his underwear once— skids, bacon strips, or clean as a whistle—then throw the damn things in the trash. Man, if Jeff only knew how dirty Oliver still felt after a rinse under Nakbe's primitive shower system and how after that, he had to slip back into his sweaty clothes. The guy would go nuts!

After drying himself, he adjusted his necklace, finally slipping into a clean—as of now—pair of underwear. He grabbed his clothes from the sunny patch where he had placed them earlier, fetched his binoculars and hat, slithered into his Crocs, and embarked on a hike through the palm forest.

Walking the trail to Structure One, he noticed red tinto trees, poisonous che che, and ceiba trees, both big and small. Oliver stopped to rest by a large ceiba, pondering the shallow roots. The Maya thought the roots traveled deep enough to reach the underworld. In truth, the most impressive thing about the trees was their conical thorns, as pointy as caution cones. Sometimes, the trees grew tall, towering over the scrub and blossoming majestically. The branches would form an unruly arc over a trunk as round as a pregnant cow.

Oliver adjusted his hat and kept walking but stopped again, fixing his binoculars high in a tree. "Just a brown jay," he muttered, moving along.

He stopped several more times—spotting a goofy crested guan, a large red-lored parrot—and all the while, he followed the dried paw prints of a jaguar.

After five more minutes, he found himself at the jungle base of Structure One, observing the hungry earth that was slowly masticating, devouring, and digesting the ruins. Oliver looked up at the canopy of jungle—thickening, eclipsing.

He grasped the rope before him and climbed the embedded wooden stairs until he reached the top. Then he stood, the wind catching his ponytail, the setting sun warming his dewy backside. His eyes searched the sky. He had it all to himself.

Oliver could see for miles, all the way to the brushy top of the La Dante pyramid at El Mirador. He loved this place, the jungle, and everything in it. *I wish I had found the stucco mask buried here,* he thought. Still, simply being here was enough. He never tired of it. It was still exciting.

Lifting his binoculars, Oliver mined the trees below, spotting an orange-breasted falcon craning his head, hunting. The bird looked fierce and alert. Oliver felt awe somewhere near his heart.

Meanwhile, his own eyes grew heavy. Still, he sat, surveying his kingdom, listening to the chatter of birds while waiting for the orange glow of sunset. The rum would have to wait.

Oliver cradled his head with an arm while his body lay cocooned inside his hammock. His eyes searched for stars through a tiny opening in the canopy of trees. After carefully adjusting his weight, he thrust out his other arm, waiting. Emil passed the rum from his parallel swing, and Oliver grabbed it, took a big swig, and then handed it back. Emil shooed a mosquito and drank. "Man, how long have we been sleeping like this? Twenty, thirty years?" asked Oliver.

"A long-ass time," Emil replied, placing the bottle beside him. "So, how was your time with Ethelene? You haven't said anything about it. Was it that bad?"

Oliver whistled, the sound looping from high to low. He peered over his shoulder towards the crew, strung through the trees like alien pods from *Invasion of the Body Snatchers*. Oliver took a deep breath, looking at Emil. "Ethelene…she still has a hold on me. She might be the most annoying ex-wife in the world. Still, we had a good time. She's something else."

Emil chuckled, imperceptibly nodding his head inside his hammock. "I always liked her. I mean, I was sympathetic to your stories—the drama. So, what did you do?"

"Well, some things are unmentionable," Oliver said flatly.

Emil lifted his arm high above the hammocks. Oliver laughed and gave his friend a high-five.

There was snickering, then silence. "We went to Yaxha. That was about all we had time for."

Emil laughed. "I bet."

"Well, we spent the next morning inside Tikal, at Temple One and Two—she had to see those at least." Oliver smiled. "Did you know that Ethelene went through a phase where she wanted to be a contestant on the television show *Survivor*? Well, the show was filmed in Yaxha years ago. So, she loved seeing that. After Tikal, I drove her back to Santa Elena and shipped her off—back to her Cosmostheology friends. And that was that."

"Hmmm."

"Are you dating anyone?"

"No. Never. Half the problem is that we're always around college students, nobody our age. Do you remember the scene from Indiana Jones where the college girl writes on her eyelids? I don't get messages, just eye rolls like I'm an idiot," said Emil.

"You're depressing. I might need more rum."

"At least you got laid. Me? I'm dryer than we'll be after we finish off this bottle."

"Emil, how's your son? I got a text from Esme, something about seeing Joseph in New York. I didn't know they had stayed in touch."

"Really? You don't say. I saw that he called recently, but he didn't leave a message. Our relationship is so strained I didn't call back. Damn, I should have. I sure miss the kid."

"Yes, you should have. It's time you patched things up. Joseph was a great kid. I bet he grew up to be a fine young man."

"He did," said Emil, almost whispering.

There was silence for several seconds, and the jungle seemed to hum louder.

"He's so good-natured, just like his mother. I wish I could overcome the fact that he hasn't done more with his life. Straight A's in high school, smart kid, you know? Now, he's working for some old lady, *and* he's not even a registered nurse. I guess I shouldn't have discouraged him in the kitchen. He's a heck of a cook and could be an awesome chef. Aw, hell. What about Esme? I know about *The Morning Show*...," Emil said, his voice trailing off.

"Man, I feel for the kid. She's really trying. She's got dreams and talent to back them up. I can't believe some of the tricks she does. You wait. She'll do it—make it. She's always known she wanted to be a magician. Where she got that? I don't know. Kind of a man's world, you know? But you should see her levitation tricks. They are mind-boggling," Oliver said, yawning and stretching.

"Well, my friend, what do you say?"

Oliver pulled the mosquito netting over his hammock. "Mañana la Muralla, mi amigo."

"Buenas noches mi amigo."

La Muralla was behind them. El Mirador waited two hours ahead. They were walking on the remnants of a Sacbe, an ancient—the first really—super-highway. It was an original interstate system of the Maya that connected the grand cities of old.

Diego walked behind, pulling the mules, heavily laden with clothing, tents, food, and water—everything they would need for their journey and beyond. In the middle of the pack of men was Gus, the cook, and two park rangers; the local trio was full of laughter and jungle stories, grand tales of jaguar encounters. Wilberth, the youngest ranger, wore a jaguar tooth necklace, a stray tooth he'd found when he was a kid. Wilberth told them it made him strong and brought him luck. Oliver hoped that it did.

The group didn't have a doctor, soil specialists, students, or scientists. Emil walked ahead and Oliver behind. Slowly, the men examined their surroundings, stopping to identify birds and laughing when a howler monkey threw a sticky turd. This time, it missed.

All around them, *ramón* trees and gnarled branches of scrub grew alongside oversized mahogany, cedar, and grand ceiba trees. A toucan flew by them, flashing happy colors, drifting through the upper branches of a mahogany tree. The big black bird disappeared in an instant. They were getting closer.

They continued with sore feet and sweaty backs until they finally came to the humble sign marking El Mirador, the cradle of the Maya civilization. Emil flashed a smile rivaling his son. Then he got down on his knees and prayed.

Oliver took off his hat and scratched his head. He visualized his favorite artist rendering of the city in his mind's eye: whitewashed streets, terra-cotta pyramids, a metropolis three times larger than Los Angeles. He shook his head. Now, there was only a jungle.

But inside the trees before them were a million ghosts: the ancient ones. Fourteen square miles of the city—pyramids, houses, structures, and roads—were all buried. Two-thousand years ago, it was the largest city in the world.

Esme

Esme opened her locker, grabbed her purse, and slammed the locker shut. She wanted a burger—again. The rabbit food in her lunch bag just wouldn't cut it. She always craved comfort food when she felt like crap and she had felt that way since returning to Orlando. It was embarrassing for her co-workers to know that she had failed. In the end, their reactions were worse than she had expected. Instead of teasing her, they were eerily silent, avoiding, staring. Most likely, they didn't know what to say. The alienation was worse than glib words of hope.

She climbed the dark stairs, exiting through the hidden door and entering the crowd of tourists. Some wore black capes and magic hats; some carried wands. Others looked overwhelmed. Overall, though, they were happy. Everyone in her vicinity walked like a herd of zebras, craning their necks, staring at the sky, waiting, and watching for the dragon to breathe fire. It was the next best thing to fireworks, sure to initiate oohs, ahhs, and applause.

Esme didn't need to see it. Instead, she kept walking, passing through the irregular brick doorway. Squinting at the sun, she felt like a faceless nobody. By now, she had expected to be famous, streaming—not powerless and fat, depressed and lovesick. She wanted to lose weight for Joseph. Still, she wanted; she *craved* a freaking burger.

She looked up, focusing on a blue balloon stuck high in a tree. Slowly, she pulled it closer with her mind, humming low, almost inaudibly. She let go of the invisible string and smiled, allowing it to float away. Her power worked sometimes, but not all the time, and a faulty power wasn't good enough.

As soon as she returned to Orlando, her power became unreliable, measly, and lame. Gone was the vortex of energy from the hotel room, the sizzling swirl of strength that had astounded them both. It was like losing a finger—it was hers. She owned it and counted on it being there forever. On the flight home, she dreamt of headlining in Vegas. Or, at the very least, starring in her own show at Disney Springs or Orlando I-Park.

But, as bad as her diminishing power turned out to be, it wasn't the worst thing that had happened when she got back. The worst thing was missing Joseph, constantly checking his Instagram and Facebook, or revisiting the selfie she had snapped of them in Central Park. Texting him over and over became her hobby. He even haunted her dreams. She knew that it was unhealthy to be so obsessed. Frankly, she didn't understand why she was so obsessed. *I'm obsessed because he's as cute as a baby sloth.* "Oh, sorry," she muttered, looking sideways at a woman in a red and white sundress.

Esme bent to the ground, retrieved a souvenir Minion, and handed it to the lady she had just plowed into like a truck. The woman looked at her skeptically. *I need to forget about Joseph!* Esme kept walking.

After a few minutes, she entered Richter's. It was summer, busy. The line was long. Still, she had to get a burger. Before New

York, she hadn't eaten red meat in years. Everything had changed there. She started ruminating.

Reconnecting with Joseph might turn out to be good— maybe great. But they didn't have a chance to consummate their relationship. Maybe, Joseph didn't even want to. Esme knew she was cute on a good day. But she was chubby, and Joseph was hot, handsome—that smile!

Plus, he was sweet and incredibly kind. He talked about Mitzi like she was his beloved grandmother. Esme wondered what Joseph was doing, and the air started popping, fizzling.

Esme looked around herself, wondering where the strange noise or vibration originated. She shuffled forward in line, listening and watching. Someone was chewing gum. She detested that sound. Plus, the people ahead of her smelled sweaty and stinky. It was hot outside and hot inside the restaurant. She could almost feel tiny molecules of grease hanging in the air. It made her feel slightly sick. Did other vegetarians go through this? The push and pull? The cravings and guilt? Probably.

Her phone pinged, and she grabbed it, swiping. A giant smile enveloped her face. It was Joseph. Attached was a photo of him at Central Park, at the zoo, standing in front of a scarlet ibis, smiling his luminous Joseph smile. *This red bird reminded me of you. Do you still like toucans? Miss you. :)*

Eagerly, she patter-punched the tiny keyboard. Joseph always sensed, somehow, when she was feeling low or thinking of him. *I'm at work. Time for a burger. I suck at veggie life. I love toucans! Miss you!*

Esme stuffed the phone into her purse and ordered her food. She felt better—happy, even. After a few seconds, her phone pinged again. She rooted for it, beaming. Her smile faded; her brows furrowed. She read the text: *Honey, I'm sorry I haven't been there for you lately. I'm going to do better. Don't give up on me, okay? I'll try calling later. I have lots to tell you. I hope you are feeling better. Please answer.*

"Mom," she said, the sound enveloped within a sigh.

Esme inhaled and blasted the carbon dioxide through her puckered lips. She knew she had to talk to her mother sometime, and maybe she had punished her mother long enough. After she heard her order number called, she lumbered to the counter, accepting her tray. It looked delicious, dripping grease, oozing cheese. She stared at her plate. *One problem at a time*, she told herself. *One problem at a time.*

Joseph

Joseph read Esme's text and slid his phone back into his pants. Before their reunion, Esme had drifted through his brain occasionally. But his life in Guatemala seemed distant, overshadowed by the death of his mother. That's why his new feelings were so unexpected. He looked at his sneakers, fingering the rosary beads in his hand. *Mother Mary, please watch over Esme. Guide her, help her to control...*

'Son, why don't you join us? Come inside. I've seen you here many times."

Joseph looked up, shifting his position on the concrete steps. "Father, I can't today. Maybe next time," said Joseph with a thumping heart.

The priest laid a hand on his head. "God bless you," he said. Turning, he drifted on invisible feet towards the golden door. Before the priest entered the church, he stopped, looking back. "Have you need for penance? I sense a heavy heart. Why don't you come later, after mass? I will be in the reconciliation room," said the priest, slipping inside the church.

Joseph reflected on his predicament; so many ideas and worries surged through his heart. He wanted to light a candle for his mother and Esme. *Maybe if I confessed…but who would believe me?* Joseph ran down the steps and zipped around the corner.

Joseph entered Mitzi's apartment, wiped his feet, and continued into the living room. Silence greeted him, prompting a relieved smile. After walking into the dining room, he placed a heavy box on the table and his backpack on a chair.

Beyond the dining room and down another hall, Joseph heard Mitzi buzz from her bedroom. When she got close, he could see her white hair, wild like dandelion fluff. She wheeled towards him, eyes dancing. "Should I reheat the leftovers?" asked Joseph.

"Not yet. Open it," said Mitzi, clapping her hands.

"What? The box?"

"Yes, you fool."

Joseph laughed nervously. "Okay. Hold your horses. What is it today? A new bicycle? Maybe a Picasso?"

"Ha! You'll see."

Joseph retrieved a knife from the kitchen and sliced the tape, peeling the box open. He lifted out a large book, twisting it in his hands. "Mitzi, do you want to cook now? What's this? You said you always hated cooking. You said the kitchen was your torture chamber."

"Kitchens equal work, hence, torture. The book is for you. If you're going to be a chef, you need to read *The Joy of Cooking.*"

"But I'm not a chef. My job is to take care of you. Are you trying to get rid of me?"

"Maybe. Joseph, you've been moping around, missing your girl. I have eyes. Here's what's going to happen. I'll hire a new full-time personal care attendant—or maybe Sara would like to switch to weekdays. We'll see. She doesn't cook like you, and I won't eat homemade tamales and barbacoa every day, but I'll survive. Go see your girl in Florida. Then, when you get back, I'm sending you to culinary school."

Joseph closed his mouth. "No, I can't let you pay for me. I don't know what to say."

"Say yes! Because I won't take no for an answer. I'm old and rich. I do what I want. My son doesn't need the money. He already owns several restaurants. You can start at one of those when you graduate and work your way up."

Joseph rubbed his mouth and scratched his cheek. "I'm speechless. I like my job here and you pay me well."

"Not anymore!"

Joseph raised his eyebrows and flashed a wild smile. "I have always dreamed of being a great chef, but..."

"I know you have. You just need a little help, a push in the right direction. Now, you *will* be a great chef. You can't take care of old ladies forever. I know you have a thing for me, but you're too young for me, too handsome for an old hag like me," said Mitzi, slapping her knee and laughing at herself. "It's settled then. And if you can't pay rent while you're in school, you'll stay here, right? Wait, how about France? Le Cordon Bleu. Yes, that's where you should go. What do you think?"

Joseph rubbed his head with both hands and ruffled his hair. "Mitzi. I'm overwhelmed. You really *are* trying to get rid of me."

Mitzi raised her eyebrows and laughed, clapping her hands again. "Now, let's eat," she said, snickering.

Joseph was shocked, stunned. Shuffling into the kitchen, he leaned on the counter, palms down, staring at the coffee maker.

He wouldn't miss his apartment or the subway. However, he would miss Mitzi. He'd helped her for so long that her apartment felt like a second home. She was like a feisty grandmother. Would Sara be able to lift Mitzi in and out of the bathtub?

Mitzi would miss him too. She was acting brave, but she was only tough on the outside, and inside she was a marshmallow—a *chef*. Joseph felt gob smacked.

He missed Esme already and wanted to see her. She tugged at his heart. But seeing her again scared him, too. "What if it happened again?" he whispered to the stove.

"I don't hear anything in there. Are you okay? Did I throw you for a loop?" called Mitzi. She buzzed over to the archway into the kitchen, watching him with round, expectant eyes.

Joseph turned. "I'm alright—maybe a little dizzy. But happy. Mitzi, you need something. I almost forgot."

"What's that?

"A hug."

Commence Cerebral Streaming–

Session Five

The mechanical stewards have been as industrious as fire ants, preparing the secondary vessel for our mission to the tiny Blue Earth. Their singular focus allows for perfect flow and organization. I, on the other hand, have chosen to utilize selective idleness. Instead, I am preparing myself mentally. We are nearing the wormhole. .

Sula is afraid.

I have passed through many cosmic doorways during my travels. The first was unfortunate; my parents disappeared inside the portal, their souls adrift, and uncollected. Still, I am not afraid.

Since then, we have made technical advances in engineering. Sometimes, when we enter the Blue Earth portal, I feel my parents' presence. It is almost as if they are trapped there, waving to me, and sending their beautiful energy. But the fate of their wayward spirits remains a mystery. Maybe, their power was redirected to the Deities, their bodies reduced to floating energy cells.

The crew told me my father was curious. The others said my mother had a most beautiful mind. My parents sailed the cosmos together, visiting the realm of meat-eaters numerous times. My mother was a commander for over two hundred years, beloved by her crew. Honorable. Wise. Adventurous!

There are *Beings* aboard HaYax that worked with my mother and father. Sometimes, I feel their keen appraisal.

Dulfim knew my parents well.

Listeners, I respect all crew members equally except my playmate Dulfim. I appreciate him ten percent more. Dulfim and I laugh like children and bond like protons and electrons while watching documentaries about the tiny Blue Earth. We play knowledge wars, and most importantly, he teaches me about my parents' exploratory life.

Listeners, I am juggling while I stream this data. The whirlwind above my head looks like a waterspout. I plan to give Sula the large opaque rock in the center for good luck. It is a piece of compressed carbon the size of a cantaloupe. It is useless, unable to record information, but on the other hand, its beauty is evident. I think my gesture will please Sula.

Good luck is considered, by some cultures (especially the meat-eaters), to be nothing more than an empty wish. The minuscule energy cells that surround us hear our prayers. I never fail to ask for *Their* help, hoping that the cells of my parents will send their protective energy. Listeners, please pray for Sula's safekeeping. On this trip our fates are linked.

Tonight, I will sleep with an imaginary smile as wide as a constellation—and yes, I've been sleeping!

Good night, listeners.

One by one, one-hundred small pieces of carbon, crystal, glass, and stones clatter into a glass tube.

Continue Universal Translation Mode—
Edit For Content—End Of Session.

Joseph

Joseph peered through the tiny windowpane, appraising the layer of white clouds resembling a slather of marshmallow fluff. He turned towards his seatmates. In the middle seat, a bald man in a parrot-head T-shirt clicked the keys of his laptop. At the aisle, a teenager slouched, listening to his phone. Both men were slaves to their devices, unaware of the deliciousness just outside.

Unlike most people, Joseph loved to fly. As a kid, flying meant quality time with his dad and visiting exotic locations; nothing bad ever happened after a flight, only good.

He'd been thinking about his childhood ever since his reunion with Esme. He'd also been thinking about his dad, wondering if this new career choice would appease him.

There was something else, too. After Mitzi's proposal, he recognized that it wasn't his dad who'd diverted his dreams—it was himself. After all, he was the one who decided not to pursue becoming a chef; he was the one who chose not to spend money on nursing or medical school. It seemed foolhardy to commit to either option when the confusion between his heart and mind was like oil and vinegar separated in a salad dispenser. His heart wanted mole, squash blossoms, and tamales in chipotle sauce. But his mind had its own agenda, whispering silent pleas about healing, balance, and harmony.

After Mitzi offered to send him to culinary school, the decision seemed easy: *Cook!* Joseph smiled, nestling deeper into his seat. Returning to the window, he wondered how close they were to Orlando.

Joseph was surprising Esme. He had texted her, casually inquiring about her plans for the following week. But he already knew everything about her, every thought, every location. Joseph shook his head, trying to dispel the whispers. It didn't work. The closer he got to Esme; the more obvious things became. It was like the radio in the cockpit: push a button, think of Esme, and become connected to ground control.

"Are you going to *Harry Potter?*"

Joseph froze, his fingers and toes tingling. He turned to the man beside him. "Did you ask if I'm going to use my power?"

The man laughed. "No, I wondered if you are going to *Orlando I-Park*—you know, *the Wizarding World of...*"

"Oh." Joseph cleared his throat. "Yes, I have a friend that works there..."

Well, folks, we're approximately thirty minutes outside Orlando, Florida, and we will be landing shortly. The weather is a balmy eighty-eight degrees in Mouse Town. The local time is 3:35 P.M. Flight Attendants will be coming through momentarily to secure the cabin. Please remain seated with your seat belts fastened for the remainder of the flight. Flight Attendants, please prepare the cabin for arrival.

Joseph checked his seat belt, moved his seat upright, and closed his tray table.

"Joseph! You're coming to see me!" Esme exclaimed.

Again, Joseph froze. He had heard the words as plain as day. He looked to his right; the transmission had been so loud he worried his seatmates could hear it, too. Joseph had sensed—before, in Central Park—that Esme had entered his mind. "Afraid to fly, huh?" said the man beside him.

Joseph turned. "No, I'm not afraid."

The man smiled. "Well, you look like you've seen a ghost. You're not going to hit me with those things, are you?"

Joseph looked at his hands, curled into fists, white and throbbing. He opened his hands, rubbing them on his knees. He hated being such an open book.

"I guess I might be a little afraid," he told the man. *Frankly,* Joseph thought, *now it was the truth.*

Esme

Esme walked, almost jogging, through the crowded maze of tourists flooding *CityWalk*, the restaurant-filled doorstep of Orlando's I-Park. She breezed past the kiosks and themed restaurants, past the co-mingling smells—burgers, Cinnabon, popcorn, Buca di Beppo, and the Chocolate Emporium—which she could smell all the way across the lake. Stepping onto the escalator, Esme had to pause, sandwiched inside a line of souls. Impatiently, she debarked at the top, swiftly moving forward until a busload of smiling faces mobbed her again.

Esme veered around them. She entered a moving walkway, staying to the left, passing. She couldn't stop smiling and couldn't wait to get to Joseph. He was here; he'd confirmed it when he landed. But she had known it somehow while he was still in the air. A percolating feeling had consumed her, almost as if her blood were boiling. Her mind hummed—she felt more potent, powerful.

Eventually, she reached her car, her mind a swirl of activity. She ditched her name tag, drove from the lot, heading for her apartment. Traffic was slow; it was rush hour. Esme rocked in her seat, gripping the steering wheel with clenched teeth. She bit her lower lip and fidgeted in her purse for some peppermints. After a few anxious minutes, Esme checked her appearance in the rearview mirror and appraised her stomach with a sigh. She concentrated on the road.

If she thought about Joseph—really focused on him— would she be able to read his mind? She tried and heard some fizzled whispers, but nothing that made sense. She kept driving, passing lakes and billboards, hotels and motels, endless stores and restaurants, exit after exit, and Orlando's downtown high-rises until finally, she reached Winter Park. Esme took a deep breath and exited the freeway, her heart swelling in her chest.

After several more minutes, Esme arrived at her apartment, parking underneath the massive arms of a banyan tree dripping with moss. She grabbed her purse, almost running up the sidewalk, but stopped. Joseph rose from his place near an azalea bush, a backpack at his side. He was smiling brightly, eyes animated. "I'm here, Esme!" he exclaimed.

Esme flung herself into his arms, hugging him tightly. She heard the air rush from his lungs and let go. They stared at each other, awkwardness suddenly clouding the air between them. Esme spoke first. "I'm so happy you're here! I've missed you! What should we do now?" she asked, her face flushed with excitement.

"Well, you could show me your apartment. You live in such a nice neighborhood. It's not what I expected at all. I guess I didn't know what to expect. It's like Orlando is a Candyland game, and this…" Joseph paused, looking around. "This is so grown up."

"I know. I love coming home and not seeing any theming—just beautiful trees and natural flowers. Everything is real, not artificial. There's a little pond behind the building. It's expensive here, but I have a roommate. She works nights and is rarely around. Oh, she works at *Orlando I-Park*, too. She's nice, mostly."

"Mostly nice is good," Joseph said, grabbing his backpack.

"I'm upstairs," Esme said, pointing at the stairway. The stairs were attached to the front of a yellow-sided building lined with shrubbery and azalea bushes.

Joseph followed Esme up the steps, and they entered her apartment. Esme shut the door. Joseph dropped his backpack. And objects from all corners of the dwelling lifted in surreal animation.

"It's happening again," Esme hissed.

"Jesus," said Joseph, groaning and ducking as a pillow flew right by him.

Amid the whirlwind, salt and pepper shakers bobbed and shook, seasoning the air. Paper napkins floated randomly like dandelion seeds caught in the breeze. Mugs, wooden spoons, and dirty plates circled, dripping water and food debris. Two blue blankets tossed and turned as if spinning in a dryer. A bar of orange soap and tennis shoes played a game of tag. Joseph grabbed the television remote as it passed by his face.

A minute later, everything fell to the floor, littering the carpet. The duo stared at the mess. "It was different this time. Did you notice that? Slower, more graceful, controlled chaos. Weird, huh?" Esme remarked, kicking at a fork.

Joseph shook his head. "I'm scared."

"You know, I mean…, it doesn't even feel like I'm doing it. But, if I'm not doing it, then who is?"

Joseph looked at Esme, then at the floor. "Diablo," said Joseph, performing the sign of the cross.

"What? No. I'm not possessed," she said, hands on her hips.

Joseph crossed the floor, pulling Esme into an embrace. She hugged him back, feeling his heart thump against hers. "I'm sorry. That's not what I meant. I know you are a good person—the best. It's just so weird," Joseph said, stroking her hair.

Esme pulled away slightly, looking at Joseph with glassy eyes. She leaned in, tilting her head and kissing him softly. Joseph responded, rubbing a hand over her back, lingering at her waist. Then he pulled away. Stepping backward, he held Esme by the arms and looked into her eyes. "Let's take things slow, okay?"

She licked her lips, diverting her attention to the floor. After a few seconds, she rubbed her hands together and spread her feet as if expecting the wind to knock her down. One by one, she lifted the debris, sending everything flying, zipping around corners, popping up and down until everything was in its original place, snug and secure. She grabbed Joseph's hand and stared at the sofa, probing, fixated. She had to try; she felt like she could move mountains. "What are you trying to do?" Joseph whispered.

Esme didn't answer. But the sofa stuttered, lifting, hovering several inches off the floor. She concentrated with her hands clenched and her abdominal muscles tight, humming loudly. But she couldn't hold it up; she felt the pull loosening. The sofa dropped with a thud, shaking the floor. Esme gasped. "I did it!"

Joseph stared at the sofa with furrowed brows, threading a shaking hand through his dark hair.

Esme loved the proximity of Joseph's warm body. They were lying in bed, giggling, and holding hands, telling stories like they were on a middle school sleepover, an empty pizza box between their feet. "I want to go there!" Joseph said, pointing at the flat screen.

"That's where I work," Esme returned, swallowing a sigh.

"I didn't know the I-Park had roller coasters! Can we go? It's probably the last place you want to go, though, right? But it looks so fun. Do you like working there?"

"Yes and no. It *is* a fun place to work. But I thought I would be in a different place now, that's all. I've been learning new magic tricks, the real kind. Trying anyway." Esme paused, rolling her eyes. "I suck at magic tricks. All I want to do is levitation. But I never know if it's going to work. Maybe, now it will. When you're around, I feel powerful. Can you help me practice? I need to do something great, something that will blow people away," she said, staring at the ceiling as if it was the milky way.

Esme sat up in bed, turning off the television. She looked at Joseph and tilted her head. "Don't do that, Esme!" yelped Joseph, rising to his elbows.

"You don't want me to use my power. That's what you were thinking. Why are you so uptight about it?"

"Why can't you just do magic? Do you know what I think real superpowers are? Gratitude. Kindness. Generosity."

Esme stared at Joseph with a scowl, and the word *barf* dangled on her lips. "Come on? If you could do what I can do...," Esme paused, dramatically sighing. "So, you're telling me that you wouldn't use it? You'd live like a normal person, give money to homeless people, and care for old ladies forever without using your superpower? Joseph, you're like a saint or something."

He looked away. Esme folded her arms, reclining on the bed. She loved Joseph, but he was annoying the hell out of her right now. Joseph placed his pillow behind his back, leaning, wiggling his toes, pursing his lips, and staring across the room. "I haven't told you about something. I have big news. *Huge* news." Joseph reached for Esme's hand and pretended to place an object in her palm.

"What are you doing?"

"I gave you an olive branch," he said, flashing his brilliant smile.

Esme shook her head and rolled her eyes, smiling back. "Tell me!"

"Well, I'm going to Mexico City, to le Cordon Bleu. I'm going to be a chef! I thought about France but decided Mexico was the right place for me. It's the cuisine of my heritage. My mother was from Mexico City. She met my dad while he was working at Teotihuacán—it's this huge archeological site. Now, I'll see it again, and I can honor my mother. It feels right."

Esme's heart suddenly felt like it was drowning in quicksand, every beat sucking happiness into a pit of hopelessness. She tried to ignore Joseph's remark about his mother, which made her think of her own mother. She tried to squash her sudden sorrow at Joseph's leaving and applied a smile to her face, a fake smile. "That's wonderful. When are you leaving?"

"I'm leaving in two weeks, and the semester starts later, in September."

Esme already knew the answer but didn't want Joseph to realize she knew. "It sounds expensive. Are you paying? I mean, I guess that's a rude question."

"That's okay. It's Mitzi. She's paying," Joseph replied somewhat sheepishly.

"Wow! That's nice of her. She must like you a lot."

Joseph blushed. "She is like a grandmother to me. Except, my grandmother never acted like Mitzi!"

Joseph looked over Esme's shoulder at her nightstand, pausing on an eclectic bowl of seashells. "I've noticed you like to collect things from nature."

He reached around her, grabbing a brown whelk shell and twisting it in his hand. "This is very pretty. Where did you find it?"

"We used to live in Clearwater. I loved to go to the beach," said Esme, looking at the shell somewhat sullenly.

Joseph grabbed Esme's hand. "You're thinking about your mother."

"Yes, we used to have fun at the beach. My mother keeps calling, and I haven't called her back. I don't know what to do because she always lets me down. I'm jealous of the relationship you had with your mother."

He inched closer to her. "I was always jealous of your relationship with your father," he said, kneading her thumb.

"Joseph, I can't believe that we lost touch. We have so much in common. For one, neither of us has siblings. I cried when I had to go home—when I left Guatemala. I missed you so much."

"I missed you too. But we're together now. We'll have to make up for the lost time."

Esme pressed her body against Joseph's, thinking there wasn't enough time in the whole universe to make up for the years she'd spent away from Joseph.

Commence Cerebral Streaming—

Session Six

I dreamt of Sula last night.

If you, mysterious listeners, have been mindful of my musings, you will know this fact is significant. I slept!

Since Sula reprogrammed my brain's arousal center, these past weeks have been as peaceful as the silent hours of children. Even so, there are nights when I only sleep for eleven or twelve consecutive hours. On those nights, my wish for a good night's rest remains as elusive as a snowflake on the plains of Pleione.

I never dream of Sula's physical appearance. I do not care about her outer shell. Still, I spun a peculiar fantasy throughout my previous confinement. I must have been contemplating my conversation with Rigel and the curious thoughts I overheard about Sula. (My readings were purely superficial, and I am not ashamed.)

Rigel was surprised at my devotion to a *Being* with such a small head. This idea is very humorous. I'm bewildered, deciphering why Rigel would think such an irregular thought. Rigel knows better than any *Being* that brain size is insignificant compared to the number of neurons, their location, and how they are connected. I am almost blushing—if I could blush—at the mere thought of the inner workings of Sula's brain. Sula could have a head as small as an earthly watermelon, and I would still be devoted to her.

Sula does have a small head, but her mind is like a million streams flowing like a neutrino particle, unimpeded by interstellar and intergalactic magnetic fields, running straight through the universe. This concept is the preeminent way to describe her beautiful brain.

My dream was peculiar. Sula was guiding a meat-eater as they navigated an unusual contraption. Sula's tall, graceful body was now short, dressed in ugly cotton garments, not spun from robotic, electronic silk or any other standard thread. Her light green skin resembled silica, and her soulful eyes—eyes that harness all the colors of the northern lights set against the night sky—shrunk to the size of a walnut.

Conversely, her delicate nose and lips increased to grotesque proportions. Her body became soft. I think she was one of them: the meat-eaters. We have studied many hybrid specimens in our laboratory during my lifetime. Honestly, it is one thing to see images of them and another to see one firsthand. Touching their spongy flesh sends shivers down my spine. If something happened to our ship during our visit to the tiny Blue Earth, I worry that the meat-eaters might devour us like cows.

Meat-eaters are very curious in appearance, with skin that changes from one individual to the next, like a chameleon. Our skin changes to a subtle gray during summer, but always, there is the underlying beauty of green.

Meat-eaters also have weird follicles on their head that can grow like a patch of sutopi weeds. Still, many others have a glossy bare head like ours—beautiful!

The mouth and groin of meat-eaters stink. They are dirty creatures. Primitive.

Listeners, meat-eaters chew a strange rubbery substance, open-mouthed as if they were dirty cows chewing a tacky cud. I dislike cows. To make matters worse, the chewing substance—harvested from the unlimited data inside our insect drones—has no nutritional value. This example is only a fraction of the meat-eater's irrational behavior. I could fill the great Pleiades crater with their foolishness.

Meat-eaters are the strangest *Beings* in the galaxy. Some hybrids use fecal matter to treat disease, which has occurred for millennia. Transferring the fecal matter of a healthy individual to an unhealthy one can cure many diseases. It is a simple treatment, but in many cases, it works.

However, even though the meat-eaters are advanced enough to use this peculiar technology, they still haven't figured out how to program their primitive toilets. The toilet of the meat-eater will flush automatically before the meat-eater finishes eliminating. Listeners, it has been observed by our drones. It is disgusting! Why would they not design a better toilet? I do not understand them.

Long pause, followed by an intake of breath and diabolical giggling...

They are, however, learning much with our help. We release *all* hybrid specimens when our tests are complete. No harm has befallen them. The meat-eaters—as ugly as they are—have souls like us. The Deities created them, and we are not in an elevated position to judge their purpose. I, Dob-Dec, cannot divine the secret of their creation. However, I have my theories. It would be very humorous if a meat-eater listened to this entry someday. I hope that if I am lucky enough to sleep tomorrow night, I will have no more dreams of monsters like them.

It is an excellent thing that I slept. We leave the mother ship tomorrow.

Continue Universal Translation Mode—
End of Session.

Oliver

A foul-tempered rain pelted the plastic roof of the camp's makeshift food shelter like a mad teenager beating his first set of drums. Swaths of moisture occasionally drifted under the awning, floating on a gust of wind, and settling over the crew's arms and legs. The air smelled humid and musty, and now and then, smoke drifted in front of their faces, exhaled from a hot breakfast hearth. Howler monkeys slept in the trees around them; all was quiet except for the sound of water. "I guess I won't need a bucket shower tonight," Emil scoffed.

Oliver took a sip of coffee. "I don't like it. The rain is early this year. I hope it's not a bad omen for the season. The new crop of students will want to pack up and go home."

Oliver stared into the surrounding jungle, barely visible in the dim light. "Can't dig in the rain. But I guess we'll take our tools anyway, even though it will mostly be a survey and look-see, huh?"

"Looters and rain. We can't control either one. At least a wet trek is more fun than building polycarbonate roofing. Yeah, we might as well be prepared—new area and all. I'd give anything for a little whiff of death: a bowl of finger bones, some sacrificed babies, bejeweled teeth. Most likely, we won't find much where we're going."

"Let's wait till after breakfast for human sacrifice references," Oliver crowed, looking sideways at his friend.

Oliver returned to his plate, lifting a fork, picking at his eggs, and pushing his rice and beans around on his plate. He stared at the whole mess with revulsion, happy for the stash of beef jerky bulging in his lower pants pocket. After scowling at his plate for several seconds, Oliver grunted and started scooping food into his mouth, gobbling it down as fast as he could, knowing that he shouldn't waste the food before him. Emil looked at Oliver and snickered over his coffee cup. "God, you're annoying," garbled Oliver.

Emil wiped the sides of his mouth and slapped Oliver's back. "You're stuck with me, my friend. What a morning. Should we wait it out? Or go."

"Go," said Oliver, gulping the last dregs of his coffee.

After a time, both men pushed themselves away from the rickety table. "Adios amigos!" Emil shouted to the outdoor room.

Muddled grunts and grumbles followed. A man ran up to them, holding out his hand. Oliver smiled. "Thanks, Gus," he said, grabbing the bananas.

"Nice," Emil interjected.

"I never thought I'd be so happy to see a banana," Oliver said morosely.

They grabbed their ponchos and pulled the plastic over their heads. Emil grabbed the backpacks that held their tools: cameras, trowels, spades, hand shovels, hoes, brushes in all shapes and sizes, dentist's probes, a notebook, and an endless supply of empty plastic bags—enough to keep a good mathematician busy for days. Oliver slipped one of the packs over his shoulder, adjusted his hat, and grabbed a pointy mattock, swinging it like a machete. Emil placed two water bottles into the sides of his pack and wrangled them onto his shoulders. Then, they waited.

Finally, Antonio stepped from behind a tarp enclosure a few yards to their left. "Ya voy!" he yelled, picking up a machete, jumping puddles, and strolling over to where Oliver and Emil waited.

"Everything okay in there?" asked Oliver.

Antonio rolled his eyes. "The revenge of Montezuma is powerful today," he said, stifling a burp.

The men snickered, watching the jungle to their right, waiting. Soon, Phillip rolled down a rutted path with a wheelbarrow. "I guess it's now or never," Emil grunted.

The men headed down a narrow trail embedded with tree roots and muddy tracks until the path dissolved into a thick jungle, a spider's web of branches. Antonio took the lead, bushwhacking a jagged path with his machete. The men fell into a soggy line, following sporadic survey markers deeper and deeper into the jungle. "Ground truthing," Emil said bitterly.

"The lidar doesn't find everything. Once we get around this old agricultural area, we should hit the housing structures. The suburbs. It would be more fun if we were headed for a new pyramid and some royal bones, huh?" Oliver remarked.

"I wish," stated Emil, rain dripping off his baseball cap. "It's all good, though. I love the infrastructure—as long as we find some infrastructure."

They kept walking. Eventually, the rain slowed, the sky brightened, and strange mounds appeared around them: square shapes, irregular walls, gumdrop hills, and holes—everything alive with plant matter, zigzagging through the trees. Oliver wandered in one direction and Emil in another. They kept bushwhacking, blazing new trails. Oliver and Emil started mapping the area, recording data, and deciding which mounds required further study. All the while, they were randomly displacing the jungle floor, poking, and investigating. This work went on for hours.

Meanwhile, Antonio built a tarp shelter, and Phillip collected the spoils. After another hour of shallow digging and poking, the men gathered, huddled under the tarp while devouring Oliver's beef jerky. They chewed while staring at the weeping jungle. Antonio and Phillip filled the tarp enclosure with laughter, swapping stories told in Spanish. Oliver and Emil talked of the day's meager discoveries. "I think we should get GPR out here. I ran into what I think is a defensive wall, and wonder what might be buried around it," said Oliver.

Emil took a sip of water. "Sounds good. I'm more interested in what we might discover in the soil around the housing structures. Right now, though, I'm thinking about the rum. I wish I had a mouthful to warm my gut. The dampness is annoying the hell out of me. How's the rum holding out?"

"Holding. But there's never enough."

"I don't think I'd survive out here without it," said Emil, wiping his hands on his pants.

Oliver rose, staring at the intermittent drizzle. He offered Emil a strip of jerky and grabbed his backpack. "Before we call it a day, I'm going to head southwest, follow the wall."

Antonio grabbed his machete and smiled like he was preparing for a day at the beach. Oliver shook his head and offered a strip of jerky to Antonio, then shoved the last bite into his mouth. While he chewed, he slapped Antonio's back, and together, the two men disappeared into the jungle.

Sometimes, Oliver stumbled, almost falling. The terrain was rough; hidden roots sprouted hands, grabbing, tripping human feet. In the air, vines sprouted fingers, continuously snagging, and snaring. Antonio kept chopping. Oliver followed, watching for spiders, worried for snakes. Above them, a pack of spider monkeys jostled the branches as if they were part of the team. "Let's not get lost, Antonio," warned Oliver.

They stayed close to the wall. Rain and repetitive whacking were the only audible sounds. Oliver stopped every few yards, leaving survey markers, taking notes, and collecting fragments he shifted from the soil.

After another hour, Oliver stopped and checked the time; he pushed a red marker into the soil at his feet and looked up at the sky through a hole in the canopy, realizing the rain had stopped. The forest was suddenly bright. Slipping his notepad into his backpack, Oliver reached for his water bottle.

Antonio thrust his machete into the earth, looking for a resting place. Oliver surveyed his surroundings, turning and craning his neck. After a minute, he adjusted his hat, looking through an opening in the trees—something glistened.

Picking up Antonio's machete, Oliver motioned for the other man to remain where he sat. He moved forward, slowly approaching the shiny object, traversing mossy stones, roots, and weeds. Oliver ducked under branches until he stood over the thing. He swiveled; there were mirrors, strange metal fragments, and pieces of glass everywhere he looked. Oliver placed his hand over his mouth, rubbing a trail around his lips. "What the hell?" he asked the air, his voice shaky, vibrating. "Antonio!" he yelled.

Oliver lowered his hand, placing both hands on his hips. "Holy fucking shit," he spat.

Commence Cerebral Streaming—

Session Seven

There is an unmistakable effervescence afflicting the crew today. Dulfim loaded the newest games into our entertainment system. Oh, how I love a new game! But games aside, this is a critical mission. Accounting for the dilation of time, we will arrive in the atmosphere of the tiny Blue Earth in the calendar year 2009. This time, it is much more than a transfer of vital supplies to our Atlantic-dwelling crew and our latent crew, living deep in the bowels of Antarctica. (Our Antarctic crew has found many peculiar creatures, including icefish. Extraordinary.)

Besides the peculiar discoveries, our latest voyage is an ongoing research and sample appropriation trip, with an extracurricular mission designed to bestow world-altering knowledge unto the meat-eaters. It is the last implementation before, in approximately two hundred years, we estimate their world will suffer mass extinction and undergo creative terraforming by our leading scientists.

The *choosers* have selected a child with a favorable sense of humor. Our futurists predict he will launch a simple vehicle—only meant for earthly pavement—high into the cosmos. How peculiar.

The meat-eaters do such whimsical and bizarre things. Sadly, they also do things most foul. But I will not ruminate on those deeds now.

Rigel has loaded the sacred knowledge, and Sula will be the intermediary when our secondary vessel is close to the targeted meat-eater. My curiosity is piqued. Listeners, it wasn't that long ago, when *only* the Deities bestowed knowledge. Now, we too, are a conduit of intelligence.

However, such serious matters do not amuse me. I have better thoughts to contemplate, like nutrition. Rigel informed me that our nourishment tablets will include the delicious roots of the green orchid. During our conversation, I overheard—yes, I was listening—that Rigel would miss me. This thought is curious and perplexing.

Thoughts of delicious flowers make me melancholy for the public gardens of my homeland. Now that I dwell upon it, if the minds listening to this data are as interested as my own, they must wonder about my place of origin. My home planet is unlike the Blue Earth ahead of us, with its deep blue waters, tropical jungles, and miles of plains leading to forested mountains and icefish. Indeed, the Blue Earth is a marvelous planet. Too good for its inhabitants. Our world is vastly different. We, as its stewards, are infinitely different.

I will begin with my dome: a public garden inhabits a perfect circle outside our living quarters, alive with imported birds and exotic flora as diverse as the most extensive jungles of the tiny Blue Earth. Outside the dome, sand rules. Our vast mountains have dissolved into multi-colored heaps that resemble a massive earthly layer cake with rust, gold, white and green.

On our planet, we never stop learning; the universe is ripe. After this trip, we will possess enough samples to replicate the Blue

Earth during the inevitable terraforming and enhance our domes' ever-growing variety.

Happiness reigns supreme on Pleione. It is pervasive, like a love virus. Every day, after our studies, we exit our classrooms to harvest fruit and vegetables to feed our community. The plants are happy to provide. Nothing is wasted; even potato peels are dried and eaten as snacks. I have a favorite food, and as you may have guessed, and it is a green orchid. Although, our green orchid is unlike those found in the Blue Earth's jungles. Our savory flower is like a Venus flytrap. What a humorous name. Undoubtedly, the meat-eaters are comical, especially in appearance.

Our green orchid eats the insects pollinating the garden, and its roots grow as tasty and nutritious as seaweed. Eating the crunchy seeds fresh is a revelation. After our harvest, we eat among the slender palms at the center of the courtyard, relishing a momentary respite from our relentless suns. Now, floating in darkness, I would be happy to feel the suns' sizzling caress.

Listeners, I wish you could see my home. The radiant colors of our gardens resemble earthly rainbows, and the giant crystal dome above acts like an intelligent terrarium with foamy clouds and a predictable cycle of cooling rain. Myriad species of birds, insects, and pollinators reside among us. However, the earthly grass animals that we have grown through our DNA database live in zoo domes. The toothy, armored dinosaurs are terrifying. I am glad they have a terrarium far away from mine!

Someday, our disc may create a zoo dome. When I visited the beastly domes as a child of thirty-three, I had diabolical nightmares for years. My brain spun monster-filled fantasies of white tigers, growling, gnashing their stained, yellow teeth, and growing white-feathered wings that lifted them to the heavens. I saw black bulls with stomping hooves, transforming into the grasses they ate, drying and undulating until they eventually blew away and dispersed over the plains of Pleione. The dreams were bizarre and astonishing.

Now, I only dream of the beauty and grace of beasts, both big and small. I can't wait to grow a zoo. There will be no bulls in my zoo. No cows.

Before I was born, space crews collected DNA from almost every creature that roams the tiny Blue Earth. We do not kill or eat animals, so we feed our zoo beasts with meat grown from our bovine DNA samples. It is a dreadful affair but necessary. I've always felt that cows are strange as they move toward you, chewing and staring. I imagine them chewing their way into my soul.

My favorite creatures, by far, are our rare and beautiful bird species. They are glorious, flying inside the domes, flashing their iridescent feathers like one of our vessels racing with the slow and primitive airplanes of the tiny Blue Earth. I feel envy when I gaze at these feathered creatures. Avifauna is the perfect example, demonstrating that head size does not equate to brainpower. Birds are very knowledgeable given their diminutive size. Our ships may be faster, but they will never be as beautiful as the feathered beasts.

Often, I think about our ability to recreate any creature in the universe, but it never ceases to amaze me that the Deities did it with no DNA whatsoever. This idea is curious. We can recreate, but only *They* have the power to create.

Sula and her family live at a forty-five-degree angle from my classroom. I wish that I could live as Sula's mate. But the stars did not align in my favor.

Our educators have supplied this mission with enough games to expand our knowledge like an earthly sea sponge for years until our return. I am curious to play the games Dulfim loaded onto our secondary vessel. And this thought is an important reminder that it is time to go.

Continue Universal Translation Mode—End of Session.

Joseph

Joseph pulled the *hojas* from the water bath, placing them on a flattened dishtowel. He selected a single cornhusk, patted it dry, and spread a layer of masa and a dollop of blood red chili sauce. Fat dripped from his fingers as the final layer of shredded pork completed the tamal. After carefully folding it, he placed it in the biggest pot from Esme's cupboards. Joseph started the process again. "Do you want me to make half the tamales without pork—just the chili sauce?" he asked, turning to where she hovered behind him.

Esme took a deep breath, raising her eyebrows, seemingly inhaling the intoxicating smell. "Maybe, but the pork smells so amazing—I never used to eat meat. Now, I keep giving in to my cravings. I can't seem to make up my mind," she said, reaching for a clean spoon and then dipping it into the pot of chili sauce beside Joseph's elbow. She placed the spoon over her tongue like it was a lollipop. "God, this sauce is good," she murmured.

Joseph stuck his pinky into the saucepan, tasting. "I was going to make my mother's mole, but I couldn't find mulato or pasilla peppers at Publix. Only ancho. When I was a kid, when we lived in Mexico City, we would go to the Mercado de la Merced for peppers," said Joseph.

Pausing, he placed his sticky hands on the counter, his eyes far away, probing the tiled wall before him like he was watching a movie. He shook his head. "We would go to the market. It was my favorite thing. The food! Esme, you've never seen anything like it. The smells, the cilantro and flowers, the plantains and yucca, the ripe bananas and cumin. The peppers! So many, all colors. Some brown, dried—as tough as leather; some as bright as a red corvette. Purple, green, so good. The fruit was the best I've ever tasted. Papayas as big as pumpkins. My mother and I would browse the stalls until her basket was full. I would carry a big watermelon in my tiny arms." Joseph cradled his arms for effect before continuing. "I couldn't wait to eat. It was such a happy time for me. My mother made the best mole in Mexico."

Joseph grabbed a new corn husk, then put it back. "At Christmas, we would have a *Tamalada*. My cousins, aunts, grandmother, everyone would come, and we'd make tamales. My grandmother is still alive. Can you believe that? I will see her first thing when I get to Mexico City. My grandmother would say, 'Alma, put down the Rompope. We must work. We must make the tamales!' My mother would drain her drink, slam it on the counter, and kiss my grandmother on the lips. They never shooed me out of the kitchen. I watched and listened. I knew all the gossip. I remember their recipes," said Joseph, tapping his skull.

He continued his work. Esme watched, massaging his shoulders, and leaning to wipe a speck of food from his cheek. "I suppose you should make a few without meat," she said slowly, unsure of herself. "But how will we know which ones are vegetarian?"

Joseph peered over his shoulder. "I will tie a corn husk bow for you. Wait a minute. Shoot. The masa has pork stock and lard. They won't be vegetarian. Will you still eat them? I'm sorry. You know, I've also felt that I should give up meat. I don't know why. I've gone weeks without meat—lots of beans. You know? It used to drive Mitzi crazy. She never knew what to expect."

Esme smiled. "We have so much in common. Okay, I give up. Just put meat in all of them. God, they smell so good," she said, reaching for the pan of shredded meat with her fingers. She plopped a fingerful into her mouth, the juices dripping onto her shirt.

Esme appraised her chest, rubbing circles over a burgeoning grease stain. She swallowed, rolling her eyes. "So good. I don't think I'm a vegetarian anymore."

Joseph laughed. "Me neither."

"Tell me more about Mexico City. I can visit you, right?" said Esme, with a high, hopeful voice.

Joseph nodded and reached for the chili sauce but stopped midway, recoiling his hands over the counter. Again, he stared at the tile in front of him with a queer expression applied to his face. "I was incredibly young, but the memories are still vivid. We left Mexico City so long ago; I think I was seven or eight...There were so many flags and Jesus statues everywhere in Mexico City. I went to the market with my mother, but with my father, I saw Diego Rivera's murals. The murals were amazing, but I preferred graffiti art, you know? My dad showed me the grand churches, but to tell the truth, I liked the small, weathered buildings better and the streets lined with jacaranda trees dripping with purple flowers. My dad would marvel at the baroque architecture while I was peering inside tiny, smudgy windows to see what people were cooking. I remember my feet would be so tired and my mind so bored. Still, my dad would drag me to the Hotel Ciudad or the Coyoacán. Mexico City is a sensory overload of colors, sounds, smells, and tastes. My dad would marvel at the *murales*, but I was too young to care about such things. Now, though, I can't wait to see everything with fresh eyes. I might make my father proud yet."

Joseph returned to his tamales. Now, his demeanor was stiff, his expression serious. Esme leaned her hip against the kitchen counter. "I wonder what our dads are doing right now..." she asked the room.

Joseph glanced at Esme, then scooped a portion of meat, lacing it over a tamal. "I think they are probably drinking rum and telling tall tales." He looked at the clock on the microwave. "Okay. They are probably hard at work, digging something with a baby spoon or scraping the soil with a Barbie comb."

Esme started laughing. "Is that what you think they do all day?"

"No, but I know it's not always fun—boring even. My dad always exaggerated. He told me stories that made it seem fun and exciting. When I first arrived in Guatemala, I feared the howler monkeys. One morning, he told me that the monkeys cried and howled because they were sad that they weren't human. He said the monkeys were cursed and under a spell. Every morning, at four a.m., they'd howl to Hun-Batz, one of the howler monkey gods. They'd cry every day, hoping the spell would reverse, hoping to turn back into humans. To this day, they still cry in vain. Hun-Batz doesn't listen."

"I like that story. Your dad is cool. I miss my dad. My mom's been calling me. I haven't called her back."

"You should call her. You only get one mother. I would do anything to get mine back."

Joseph raised his right hand, and without touching his shirt, he did the sign of the cross.

Esme shifted her feet. "My mom is so weird. Your mom was sweet. I remember her. You never met my mom. All she cares about is Cosmostheology."

Joseph wrapped the last tamal and placed it in the pot. Heading to the sink to wash his hands, he felt terrible for Esme. Joseph wished that she would think of her mother with more kindness. However, he knew how she felt. There was a hidden chamber in his heart where blood didn't flow. That's where he kept the lousy energy—the negative thoughts about his father.

"I knew it. You're not perfect!" Esme exclaimed. "I heard what you were thinking about your dad in your heart of hearts!"

"Don't do that! I don't read your thoughts."

"But how could you? *Can* you read my thoughts?"

"No, of course not," Joseph replied, drying his hands, and looking at the floor. Let's change the subject. Are you hungry? Should I steam the tamales?"

Esme embraced Joseph greedily. "I'm starving. Besides, I can't wait to perform tonight. I'm *Jade* when I work. Did you know that? It's my magic name, my performance name. Isn't it beautiful? My dad wanted to name me *Jade*, but my mother picked *Esme*," she said, rolling her eyes. "You'll film me, right? Watch me?"

Joseph turned and gave her a gentle, tentative kiss. "I will always watch my Esme."

Joseph held his phone at chest level, biting his lower lip in concentration. He started filming. In front of the phone, Esme interacted with a modest crowd. She was no longer performing any magic tricks—only levitation. Which, he supposed, was the highest form of magic there was. Except, it wasn't magic at all. It was real.

At the very least, Joseph was relieved that she had taken his advice and was using a deck of cards instead of heavier objects. All magicians utilized cards. No one would suspect a thing.

He smiled behind the phone when Esme knelt, extending a splayed fan of cards in front of a little blond boy in a Mickey Mouse shirt and matching hat. The boy jerked away, smashing his rosy face into his father's kneecaps, grasping tiny arms and sweaty fingers around his father's calves. Esme rose and shuffled her cards. She surveyed the crowd dispersed over the sidewalk near Café Cascabel on International Drive.

Esme looked sexy, he thought, with her auburn hair backlit by a steamy, setting sun. She was wearing a puffy, white cotton blouse with turquoise embroidered roses and a mini denim skirt with a frayed hem. Joseph's eyes trailed Esme's white, creamy legs to the toes she had painted cherry red. He looked back up, waiting for her next move.

This time, Esme splayed the cards before the father's outstretched hand. The man selected the queen of hearts, holding it up for everyone to see. Esme backed up five feet and smiled. "Now, put the card into your pants pocket," she instructed.

Joseph kept filming, watching as Esme retrieved a tiny wand from the back pocket of her skirt. She pointed it at the man, swirling it like she was casting a spell. The crowd tittered, and so did Joseph—he couldn't help himself. She was good at this.

The crowd gasped when the card flipped from the man's pocket, floating over his head. All eyes watched the card rocket into the sky, then stream into the mother's purse. The blond woman reached into her bag, retrieved the card, checked for strings, then held it up for everyone to see. Joseph knew there were no strings. No tricks.

Murmuring voices dispersed through the crowd. *By the looks on their faces, they've become enchanted with my Esme.* People clapped, some shook their heads, and a few scattered to their cars. Still, the crowd grew.

Esme approached a little girl with brown hair and dimples. Then she knelt, displaying her cards like a fan of turkey feathers. The brown-haired girl squealed with delight, selecting the four of clubs. "Can you place the card on your head?" asked Esme, rising and backing away.

The girl giggled and, sticking out her tongue, placed the card on her head. The card immediately slipped off, falling to the ground. The girl's happy expression vanished as she knelt, picking it up with serious eyes like she had just committed a crime.

Esme laughed. The crowd laughed. The little girl's mother took the card from her daughter's sticky fingers and placed it back on her daughter's head. This time, it stayed.

Esme wiggled her wand. The crowd watched as the card spiraled, swirling as if caught on the breeze. Slowly, the card danced, landing on the Mickey Mouse cap of the shy little boy. His father grabbed it, knelt, and showed it to his son. The boy's eyes expanded.

Esme continued her games until the sun set over Orlando. The lights of International Drive flickered to life: restaurants by the dozens, whizzing headlights and taillights, streetlights, hotels, billboards, and dozens of phones. The crowd of tourists morphed from large to small and back again as people walked the sidewalk and passed the show.

As darkness settled over the town, Joseph stopped filming. His hands slipped into his pockets as he watched with a luminous smile at the back of the crowd. The previous misgivings melted into pride and admiration for Esme. Maybe, it wasn't his place to interfere with her career or prevent her from doing what she loved. Although, he would always worry.

Joseph's heart skipped a beat when an ear-piercing squeal erupted in the street. Tingles shot down his arms to the tips of his fingers; his hands flew from his pockets. Somewhere ahead of him, tires screeched, and drivers leaned on their horns. The crowd in front of him screamed and flailed. Joseph realized what was happening, his heart thumping like a drum. Without hesitation, he closed his eyes and pushed at the air ahead of his chest with his palms. His ears exploded with an alternating tone. Utilizing the power deep within his brain, he grabbed control of the errant car—the one careening into the crowd towards Esme. He lifted the car into the air, tires spinning. The startled driver stared from her side window as if caught in a nightmare. Joseph gripped the vehicle in a mind-meld, hovering the car over the crowd, with dirt and debris falling like raindrops from the rotating tires. Joseph felt like he was no longer on Earth. Now, his body was a rotating ball of neurons exiled to inner space. Squeezing his eyes and clenching his fists, he floated the car like a toy, as light as a feather, placing it in the parking lot of Café Cascabel.

Joseph opened his eyes.

Initiate Cerebral Streaming—

Recording Session One

My father named me Sula. On Pleione, this designation means *healer of souls*; and I feel blessed to occupy my life practicing science and care.

Whenever I travel without my family— my mate, children, and beloved parents—I *still* feel close to them. I always know when they are thinking of me; the energy from their messages transforms the air I breathe. I hear the humming of insects, and my skin tingles. Their energy replenishes me.

Today is different; my thoughts are colliding like an energy collision of charged protons. First, the neural fish swim toward fear. Then, they turn the corner and wiggle toward excitement. This cycle continues until I fall asleep. Dob-Dec assured me we would be safe. I trust his judgment.

Dob-Dec has been streaming his thoughts, keeping a mental log of our mission. He suggested it might be therapeutic for me, too, as we approach the electromagnetic doorway. It is humorous that Dob-Dec is giving me a prescription for peace when I am the healer.

I have treated Dob-Dec several times on this mission. He is prone to mysterious accidents and peculiar ailments. His misfortune is an anomaly since we have nearly eliminated illness and pain among *Beings*. Dob-Dec often acts like a child of thirty, playing simple games and always curious to learn the things he does not know. Someday, he might understand the nature of the universe—if he lives long enough.

Dob-Dec is fascinated by the formation of gravitational wormholes, or electromagnetic portals, like the one we will pass through soon. Yesterday, everyone had such animated conversations about portals that they created a vortex with their nourishment tablets. The wafers were flying everywhere *except* into the mouths of the crew. The contagious laughter calmed my soul.

I'm not laughing now. I fear the unknown. Several thousand years ago, portals were simply a quantum passage into the dimension of Deities. We did not utilize them for travel. Only the most extreme and curious crews entered until a ship returned. Now, intergalactic travel is commonplace. Still, I am afraid.

Even so, I am eager to enter the Blue Earth's atmosphere and see it in person for the first time. I have traveled to many planets, but never one so distant. Soon, I will understand the world of human-hybrids firsthand.

Rigel has given me a curious assignment: a cerebral interaction with a human male. I've decided to present myself as a Felidae, as hybrids do not eat cats. They do, however, exhibit irrational behavior. They are flawed, inferior, imbalanced, emotional, and servants to their technical devices. Hybrids have adequate intelligence but still do not protect Earth.

They wage war like hornets.

Even so, we may not fully comprehend their relevance in the universe. Humans do not understand the power of sound, but I have heard them sing with the voice of Deities. Now I believe they *do* have merit.

My tales of Earth will electrify my children. They hope to see the small planet for themselves someday. But then again, all children want to travel to Earth when they are grown. It is unfortunate to contemplate what happened to Pleione's children, the young minds that traveled to New Mexico alone. Now, *Beings* must reach their fiftieth year before solo space travel is allowed.

Rigel has ordered a thorough analysis of the effects of living underground in Antarctica. I was surprised when Rigel assigned me to the secondary vessel. There are other *Beings* qualified to assess the health of the earthly crews. A remote evaluation is standard. Planet Earth is not my area of expertise, as I have never seen a hybrid. But I will defer to Rigel's supreme wisdom.

I overheard a superficial thought during a conversation with Rigel before we departed HaYax. Now I suspect that Rigel aspires to make Dob-Dec happy. Perhaps Rigel loves Dob-Dec. But then again, all *Beings* love Dob-Dec.

We are playing his favorite game tonight, a children's game. Dob-Dec has a young heart. Although, *tonight* is a misleading term. I yearn for the warmth of the suns, the cacophony of smells, and the tastes from my dome. The nourishment we glean from the solar gardens inside HaYax—our mothership—along with a mix of nutritional wafers, tablets, and dehydrated snacks, cannot compare to the fresh delicacies we grow at home: plumeria blooms and green orchid roots, mild runga fruit and the spicy flesh of curooga pears, looping shunts, pink grapefruit, and other exotic varieties imported and grown from Planet Earth. I crave lapock shoots as green as the sands of the Pladoon plains.

My tongue is growing restless. I miss the pop of Kapa seeds inside my mouth! We have hundreds of Kapa cobs in our dehydrated packets and a seemingly endless array of Meera and dried Adara peel. We are saving these treats for the Antarctic and Atlantic crews, along with a myriad supply of nutrition they cannot find on the tiny Planet Earth. I would never appropriate their treats. Fear has stimulated my appetite, but I must not dwell on nutrition. Before I leave my quarters, I will meditate with my family. Farewell, listeners.

Resume Universal Translation Mode—
End of Session One.

Oliver

Oliver sat amidst the dirt and debris frosting the top of La Danta, his hair damp from sweat, and his shirt adhered to his chest. He watched a turkey vulture soaring in the distance, distracted, and lost, thinking about the thin metal fragment lodged between his thumb and forefinger. It felt like a chip from a cheap aluminum can; he'd never seen anything like it. The braille-like lettering resembled strange hieroglyphics. Possibly, it wasn't even metal at all.

They returned to the debris field the next day, and upon further excavation, they found bones. The bones were a mottled green and strange, not human or animal. Oliver suspected—or knew—what the scene contained, but he didn't know what to do about it. He still hadn't reported his findings. Emil agreed.

They spent two weeks threading the tree-strewn perimeter and carefully cataloging fragments. Findings included thousands of shards of glass that reflected light in a strange, rainbow-like way, plus tiny irregular bones, and unusual metal fragments. The duo hauled samples—just a few small pieces—back to camp and didn't tell a soul. A discovery this extraordinary needed to stay contained.

Oliver hoped that Antonio and Phillip would keep their secret until the samples Antonio absconded from the camp were returned from analysis. But Oliver didn't need confirmation to know what he was looking at: the scene contained scattered remains from an alien spaceship. Oliver's pulse quickened just thinking of the word: *Alien*. He hadn't had a good night's sleep since he found the debris field. *What if there was drift? What if the ship bounced?* Debris could be scattered for miles. Oliver felt like a kid at a carnival. "Damn, this is going to change my life," he whispered to the winds.

Oliver made a fist, crumpling the enclosed material. Then he opened his hand, holding his palm flat. The material sprung back, flattening like it was eerily animated. His pulse raced as he pulled an unusually long finger bone from his pocket, slipping it from a plastic sleeve. *Does the Guatemalan government have rights to the contents of an extraterrestrial crash on their soil? Who investigates? The ICAO? The United Nations? Guatemala?* Usually, the country of origin would oversee the investigation. But, in this case, there was no country of origin.

Puffing and grunting sounds, then scrabbling erupted behind his head. He twisted around and eyeballed a red Yankee's baseball cap, then Emil's head. Emil crested the pyramid and stood, surveying the view. After a few quiet seconds, he shrugged the backpack off his shoulders, slapping the dust from his hands and pants. The man sat beside Oliver, emitting a sigh for the ages. "Beautiful. Never get sick of sunset up here," Emil huffed, crossing his legs.

"You smell ripe."

"So, do you, my friend," Emil replied.

Oliver opened his palm, displaying his treasure. Emil grabbed it, rubbing the bone with his finger. "I know we're on the same page here. We know what we're looking at, right? So, now what?

The crash isn't that old, maybe ten, fifteen years. We were here the summer of 2009—2010, too. I don't remember hearing a crash, though," Emil stated, handing the bone back to Oliver.

Oliver accepted the bone, closing his fist around it. "Analysis is key. Maybe we're wrong. Maybe, it's NASA or some other secret government aircraft that crashed. But why would they be flying over Central America? And that still wouldn't explain the bone fragments. It would be irrefutable if we found an elongated skull with super-sized bug eyes."

"Maybe animals ate the skull."

"Or *skulls*."

"Would foxes do that? Coyotes maybe? There're no wolves here. We need to keep looking for more bones."

"If we keep going to the crash scene, we'll need to explain or show field results. Maybe we should tell Esteban the truth," Oliver said, scowling.

"I want to keep this between us until we get the results. I hope Antonio doesn't talk. I'm worried about looters making off with our little green men."

"By the look of this forefinger, they weren't so little," Oliver stated, rolling the bone between his fingers. "No evidence of fire. The bones don't seem charred. That's weird, too, with a crash this catastrophic."

"Maybe they don't use fuel."

"Maybe not. Man, that's what's so exciting about this. The unknown! It's going to be a circus down there if the results indicate it's extraterrestrial," said Oliver, pulling the metal fragment out for inspection. He showed it to Emil.

"We don't need an Egyptologist. The writing isn't hieroglyphics or Mayan glyphs. It looks similar, though."

"What do you think they were doing here? Best guess?"

Emil removed his baseball cap, wiping his brow with a handkerchief. Then he returned the hat to his head and threw out his arms. "Enjoying the view! What else?"

The men laughed. Emil lifted two *Gallos* from the sides of his backpack, handing one to Oliver. They clinked bottles. "To aliens!" Oliver shouted to the sky.

Emil reached into his pocket, retrieving his crocodile bottle opener. He popped the caps. They both took a long pull. "Warm. But good," Oliver said.

"Damn good."

Oliver stared at the soil between his knees as if he'd just discovered King Tut's cavernous, golden tomb. He reached down, flicking plant matter off the curved piece of metal, then rubbed his hand over the mysterious symbols. They looked like watermarks drying on cement; it was as if they were organic, unrelated, and random.

Picking up his spade, Oliver traced around the metal's irregular perimeter. It glinted like a foreign hubcap sunbathing in a tiny spot of sun. The shard was the size of a piece of bread, the biggest scrap he'd found yet. Oliver left the remnant embedded in the topsoil and used his right arm to wipe his brow. Shifting his weight, he grabbed his camera and snapped a photo, then left the object framed in the dirt and moved over to the jungle floor's next lumpy square. *The chunkier, the better,* he figured. Oliver kept hoping for a head-shaped form—the skull of an alien. He felt competitive with Emil, wanting the big find all to himself.

As if on cue, Emil approached, slinking between the spindly trunks of two jiote trees; the man carefully planted his steps like he was playing a game of hopscotch. Eventually, Emil crouched beside Oliver. "It's weird. It's mostly small pieces, almost like the craft was made from shatterproof glass."

Oliver looked at Emil. "I know. It's what we're not finding that bothers me. Where is the hulking shell of a spaceship? Where is the engine? The insides of the ship? The pieces with writing—or symbols—are different. They must be made from another form of metal. The outer shards broke into larger, more irregular shapes. I guess that would make sense. Possibly a cheaper, nonfunctional part of the craft. Decorative."

"Possibly. You know, it's almost like the ship self-destructed to prevent reverse engineering by the likes of us," Emil said, wiping his mouth with the back of his hand.

"And another thing," added Oliver. But he stopped mid-sentence to grab his shovel, crossing to the wheelbarrow with a load of spoils, and returning. "There's no holes, screws, parts, joints, nothing. It's almost like they made the ship with a 3D printer."

"Interesting thought," said Emil with a shoulder shrug.

"Any more bone fragments?"

"Nope. I'm beginning to think an animal stole the bones. They could be anywhere. They're probably in Belize by now," said Emil twisting his hips and staring off into the surrounding jungle.

"I bet the aliens self-destruct too. You know, like spontaneous combustion. To prevent us from doing an alien autopsy," said Oliver with a foolish smirk.

"Ha! Now you're getting silly. But who knows…Maybe?"

Oliver fell back onto his heels. "You know, last night, I had a nightmare. I was battling a giant, drooling lizard. It didn't end well.

Man, I woke up sweating—even more than usual. What do you think they look like? I try to picture them, but all I see is movie magic."

"I don't think they look like movie monsters. I think they look like the little green people we've always imagined. But now we know they're bigger and taller, which makes sense because zero gravity elongates the spine. Perhaps, they are graceful, beautiful beings. I wish we'd find more bones to complete the physical puzzle. They've got to be out there, don't you think?"

"I know they are. But will we find the missing pieces before the circus? Every time we come here, it's one more nail in my career coffin. But this is so damn big I don't care."

Emil looked up into the jungle canopy. "Best keep working. We're running out of daylight."

Oliver watched Emil squeeze through the trees, before returning to his own patch of ground. Slowly, he picked at the surface layer with a trowel, peeling back the earth, shifting it horizontally, and leaving the contents where they lay.

Another hour passed and Oliver fell into a quiet rhythm, sweating profusely while listening to an ongoing soundtrack of jungle sounds and the occasional outburst from Emil across the way. The repetitive mewling of a toucan in the distance soothed his soul. He felt happy, never more content in his work. It almost didn't bother him that for the last hour, he hadn't found a damn thing.

Meanwhile, Emil was hooting and hollering every ten minutes, but Oliver knew there was *no* way he was working that fast or discovering that many things. Oliver suspected Emil was taunting him and snickered under his breath.

After scouring another weedy square of earth, Oliver carried his spoils to the wheelbarrow and moved over, appraising the new ground with a curious brow. There appeared to be something buried in this section. But it could be anything: a rock, a dead animal, a piece of a spaceship, or maybe a precious skull.

Oliver's heartbeat accelerated.

Carefully, he peeled back a thin layer of earth, smearing the soil away from the smooth surface of an unusual object with his hand. Oliver stared at the thing, then fumbled in his pocket for a paintbrush. He flicked the clear surface like he was brushing dust from the Mona Lisa herself. A strange light illuminated his face from below. Oliver rubbed around his mouth, swallowing, his pulse beating rapidly in his neck. "Holy fucking shit," he whispered.

Oliver's hands hovered over the object; it took every ounce of reserve to leave it where it lay. He rocked back and adjusted his hat. His face felt wet. But when he appraised the sky, it was clear, with an orange glow settling over the jungle. Cicadas roared. Oliver brushed his cheek with the back of his hand, realizing that tears were streaming down his chin.

"Emil! Goddamnit, Emil!" Oliver shouted.

Directly across from him, twenty feet away, Emil stood. "What? Did you find a goddamn skull? Fuck me."

Oliver stood, staring at his friend. "No, I found something better. Get your ass over here. You won't believe what I just found."

Commence Cerebral Streaming—

Session Eight

The secondary vessel will enter the Blue Earth wormhole in twenty-nine hours. Soon, I'll collect an endless array of new samples and specimens. My heart is ticklish, thinking about the impending release of new and improved insect drones the size of earthly mosquitos. Knowing I will soon see the Blue Earth again is uplifting; it energizes me. I can't wait to witness the endless diversity along the parallel energy lines: jungles of green foliage teaming with fragile life, ice mountains, cold and bright, and abundant water. There is always more to learn and discover.

Listeners, we must be cautious with our work. I am grateful that it is not my position to study meat-eaters. There is no light-refracting cloak suitable to calm my fears. Our ocean and Antarctic crews are brave, working hidden among the volatile hybrids. Meat-eaters are not as scary as cows. Still, they unsettle me. They are unpredictable creatures with brains as inflexible as stone.

We have watched meat-eaters fight inside rectangular rings for no reason whatsoever. To make matters worse, they now fight in large octagons, like beasts in a zoo. Their violence inside these rings is not instigated by anger. This concept is most bizarre. I have seen documentaries of the many wars of the Blue Earth, and the footage is most frightening. Potential interactions with the meat-eaters are so dangerous that we have limited our missions, sometimes sending only drones or synthetic crews. Most of all, we rely on our stations—our brave Blue Earth *Beings*.

Over the centuries, we have tried to educate meat-eaters, to elevate them. Still, they act like angry monkeys. This subject is depressing.

We had much distraction and fun aboard our little ship tonight. We played many games. The flight crew was too busy preparing for our mission to play with us. Still, we had fun. Sula and I played the levitation game, beloved by the children of Pleione. I still love to play it.

I am not acting condescending when I say that you, the listener, cannot play this game (especially if you are a meat-eater). It is an undisputed truth. I will issue instructions: First, the players go to separate quarters. We are permitted to read each other's minds. (The joy!) We may enter our opponent's mind—my heart bounces at the thought— to deceive them.

After the players separate and apply a blinding apparatus, we take turns levitating objects into the other player's zone of solitude. We can send unseen objects spinning around our opponent like a meteor, but the other player cannot physically touch them. The opponent could easily guess the thing without seeing— that is not the trick. The trick is to fool the other player's brain into thinking the object is something other than what it truly is. It is most challenging to levitate objects and bend minds simultaneously— but oh, so fun! It was almost impossible with Sula because she has the most flexible brain.

I won when I levitated an ancient, tiny basalt stone around Sula's head like a buzzing bee, convincing her it was galaxite. She laughed on the inside when I placed the rock into her hand. I hope I calmed her mind since I know she has battled fear. Sula's safety and happiness are paramount.

Now, I must sleep. I will prepare my mind for the work ahead.

Universal Translation Mode—End of Session.

Joseph

Joseph thanked the young Uber driver and stepped from the car, feeling somewhat lost as the car sped away. He stared across the street at the cream-colored structure with three arched doors. St. Margaret Mary Catholic Church was beautiful and welcoming, unlike a New York cathedral with its warm, rough stucco, red-copper roof tiles, and lush greenery. Joseph removed his sunglasses, squinting. After staring for an eternity, he stashed his book under his arm and looked both ways. This time, he was going in—he had to.

A subtle fingerless push lingered near his shoulder blade, even though no one was behind him. He figured it was his mother urging him forward. Finally, he crossed the street, and walked to the center door. He entered without hesitation.

An audible intake of breath followed as Joseph appraised the room. Beautiful blue windows illuminated both sides of the church, like long slits framing a starry night sky. The windows cast a heavenly light over the empty wooden pews, with dust motes floating gracefully amidst the sunbeams. Joseph stared at the pulpit and, above, at the bright metal sun surrounding the bowed head of Jesus. The figurine was hanging on the cross with a solemn expression. "Jesus died for my sins," Joseph whispered.

He swallowed, completing the sign of the cross.

Joseph walked down the aisle, feeling pulled in opposite directions—he didn't belong here. Twisting around, he looked over his shoulder, half expecting to see a trail of fiery footprints in his wake. Joseph felt too bedeviled to be at church. Still, he wanted to confess. What would it take to quiet his heart? Joseph imagined his mother's hands on his shoulders, urging him forward, and he imagined her whispering sweet words to calm his breathing, which was loud like he was doing push-ups.

He stopped at the end of the red carpet, looking up at a large flat-screen television hanging above his head. On its screen were images of the car he intercepted, floating through the air with rotating tires amid screams of confusion and anguish, like a news report. Joseph blinked. Now, the television was black, empty. Maybe, he was going nuts.

Moving towards the confessional, he pulled the curtain aside. He sat, emitting the sigh that typically precedes the most solemn tasks.

"Hail Mary, Full of Grace," said the priest, adding, "That sigh sounds ominous."

Joseph heard the priest adjust his seat as if steadying himself for battle.

"I hear you, my child," the voice compelled.

Joseph cleared his throat. "Father...." He stopped, buttoning his lips, his mind racing, eyes darting. Unknowingly, his face contorted—he didn't know how to describe his demons. *The priest will never believe me!*

"Whatever you have done, He knows. His mercy is infinite. He knows your sin, and He's waiting for you to unburden yourself—Go ahead, my son."

"Father, I don't know where to begin. I'm worried you won't believe me. I'm...I'm not insane. I know this will sound crazy, but I'm telling the truth. I would never lie to a priest."

"I'm listening."

"I can do strange and powerful things. I've had this ability ever since I was a kid. I can move things with my mind. Now, I can read Esme's thoughts too. I try to block them out, but I can't. The other night..."

"Son, who is this Esme? Is this your wife?"

"No, my friend. I mean, I think of her as a sister. We're very good friends. Maybe, like girlfriend and boyfriend. I can't decide. I don't know."

The priest sniffed as if stifling a chuckle.

"Son, how does Esme feel about you? Does she feel the same way?"

Joseph shook his head. "No, Father, she loves me with all her heart—in a carnal way, like man and wife. But I don't take advantage. We haven't done anything yet."

There was silence and shifting of fabric. "Hmm...I trust you, son. Continue."

"The other night, I moved a car with my mind. It flew like a paper airplane tossed by the hand of God—or Diablo. Esme can levitate objects, too. Our power is so strong it defies the law of physics. It scares me! I don't want a superpower. But, my Esme, she loves it. She uses it all the time. Father, I've never moved anything that big or heavy. Only, well, I moved Mitzi once and kept her from falling. I mean, when I was a kid, I did things. I experimented then, but not anymore. Father, do you think the devil possesses me? I only use my power for good."

Joseph wiped a tear from his cheek.

There was a long pause. Joseph could hear the sleeves of the priest's robe, fabric rubbing, and the man breathing. "Son, you say your girlfriend also possesses this ability?"

"Yes. I'm so scared for Esme."

"Pray, my child. Prayer helps," said the priest, his voice growing quiet.

Joseph could hear the man scratching his whiskers. "I believe you speak the truth as you see it. Still, this matter, well... Maybe you should also talk with a psychiatrist. I'm somewhat at a loss..." The priest paused, clearing his throat. "What you are describing... I don't think the devil possesses you. If this were true, if you and Esme have a superpower, it would be a gift from God. Do you believe in miracles? If what you're saying truly happened, then God intervened, performed a miracle, and you witnessed it. Possibly, He worked through you. He has a plan for you. I know He has a plan for this Esme as well. Son, I'm going to pray for wisdom silently. Suppose you'll humor me and wait? I need His help."

Joseph fumbled with his book, set it aside, and raked his hands through his thick, black hair. He thought about what he'd told the priest about Esme, that she was like a sister to him. On top of everything else, he felt guilty, like he was leading her on. How could he disguise his feelings from her? She could read his mind, too. Maybe she already knew how he felt. It boggled his mind that they both possessed this power—this unbelievable ability. Joseph's shoulders stiffened. He felt out of breath; he needed fresh air. Suddenly, he wanted to see the sky. He exited the confessional and raced up the aisle but stopped at the door.

There was loud shuffling in the other confessional. The priest exited through the curtain and entered the other side, finding it empty. The man turned on a dime, his robe swirling as he followed Joseph through the church. The priest spotted Joseph standing at the center of the middle, arched door. The priest stopped in front of the pulpit, staring up the aisle. "Son, where are you going? You left this!" the priest exclaimed with a raised arm.

Joseph's shoulders stiffened when he saw his new Bible clenched in the priest's hand. Slowly, he raised his own hand, holding his palm flat. Across the cavernous room, the Bible ripped from the priest's grip and floated as if carried by the delicate hands of an angel. The priest gasped.

After a few seconds, the Bible landed softly on Joseph's outstretched hand. The two men locked eyes. Joseph could see the wheels turning inside the man's ghostly white face.

"I'll keep you in my prayers," said the priest, his voice vibrating like a broken record.

"God be with you and this Esme."

Joseph bowed his head.

Esme

Esme didn't know where Joseph was...exactly. She had overheard muddled brainwaves: thoughts about churches, parks, prayers, and bright, blue windows. Then Bibles and traffic. It was a jumble of ideas, almost like she was being re-routed around Joseph's brain. Even so, she gleaned that he wasn't at the apartment and somehow struggling wherever he happened to be.

All day, while she shuttled sweaty guests into the queue at *Orlando I-Park*—mechanically going through the motions, her mind adrift—she kept receiving pings and pangs, or radio-type signals, about the emotions riding through Joseph's brain.

She didn't like what she was hearing.

When her shift ended, she grabbed her purse, slammed her locker, and raced through the crowds. People of all shapes and sizes from all over the world surrounded her, but she ignored them. She threaded through the maze of arms and legs, barely registering the familiar olfactory trail of popcorn and beer, chocolate and sunscreen, hotdogs and cotton candy, chlorine, and hamburgers. All she could think about was Joseph.

Esme stepped onto the moving sidewalk before her and shrugged her shoulders. *Okay, I'm obsessed.* She admitted to herself, but she could do nothing about it. She loved him—crazy, mad, committed like she was wearing a straitjacket, head over heels, end of the story. The worst part was he was leaving, and they hadn't done it, yet. She was an aching, simmering pile of need and want.

Esme exhaled, stopping her footsteps. Still, she moved, drifting forward on the mechanical sidewalk. She reached the end, stepped off, grabbed her phone, and texted Joseph. *Where are you?*

Esme watched the screen, then dropped her arm. She walked among the shadows of strangers in a daze. Thoughts of the night of the accident settled in, mixing with the wonderings about Joseph.

The reality that she had saved the lives of strangers—not to mention herself and Joseph—blew her mind. Somehow, she did it. Before she had barely perceived a threat, her powers lifted that out-of-control car to safety. No one got hurt. She had relied on Joseph's testimony, his erratic, chaotic story. Still, she only remembered the aftermath: Joseph hugging her like a boa constrictor, his fluttering heartbeat, and his salty, sweet smell. Always, he smelled delicious, like Zest soap and cinnamon. She'd been sure they would do it that night after the roller coaster of adrenaline and excitement. And yet, nothing but kisses followed. She would spontaneously combust if they didn't consummate things soon.

Ping!

Esme stopped short of her car, lifting her phone. *I'm at Disney Springs. Be home soon. Thinking Quesadillas.*

Cute thoughts of Joseph standing at the stove overwhelmed her. Esme feverishly clacked the keys. *Why Disney Springs?*

A surprise for my Esme.

Esme's heartbeat accelerated. *Wait there. I'll meet you by the volcano.*

Okay. I'll wait. Drive safe. Joseph texted back.

Esme's fingers hesitated; she desperately wanted to apply a dozen heart emojis. Instead, she typed, *See you soon.*

Esme unlocked her car and jostled in. *If only I had the power of persuasion. That's the superpower I want right now.* She started her car.

Esme zigzagged down the sidewalk, caught in another undulating, over-populated crowd of miscellaneous souls. She turned at the Lego dinosaur, heading for the Rainforest Cafe and its predictable, spewing volcano. When she arrived, her head swiveled like a bobblehead, searching the crowd for Joseph's handsome face.

She spotted him standing at the edge of an artificial lake beside the restaurant, holding a bag from Chapel Hats with his back turned. Esme dodged around a mom driving a stroller like Mad Max; the woman rolled over Esme's left foot. "Ouch!" Esme muttered, looking up to find Joseph walking towards her.

Now, he was hiding his purchase behind his back. "Esme, you got here so fast!" Joseph exclaimed.

"I was close to my car when I texted. What do you have? Can I see?" she asked.

Joseph looked over his shoulder. "Should we find a bench?" he asked, grabbing her hand.

They walked side by side, backtracking through the crowd. Finally, they sat in the back row of curved, stone seats permanently arranged for musical concerts. In front of them, a band was setting up musical instruments on a circular swirl of cement. "I planned to surprise you, but you surprised me. Well, here you go. Open it. You'll see," Joseph said, his face beaming. He reached for the circular black bag, handing it to Esme.

Esme smiled with teeth, one side of her face highlighted by the sun, her hair a luminous shade of red. She unzipped the bag and pulled out a tall, black top hat. She laughed.

"You already have a magic wand. Now, you'll have a magic hat. Every magician needs a magic hat, right?"

"Oh, Joseph. I love it!" Esme exclaimed, pausing to stroke the purple velvet rose and soft, white feather attached to the side over a wide, purple velvet ribbon. "It's so pretty."

Joseph grabbed the hat and placed it on her head. "This is like your *Superman* costume. You'll put on your hat when you are ready to use your superpowers."

Esme hugged Joseph, causing the hat to slip off her head. Joseph grabbed the hat before it fell and held it behind her shoulders. He saw tears streaming down her cheeks when he pulled away. Joseph smeared them away with his fingertips. "I know, Esme. I'm going to miss you, too."

Esme shook her head. "Not as much as me," she said, sniffing. "So, you're okay with me using my powers now? I thought they scared you. Where were you today? I mean, other than here. I felt and heard things. You seemed upset."

His eyes darted towards the band, then back to Esme. "I went to confession." He looked down, reached into the pocket of his jeans, and pulled out a strand of beads. Now, Joseph's face was a mask of seriousness. He grabbed Esme's hand, placed the beads into her palm, and closed her fingers around them.

"I will always worry about you. But I realized something today. Your power isn't demonic. But humor me, okay? These rosary beads were my mother's. Hold onto them, okay?"

"But, what about you? What will keep you safe?"

Joseph looked away, over his shoulder, into the crowd walking back and forth behind them. "I need to tell you something..."

The band erupted into song. Esme covered her ears, the rosary dangling in her right hand. "What? Tell me!" she yelled.

He blinked. "Later. Not now," he said as loudly as he could. Joseph placed the hat back on Esme's head and pulled her to her feet. "Let's get something to eat. We'll have a special dinner and make memories tonight. Memories to sustain us!"

Esme wiped her tears away, thinking, hoping for a happy ending. She looked at Joseph. He was blushing.

Esme kissed Joseph again; his mouth tasted like peanut butter toast. She closed her blurry eyes, eyes that resembled a raccoon's—all smeared with mascara, blue-gray eyeshadow, and salty tears. She pulled away, tossing him an imploring look. Joseph used his thumbs to blot out the wetness from her cheeks, finishing just in time to catch a tear on his own cheek. He rubbed his chestnut brown eyes with a closed fist and blinked, causing his thick black eyelashes to stick together like hairy spider legs. Joseph pulled Esme's head onto his shoulder. They sobbed in unison, holding onto each other like Velcro. Joseph rubbed her hair. "I'm sorry that we didn't, well...you know. I wasn't ready."

Esme moved her head up and down in a nonverbal response near his armpit. She stayed embedded, almost glued to his shoulder. "I could drop you off at the airport," she mumbled.

."I don't want you to be late for work. Besides, it's so difficult saying goodbye. We should rip the Band-Aid, part ways, and not look back."

"That sounds dreadful," Esme muttered into his shoulder.

Joseph laughed awkwardly, his eyes following something over Esme's shoulder. "What was that?" he asked the air.

"What was what?"

"I thought I saw something."

He shook his head, pulling away from her. Grabbing Esme's hands, he gave them a final squeeze and then let go. Esme sucked in her breath at the finality of Joseph's action. She watched him grab his backpack, check his phone, and shove it into the back pocket of his pants. Meanwhile, her heart felt like her stomach was digesting it. "The driver will be here in five minutes," said Joseph, walking towards the front door. She followed him like a shadow. He stopped and turned. "Esme, look!"

Esme gasped. "I'm not doing that, Joseph, honest!" she exclaimed.

Joseph lunged for the wallet that was floating in front of him. It zigged from his grip, hovering over the sofa. Darting for it, he grabbed and missed. The wallet—his wallet—skidded around the corner and entered the kitchen. He looked at Esme. "I'm not doing it, Joseph!" she exclaimed again.

Joseph tiptoed toward the kitchen, peering around the corner like hunting a mouse. His wallet hovered over the garbage disposal. "No!" Joseph cried. "Here!" he commanded, slicing his palm through the air. The wallet flew into his hand.

Joseph shook his head and snickered. He looked at Esme; her face wore a sheepish, startled mask. She shrugged her shoulders and swayed her arms. Joseph held up his wallet, jiggled it, and deposited it into his pack. "I better go. Esme..." He paused. "I love you."

"I love you, too!" she said, almost hurling the words toward him.

Joseph walked to the door and opened it. He stood silently for a few seconds, then stepped out and closed the door without looking back.

Esme broke into sobs. *How am I going to work like this? My make-up is a mess.* She stood with arms akimbo, watching the door for over a minute. Sucking in her sobs, she pulled up her sleeve to wipe her face. She turned her head towards the kitchen, remembering something odd that Joseph had said. He had spoken to his wallet. *What did he say?* "Here," she whispered. "He said, '*Here,*' and it must have worked."

Esme twisted her head back towards the front door, confusion *almost* overshadowing her profound sense of loss. "Weird..." She looked down at her stomach, sucking it in. Sometimes, it seemed like Joseph was attracted to her. Other times, she heard something different.

If she stayed home, she'd ruminate all day long about Joseph. But going to work seemed impossible. She stepped toward the bathroom but quickly backtracked, shuffling to the sofa to retrieve her phone. She would call in sick.

The doorbell rang like a heavenly bell. Esme sucked in her breath, throwing her phone into the cushions. She ran to the door, swung it open, and screamed.

The woman on the other side exhaled a huff of annoyance and shrugged her purse higher onto her shoulder, covering her eyes with a perfectly manicured hand.

Esme stared. "Mom! What are you doing here?" The words finally escaped her lips.

Oliver

The jungle awakened—night creatures emerged from their hiding places, scampering through the low brush, and above, bats escaped their cavities, swooping through the dusk on leathery wings, as silent as an owl. An electric buzz of cicadas spun a desperate song in the background, droning with an unstoppable velocity. Like clockwork, mosquitoes closed in.

Oliver swatted his arm, barely registering the bite. He and Emil remained frozen, rooted to the ground. They knelt as if in prayer, their faces bathed in a rainbow of refracted light. "What is it?" Emil whispered.

Oliver curled his fingers inwards, his hands hovering over the object. He shook his head as if dispelling a horrible thought and retracted his arms. "I think it's a black box. Or at least a version of one."

"It certainly isn't black."

"That's an understatement. What do you think? Should I pick it up?"

Emil stared at the smooth and seductive box; he licked his lips. "I don't know. It's almost as if the thing is alive. It emits light like it has a power source. Incredible, fucking incredible," Emil repeated in a hushed tone.

"I wonder if it's always been glowing like this. Or if we disturbed it and woke the thing up?" Oliver rubbed his hands on his pant legs and fixed his gaze on Emil. "I'm doing it," he stated.

Oliver stretched his arm, touching the top of the glass with his thumb; it felt cool to the touch. Quickly, he brushed more dirt off the top. "Well, it didn't shock me," he said, inching his knees closer.

Holding his breath, he bit his lower lip and grabbed the box, lifting it and setting it down again. He exhaled. "Well, it's cold and heavy. No electric currents." Oliver laughed nervously. "I don't know what I was expecting."

"I know what you were expecting. An exploding laser beam targeting your eyes and burning right through your goddamn skull," Emil said, poking Oliver in the center of his forehead. Emil adjusted his baseball cap. "Or an explosion! A booby trap like in the movies!"

The men started laughing until their sound dissolved, replaced with silent reverence, and seconds floated between them. Oliver laid a hand over his heart. "My heart's still racing. I don't think I've ever been so scared and excited at the same time. Now what?"

"We take it! No way we're letting it get pilfered. As exciting as this is, I'm getting a bad feeling. We know this is alien tech, right? We also know they died here. It's like an alien cemetery, and we're disturbing it and taking something precious."

"We don't know that. Maybe, to the aliens, it's nothing—just a big chunk of glass. Besides, it's not exactly a graveyard. We only found one set of finger bones and a few tiny fragments. Some of them could have lived or escaped the crash somehow," Oliver mused, sitting back on his heels, shifting his face into darkness.

"I wonder if we should just bury everything again. No report. No circus. We'll be the only ones to ever know about the crash. We've documented everything. Well, everything that we've unearthed so far. We could keep a few souvenirs...Maybe everyone—humanity, I mean— would be better off. This sci-fi shit is scary, serious proof of alien life."

"We haven't received the test results. But yeah, pretty damn definitive," said Oliver. Looking over Emil's head, he half expected to find a spaceship hovering over them.

Oliver held his breath. The weight of the situation felt heavy on his shoulders. He remembered to breathe again and inhaled. "Let's not forget, Phillip and Antonio, know about this, and any future archaeologists or locals that dig in this area could unearth it again." He paused, swatted a cloud of bugs, and moved his face closer to the light emitting from the box. "But then again, why would they? I only stopped here because there were metal fragments that caught my eye. Most visitors would move farther down the wall," said Oliver, his voice growing quieter.

Emil stood. "Hell, I don't know what to do. But it's getting dark. The mosquitoes will eat us alive if we don't get back. Let's sleep on it. Decide tomorrow."

Emil laid a hand on Oliver's shoulder. "We're keeping the box, even if it kills us in our sleep."

"Emil, if this thing kills us, we'll die happy." Oliver moved forward, slowly lifting the box like a grenade. He looked at Emil and smiled. "Looks like we won't need a flashlight."

Oliver sat on a bench in the dining tent, hunched over the table, listening to the repetitive plunk of rain on plastic. He looked down into his coffee cup, swirled the contents, and took a pull. "Goddamn it," he muttered. "Why couldn't it have been another Kinich Ahau jade head?" he whispered into his mug.

At first, he could barely control his excitement over finding the crash scene and the intriguing contents. Now, it was all a big fat mess. Frankly, he didn't know what to do. There was no handbook on alien discoveries, no rules on what to do with whatever the damn thing was under his cot. He didn't know how he was going to hide it. *What if it's a weapon?* Oliver shook his head, feeling like he needed a dose of Pepto Bismol to calm his stomach. This discovery was supposed to be his meal ticket. Now, he was on the verge of hiding it from the world.

"Buenos días, Señor Wright."

Oliver looked up. "Antonio! You're back!"

Antonio sat down beside Oliver, water dripping from his hair and arms. The men looked up simultaneously as Emil swooped under the tarp, wearing a flapping plastic cape that resembled a flying nun's habit. Emil flicked the rain off his makeshift umbrella, sat across from Oliver, and nodded. Oliver knew what that meant.

"It's alien," Oliver whispered.

"Yup. The bones don't contain human DNA. And the metal, well, we need to get rid of it fast because it's irradiated. There's bismuth and magnesium; nobody can combine those elements on Planet Earth. There are trace amounts of zinc, tungsten—from meteorites—gold, and a small amount of europium, and the rest of the properties don't exist on Earth. Not even *on* meteorites. Oh, and there's trace amounts of mercury, too."

"Mercury? Dammit," Oliver exclaimed. "Well, I guess we know what we're doing today…Erasing one of the most exciting discoveries since Tutankhamun."

"If I had a beer, I'd be crying into it," Emil muttered.

"Sí," said Antonio.

Oliver looked beyond the tent at the mud, the puddles, and the vertical pellets that showed no sign of ebbing. He rubbed his whiskers. "So, this is how it ends, huh? Just like it started. In the goddamn rain."

Emil and Oliver looked at each other; they knew it wasn't over. The glass, or crystal, which breathed light wasn't going anywhere.

Esme

"Mom, what are you doing here?" asked Esme, shutting the door behind her mother's back.

Ethelene frowned and wiggled the strap from a wicker purse off her shoulder. After regarding Esme with a look akin to resentment, Ethelene spotted the sofa, walked to it, and plopped down, her dress billowing and deflating. "What kind of question is that? And what a way to greet your mother. Frankly, I'm sick of being treated like a monster. I may not be the mother of the year, but I'm no Joan Crawford."

Esme looked at her mother sulkily, wondering who Joan Crawford was—exactly. Ethelene knitted her brows. "I've been calling and calling. I'm sick of the silent treatment, too. So, here I am." Leaning forward, Ethelene slapped her bare knees. "I wanted to catch you before you went to work."

Esme felt like a cornered shrew. "Mom, *shh*...Don't talk so loud; my roommate is sleeping." Esme lowered her voice, too. "I'm not going to work today. It's a long story—shit. I need to call in. Hold on," Esme said, flapping her arms.

Ethelene turned, reaching behind her back. "Is this your phone?"

Esme appraised her elder's cute sandals with cork heels and a peacock-themed sundress. Her mother was irritatingly gorgeous, with blond, fringy blue eyes and legs like a teenager. Plus, she was thin as a cracker. *Whose mother looks like this?*

Esme retrieved her phone. "Thanks," she muttered, lumbering off towards her bedroom.

With each footfall, Esme could feel steely blue eyes penetrating her back. She felt guilty. She'd been so obsessed with Joseph that she had completely ignored her mother's relentless calls. True, Ethelene sucked at motherhood. Even so, Esme wondered if she deserved the brutal, silent treatment of the last month. Or if she should listen to Joseph and forgive her.

Esme closed her bedroom door and called in sick, even though she figured she'd rather work than deal with her mother. After a few minutes, she wandered back into the living room and sat on a big, fluffy orange beanbag chair opposite the sofa. Immediately, Esme regretted the unflattering position. She looked up at Ethelene.

"Have you been crying?" Ethelene asked, digging into her purse for a tissue, then leaning towards Esme.

"Mom, I don't need that. I'm not crying anymore."

Ethelene huffed, shoving the tissue back into her purse. "Well, you look like a raccoon. Why were you crying? What happened? Does it have something to do with your television appearance? You know how sorry I am about that, right?"

Esme had shoved that disaster down into the depths of her soul. Thanks to her mother, she had to think about it again when she already felt like bird poop. "I'm going to miss Joseph," said Esme with a sigh.

"Joseph? Do you mean Emil's son? What did he do? I'm confused."

"He just left. He came to see me. Mom, you won't understand, but I love him, and he's going to Mexico City—to Le Cordon Bleu. He's studying to be a chef, and I don't know when I'll see him again."

Esme felt tears prick the back of her eyeballs just thinking about Mexico City. She missed Joseph so much, and he'd only been gone for a few minutes. She knew this sounded crazy, but it was a fact.

"Honey, you love him? Really? Hasn't it only been a month or so since New York?"

Esme glared at her mother. Ethelene held up her hands in defeat. "I'm sorry. I shouldn't have said that. It's your heart," said Ethelene, crossing her legs and settling back into the cushions. Ethelene shook her head as if resetting the conversation. "Tell me more about this, Joseph. How did you end up together in New York? Have you been in contact all these years?"

Esme smiled at the memory, thinking about the hotel room and the fury of objects spinning like satellites around the Earth. Meeting Joseph again and feeling the raw power at her fingertips— or wherever her power came from—had been the most exciting thing in her life. Esme looked at her mother, mentally subtracting all the juicy parts of the story. "He saw me on television. His client, Mitzi—he was a personal care attendant, you know, before—was watching *The Morning Show*, and Joseph recognized me. We were best friends in Guatemala. We played together, like Timon and Pumbaa, exploring the jungle. We had so much fun!"

"Your dad let you run around the jungle alone?" interrupted Ethelene.

"Mom, if you hadn't been on a Buddhist retreat, I wouldn't have been in Guatemala at all!"

Ethelene sucked in her breath. "I was seeking enlightenment on a sacred mission, visiting the Sri Maha Bodhi fig tree. Well, the new tree, anyway. It was a very important trip for me!" Ethelene exclaimed with a scowl.

Esme flapped her arms and rolled her eyes. "Everything was more important than me. Besides, I wasn't alone in the jungle—I was with Joseph. He's so handsome now. You should see his eyelashes. He cooked for me—his food is amazing. He's going to be a great chef. Well, he already is," she added, her voice receding.

Esme looked to her right, at the shelf by the window. She cocked her head, intrigued by one of her conch shells. It was inching down the shelf like a centipede. Esme looked at Ethelene with wild eyes.

"But how did he find you in New York? Did he have your phone number?"

Esme inhaled. "Why are you asking me all these weird questions? I think his dad told him how to find me or something. All I know is that it was just like old times as soon as we met. How am I going to survive without him?" asked Esme, knowing there wasn't an answer—a good answer, anyway.

Esme looked back at the shell and scrunched her forehead. "What are you looking at?" asked Ethelene, patting the cushion beside her. "Honey, come sit beside me."

Reluctantly, Esme stood. Simultaneously, the seashell flew off the shelf, hovering like a drone between the two women. Ethelene gasped. "You're CT!" she yelled, pointing like it was an accusation.

"What's that?" asked Esme, reaching for the seashell.

The shell darted, spinning around Esme three times before returning to the shelf. Ethelene stood too. "Oh my God, Esme. It's not a magic trick; you're operating at *celestial*. You've reached the highest level in Cosmostheology! How could this happen? What's that weird humming sound?"

Slowly, Ethelene moved towards the shelf. She reached out, touching the shell. Ethelene turned. "You've been liberated from the physical universe. You can physically control matter, energy, space, and time. I can't believe it," she muttered. Her blue eyes were as big as blueberries.

Ethelene returned to the couch and sat carefully on the cushion. She turned to Esme. "Honey, I didn't know you studied Cosmostheology, too?"

Esme's mind foraged for answers. She had to think of something. Confessing wasn't an option, not before she told her dad—maybe not ever. "Mom, I'm not a Cosmostheologist. It's just a magic trick—one I've been practicing. It's no big deal," said Esme, swallowing.

"It didn't look like nothing to me. Esme, it's amazing. You're amazing!" Ethelene swooned.

Finally, Esme sat beside her mother, smiling for real. She'd always been proud of her abilities—the special ones. *God, it's so hard hiding the truth.* "Joseph took videos of me the last time I performed on International Drive. Would you like to see them?"

Ethelene beamed. She grabbed Esme and hugged her. "I'd love to see them!"

"Mom, I did it. I posted the videos on YouTube," said Esme, walking towards her mother with wet hair, wearing a fuzzy, green robe.

Ethelene dropped her phone and repositioned herself on the sofa. "I wondered what you've been doing all this time. Just wait. I bet you'll get noticed by another agent. Honey, are you going to finish getting ready? I'm starving," said Ethelene, cocking her head. Her blue eyes followed something behind Esme's back.

Esme turned and discovered her black velvet top hat floating behind her butt like a tail. Esme grabbed it and spun towards her mother with a look of surprise. "Honey! You are blowing me away with all these tricks! How did you do that? Can I see the hat? It's beautiful."

Esme glanced over her shoulder at the empty hallway, then walked over to her mother. Sitting beside her, she placed the hat on her mother's lap.

Ethelene inspected it, brushing her hands over the soft velvet, grabbing the feather, and threading her fingers through it, base to tip. She turned to her daughter. "This is perfect. Why weren't you wearing it in the videos?"

Esme grabbed the hat and rotated it in her fingers, potential tears burning her eyes. "Joseph gave it to me before he left. Isn't it amazing? I love it." Willing the waterworks away, Esme shook her head. She looked back at the hallway. "Why do you keep looking down the hall? I'm beginning to think your roommate is a ghost," said Ethelene, poking her daughter in the arm.

"No reason. Okay, I'll go get ready."

Esme stood and turned to go but felt a sudden pull at the corner of her robe. "Honey, I'm glad that we're getting along. Have you forgiven me for being a crappy mom? For everything?"

Esme nodded, then thought better of it and swung her head sideways. "Do you know what it was like to be on live television? It's a big deal! You never even called to tell me I'd be great. Or to congratulate me on getting such a great gig. That's what most moms would do, you know."

Esme flopped onto the sofa beside her mother, scowling.

Ethelene straightened her spine. "Mom, do you know what it was like to fail in front of everyone? If it weren't for Joseph, I don't know what I would have done."

Ethelene inhaled, grabbing for Esme's hand. Esme pulled it away. "Mom, don't," she huffed.

"I've thought about how I've been absent over the years, ever since I saw your dad in Guatemala. Well, not always physically absent, but in a different world with Buddhism and Cosmostheology, apart from you. I regret not encouraging you more. I forgot to congratulate you when you got that jerky agent—sorry. You're so good; I didn't think you needed encouragement." Ethelene sighed. "I regret going to Guatemala and not acknowledging your big day. I know I haven't always been there for you. I did call after, though. But you wouldn't talk to me. I thought I was doing something important in Guatemala...Maybe I was. But whatever I did, it wasn't—it *isn't*—more important than you. That's why I'm leaving the church. I need to find myself. I need to do some soul-searching."

Esme peeked at her mother's face from beneath her eyelashes. A tear slipped down Ethelene's cheek, over her perfectly buffed face and rosy blush, dripping over her glossy, red mouth. Esme grabbed her mother's slender hand and squeezed it tightly without looking at her.

Joseph

Abandoning Esme was the hardest thing he'd ever had to do—more complicated than his confession at church because he loved her. However, he wasn't sure what box to check: carnal love, like man and wife; affectionate, sibling love; or a tried and true, deep, forever-friendship. They'd known each other since childhood. Why was he so torn?

Joseph tried to hide his romantic confusion from Esme. But he certainly wasn't an expert at brain centrifuge. The weight of her tears grew heavier with each passing mile, as did the strange pull that lassoed them together. When they parted, the rope tightened, constricting. Why did they have this weird connection? What could have caused their mutual superpower? Guilty thoughts plagued him for withholding his matching abilities from Esme, but he didn't want to burst her bubble. She felt like a superhero.

Esme believed she had saved all those people in Orlando. If she knew that he'd been the one to levitate the car to safety, she'd be crushed. Still, he should have told her everything. Being honest was the right thing to do. They had been apart for years without receiving messages, which confused him. But he couldn't change the fact that now he could feel Esme's sadness, almost like he was watching a rhythmic screensaver. The messages seemed to float into his brain as quickly as text messages, as fast as email.

The first time Joseph levitated an object was after his mother's funeral. He'd been alone in his room, shaking with anger, his emotions bubbling over like a forgotten pan of soup. A crystal skull—a replica his father had given him for Christmas—flew into his bedroom wall. Beads of blood materialized on his arm from flying specks of glass. His father had burst into the room like a cartoon roadrunner, eyes blazing. Without an explanation, Joseph admitted he had thrown the skull while overcome with anger. Emil had backed out of the room with slumped shoulders.

Joseph's eyes morphed into saucers. Out of nowhere, a hollow feeling of déjà vu swept through him. Information flooded his cortex and he felt pressed against his seat. Looking out the window didn't help. Joseph breathed in and out, staring at the layer of soft, fluffy clouds. Someone poked his arm. Joseph looked at his seatmate.

"Would you like something to drink?" asked the flight attendant, handing a plastic cup to the woman at his elbow.

Joseph smiled self-conscientiously. "Oh, sorry. Coffee and two creamers please."

Joseph appraised his seatmate, a middle-aged woman with a friendly face and a tiny white dog wedged between her feet in a soft-sided carrier. Thank goodness the lady had spent the flight staring at her phone because he was too distracted to converse. Joseph accepted his coffee from the flight attendant.

After taking a sip, Joseph regressed into his thoughts again. He couldn't solve the puzzle—not yet. However, his power—their power—had something to do with Guatemala. The connection became clear only minutes ago. Joseph had felt the green heartbeat of the jungle, seen Esme running through the trees, and knew an answer was chasing them. Without thinking, Joseph raised his hand as if parting an invisible veil. The answer was as close as his fingertips, but he still couldn't reach it.

Joseph knocked on the door and used his key to enter the apartment. As always, he wiped his feet, shrugging raindrops from his shoulders and blowing a wet tuft of hair out of his eyes. "Mitzi, it's me!" he yelled from the entryway.

The television hushed to a gentle murmuring; he heard a scuffling of papers. After that, he heard Mitzi's electric wheelchair zoom down the hall. He laughed when he saw the smile on her face. The woman splayed her arms. Joseph trotted up, placed his sack on the floor, and kissed Mitzi on the forehead. Then he leaned low to bestow a grand hug. "Oh, Joseph. I missed you something terrible. What am I going to do when you're in Mexico City?" Mitzi croaked.

"It's not too late to pull the plug. I can stay with you."

"Not a chance. Next time I see you, you'll be wearing chef whites. And don't forget to take home the book I gave you. So, what do you have in the sack?" asked Mitzi, leaning to peek inside the bag.

"You're going to like it. I have everything I need to make barbacoa enchiladas with mole sauce. And for dessert, I'm frying cardamom doughnuts with a mango glaze. The dough is ready. I even have peanut oil. Oh, I have something else, too."

Joseph reached into the sack and pulled out a large, oval bottle. He twisted it so Mitzi could read the label. "I found this in Winter Park, at a farmer's market by an old train depot."

"Black mangrove honey," Mitzi read aloud. "I've never had that kind," she added, licking her lips, and looking up into Joseph's eyes.

"Mitzi, don't cry," he implored, grabbing her hand.

Mitzi shook her head and wiped her cheek. "Now, look what you made me do. Did you have to check your bag because of me? You are too sweet for your own good," she said, sniffing and chuckling self-consciously. "That reminds me. How did things go with that girl of yours? I bet she's stuck on you like Elmer's after eating your tantalizing food."

Mitzi placed the honey jar between her legs and reached up, pinching Joseph's cheek. "Plus, you're not bad to look at, either. That girl must have been sad to see you go."

Joseph blushed. "Yes, she was sad. I'll miss her too, but it won't be for that long. And besides, maybe Esme can visit me in Mexico. Plus, there's always FaceTime. Mitzi, should we head inside and sit down?"

Mitzi laughed. "I'm already sitting!"

"Here you go," said Joseph, placing the entree on the table between her outstretched hands. He rotated the plate, pointing at the black beans. "Have you ever had pepitas?"

"I'm not sure. Are they pumpkin seeds?"

"That's right. I topped the beans with toasted pepitas and pickled red onions. There's annatto rice with spring peas and mixed vegetables, and the enchiladas are sprinkled with cotija cheese, sesame seeds, and cilantro. The mole sauce is as close to my mother's as I could get. I used almond butter instead of peanuts, and to balance the bitter chocolate, I added pureed plantains—my mother always used raisins. My secret ingredient tonight is espresso to make the chocolate shine!"

Joseph filled Mitzi's wine glass, then his own.

Mitzi grabbed her knife and fork. "It looks like I chose the right investment—you!" She took a bite of the enchilada and a big slurp of the dark red wine. Joseph raised his glass, too. "The wine is from Argentina. A Malbec..."

"Joseph, sit down and eat before it gets cold!" Mitzi interrupted.

Joseph pushed Mitzi's wheelchair closer to the table and sat beside her. He started eating. For a few minutes, the only sound was a sprinkling of rain against the windows in the living room and the low mumbling of an unknown television show. Joseph let his mind wander, his fork pausing beside his beans. Thinking about Esme was becoming his brain's automatic setting. For the first time, he was having trouble concentrating; he'd almost forgotten to put the dark chocolate into the mole sauce. Joseph thought about using FaceTime to communicate with Esme—he didn't need FaceTime. Already, he could see and hear her. Ethelene, Esme's mother, was there, and Esme was still upset. She seemed confused and...

"Joseph? What's wrong? You're not eating. Do you feel guilty about the meat? You'll need the protein to keep up with all your new girlfriends in Mexico," Mitzi said, winking and chewing.

Joseph smiled and laughed. "I've been eating lots of meat," he said, rubbing his stomach, then taking a small bite. "I think I've even gained weight. No, I was thinking about Esme. I worry...But, enough about me. How are things going with your new personal care attendant?"

Mitzi raised her eyebrows.

"You don't like her? Maybe I shouldn't go," proclaimed Joseph, dropping his fork.

"Poppycock!" Mitzi exclaimed, slapping Joseph's hand. "Don't worry, kid. It will take time to get used to someone new. It's *him*, by the way. I like him just fine. I'm not too fond of his tattoos, but he's strong. We do all the stretches that you wrote down. Plus, he can open a can of soup, and when I want something else, I order food delivery."

Joseph's shoulders relaxed. Scraping his plate, he scooped a large bite of enchilada into his mouth but still managed to smile, "I bet the soup isn't as good as my pozole. Tattoos, huh? What do they look like?" Joseph garbled with a full mouth.

Mitzi took a big sip of wine and cackled. "They're hideous and hilarious, too. The poor kid tattooed every critter he ever had— dogs, cats, all up and down both arms. There's even a rat." Mitzi rolled her eyes. "If I had a pet rat, I'd put that one somewhere invisible, somewhere the sun don't shine, if you know what I mean."

They both started laughing.

Twenty minutes later, after Mitzi had eaten the last bite of enchilada and scraped every bit of mole sauce from her plate, she paused, her expression serious. She leaned forward, grabbed his hand, and said, "Joseph. This meal was one of the best meals I've ever had. And I don't mean the best Mexican food I've ever had. I mean the best *food*, period. You are going to make your mother so proud—up in Heaven. Your dad too. You just wait. Someday, you'll have your own restaurant, and if I'm still around—and I damn well better be—I want you to get me a ticket to the James Beard award ceremony when you win best new chef!"

Joseph smiled with his eyes, pushing his wine glass around in a circle. "Now, pour us some more wine and fix those damn doughnuts!"

"Yes, Mrs. Ferndale," Joseph said.

Joseph hated taking the subway in the rain. The smell of wet dog permeated the air, and the floor of the car sluiced with detritus and muck. He rubbed his knees and yawned, listening to the rails' soundtrack—a whistling and irregular screeching that sometimes resembled a tortured cat.

After an epic stretch, Joseph wiggled his toes and gripped the corners of his book, feeling the crisp, new paper, smelling that new book smell. "What you got there? In the sack? It smells good, man, better than farts and piss," said a man with an orange T-shirt and dreadlocks hanging heavy in a giant coil down his back. The man leaned towards Joseph, twiddling his pointer finger.

Joseph smiled. "Leftovers."

The man stood and stumbled to the door of the car, waiting. When the car stopped, he turned his head. "How 'bout you come cook for me, huh?" The man patted his satchel. "I give you something good in exchange, guaranteed to give you more joy than that big book."

Joseph snickered and shook his head. When the train stopped, the man departed the subway car and burst into song, the sound echoing behind him as he disappeared into the shadows.

The doors closed, and Joseph returned to his book, smiling, and inhaling the fresh, inky smell. He leafed through the pages, pausing to rub his fingers over the intoxicating photographs. They inspired and intimidated him.

He had never prepared most of the food he saw, like sea scallops with lemon-herb beurre blanc, black cod in sake-miso marinade, strawberries with vanilla bourbon zabaglione. *What is a Zabaglione?*

Joseph paused over a photo. "Easy Black Bean Soup. I could make that with my eyes closed," he whispered.

He skimmed, turning page after page, laughing at the recipe for devil's food cake cockaigne. "Cockaigne?" Joseph muttered aloud.

The woman across from him giggled. The man on his right shuffled his papers and guffawed. Joseph kept paging, mesmerized by the glorious food.

Eventually, he found himself mostly alone with just his book and his thoughts. He closed the cover, checking the time on his phone. It was late; he would soon arrive at his stop in Queens. Joseph slipped the book into his sack and slouched, his mind blank and sleepy.

After a time, he jolted awake. Joseph covered his ears as a confusion of brainwaves blustered inside his head. Helplessly, he stood. Then he sat down. It was Esme.

Again, Joseph stood, grabbing the greasy railing above him, "Joseph! Help me!" He heard her scream.

Initiate Cerebral Streaming—

Recording Session Two

I am breathing in unison with my beloved family. Now, they are light years away, learning under the Deities' watchful eyes, safe on the undulating sands of Pleione. We (the crew) of the secondary vessel are at peace now that we have safely pushed through the worm hole.

It was an experience unlike anything I have felt in space. I simultaneously underwent a forward and backward momentum, as if my soul and living body detached. The colors were new to me. It was dizzying.

After the event, Dob-Dec grasped my hands, levitating us toward the upper limit of our little ship. We moved as if listening to the voices of angels; everyone laughed, our minds racing with excitement. We were too jubilant to refrain from thinking as one interconnected unit, a chain of happy thoughts, a jumble of positive energy, passing from one soul to another like a virus.

I speak for all when I say we are excited to start our research and take the first step toward completing our mission. Today marks our journey's center point. The distance from Pleione is extreme. Even so, when I close my eyes, I can smell our garden's sweet, spicy aroma; I feel my mate's loving hands stroking my back; I see my children's eyes, watching me with their luminous black orbs. My children want to absorb every detail of my travels. I yearn to bestow my newfound knowledge firsthand. Although, I must stay focused on the here and now.

After we arrived, we feasted on the deck while watching the Blue Earth in the distance. It is a water-filled planet, unlike our own. On return trips, as our world comes into focus, I always marvel at the swirls of gold, the dusting of amber, and the brush strokes of olive and rust that envelop our planet like the eye of a solar storm.

But, staring at the Blue Earth I know the truth: it is the most breathtaking planet in the galaxy. The planet holds an endless diversity of life. It tickles me to imagine feeling the grass beneath my toes, breathing the Earth's crisp oxygen, wading knee-deep in the cool, blue-green waters. I worry the water may freeze my toes!

But there are always opposite but interconnected forces when traveling through space. We experienced a glitch after our journey through the worm hole. Before the malfunction, I was asleep in my chamber when suddenly, my body levitated from the bed. I found myself floating amidst a debris field of loose objects: crystal medical records, under linens, and dried nourishment tablets. Water droplets floated like research drones. At first, I thought Dob-Dec was playing a trick on me, until the vibrating sound of the alarm. I caught myself before falling, planting my bare toes on the opaque glass of my chamber.

Dob-Dec arrived at my portal almost instantaneously; his mind zeroed in on my health status (I would never report his omission), a deep crimson color reflected within his eyes. I was relieved to discover that all crew members were safe. Our ship lost its gravity field momentarily. Following a thorough systems analysis by the crew, Lyra assured us that all mechanical systems are functioning normally. Still, it was perplexing.

Now, the Blue Earth is growing more prominent—just like our minds.

Resume Universal Translation Mode–
End of Session Two.

Commence Cerebral Streaming—

Session Nine

Descending into the bowels of the ice cavern was surreal. At home, our world sizzles under the glare of unforgiving suns. The silica mountains that dominate our planet resemble a peculiar rainbow: olive, rust, creamy white, and brown. It travels this way forever. The tiny Blue Earth is a planet of extreme opposites. In Antarctica, all is white except tiny black penguins dotting the ground like whiskers on a meat-eater. Frozen—there is nothing frozen at home. Blue Earth has water in abundance. At home, we distill our water from hydrated minerals. The meat-eaters don't deserve this fertile world.

I watched the glistening walls from the viewing station with an accelerated heartbeat. At first, the striations of ice resembled a frozen waterfall, twisting and undulating, almost like traversing a bright white wormhole. As we traveled farther underground, the cavern narrowed into a rocky limestone tunnel.

When we neared the bottom, the Antarctic crew extinguished their lights, and we did too. We remained inert, waiting in complete blackness. After we reached the cavern floor, the Blue Earth crew illuminated the cave in a bright explosion of light. What we saw increased the size of our hearts twofold. Wonder and delight swept across Sula's eyes in flashes of green and blue—I could see the amazement without listening.

Crystal gypsum daggers as tall as aspen trees covered the floor and rocky ceiling like lightning bolts. The *otherness* of the cavern changed the way we breathed. I grabbed Sula's hand and squeezed it, but I am not ashamed.

The Antarctic crew treated us like earthly queens. We feasted on the new provisions, even partaking in a fermented juice snatched from the thirsty mouths of meat-eaters. Oh, how sick I felt! Afterward, we toured the facility in the cavern's deepest region, discovering that much has changed since my last visit. Now, a gypsum disc radiates over the Earth crew's vessel like a protective eye. It felt like home—only colder.

Sula performed vigorous examinations on each Antarctic crew *Being* and did not tour the facility or participate in any of our stimulating games. As predicted, all crewmembers passed; living deep within the tiny Blue Earth has produced no ill effects. Our planet contains similar elements. It is close in chemical composition and yet, so different.

We resided with the Antarctic crew until the following night. There was a palpable sadness and a contagious fear for our safety when we parted. Traveling the parallel lines of the Blue Earth is not without risk.

Since the arrival of nuclear weapons on the tiny Blue Earth, we have often sent synthetic hybrids and drones to gather information. It is infinitely safer, as the meat-eaters are violently protective of their air space. However, if you've been listening to my data, you already know this was a highly anticipated mission with a crew of souls.

Now, we must reach the ocean crew deep in the waters of the Atlantic. We will utilize our shields and pray for guidance.

Before we departed the ice cavern, I levitated to the irregular ceiling, collecting a small sample of cave crystal to commemorate our visit. Listeners, it would be most pleasing to sneak away from mission protocol long enough to levitate to the underside of China's Beipanjiang Bridge; I would sign my name on the bottom like earthly graffiti. This thought is profoundly humorous. The meat-eaters would never forget me.

I will give the stone to Sula. But first, I must shape and insert my data. I will not tell you, the listener, what I plan to inscribe. The message is private, and I know you, the listener, cannot read my mind. This too, is humorous.

Delete Forbidden Content—Continue Universal Translation Mode—End of Session.

Esme

Esme awoke and looked around. Her bedroom looked weird, like a dark, blurry image from a drone. She lay floundering like a dying fish, not knowing what was happening, until she realized she was floating four feet over her bed and screamed for Joseph. Then her arms backpaddled, and she fell. The air burst from her lungs; she looked wildly around the room, gaping at the dark.

Ethelene burst through the door and flipped the light switch, discovering Esme flailing in her crumpled sheets. "What's going on?" shouted Ethelene.

Esme looked at her mother standing in the doorway wearing an old, oversized T-shirt. The shirt looked amazing on her. Esme sighed. "I had a nightmare," she said, leaning on an arm.

"Did you fall out of bed? I heard a thump," said Ethelene, crossing her arms.

"I guess. Mom, do you want to sleep in here? With me?"

"You *guess?*" asked Ethelene with a shoulder shrug. "I'll go get my pillow."

As soon as Ethelene left for the living room, Esme's phone

rang. She dug for it, finding it under the sheets. "Joseph!" Esme expelled into the glass.

"Are you okay? What happened to you?" he asked, his voice vibrating as if he was walking.

Esme couldn't believe it; she struggled for words. "How did you know? I think...I mean, I did call out for you. So, you heard me?"

"I had a feeling...."

Can Joseph read my mind, too? Esme looked up at her mother, who was waiting in the doorway, and lowered her voice, even though her mother was clearly within earshot. "Joseph, don't worry, I'm fine. It's just...Well, do you remember what happened when you left? With your wallet? It's like that, except weirder. I don't know what the heck is going on."

Esme looked at her mother. "I miss you. I'll call you tomorrow. Okay?"

There was a long pause. "As long as you're okay. Your mother is there, right? So, you're not alone."

"Yeah, she's here. How did you know that?" Esme said, tingling all over. She looked at her mother again.

Ethelene raised her eyebrows.

Now, Esme didn't want to hang up. She *needed* to hear Joseph's explanation, but not in front of her mother. Reluctantly, she said goodbye and set her phone on the nightstand.

"Honey," Ethelene said, rounding the bed with her pillow and sitting down. "I feel like you're not being honest with me. Something is going on with you—something big. Tell me. Maybe I can help."

"Mom, it's too weird to explain, and I've never told anyone— except Joseph. Frankly, I'd barely know where to begin."

Ethelene reached across Esme's face, brushing hair from her eyes. Shortly after, both women pushed their pillows against the headboard and settled in, staring around the room vacantly. Esme blew a fissure of air, finally succumbing. She felt like she'd explode if she didn't unload something about her life. Maybe it was time to tell her parents the truth. Ethelene grabbed Esme's hand and rubbed the soft spot between her thumb and forefinger, waiting.

"I used to like that."

"I know."

Esme took a deep breath. "If anyone might understand what I'm about to say, it would be you."

Ethelene curled her legs and snuggled closer. "Why?"

"Because you already believe in weird things."

Ethelene shouldered away, looking hurt, but then she burst out laughing. "Yeah, I guess you're right."

Esme inhaled and blurted, "I can move things with my mind."

"Like magic, like David Copperfield."

"No, that's not real. David Copperfield is a magician."

"You're a magician," Ethelene countered.

"No, Mom. You were right before. It has nothing to do with Cosmostheology, but I can move things with my mind. It's not a trick. It's *real.* You know—powers, universe, space, time—whatever. I don't know how. I just can."

Ethelene stared at Esme with intensity, almost like her blue eyes could suck out Esme's soul. "That's amazing. I've never known anyone—even in Cosmostheology—who mastered the art of levitation."

"Mom, it's not Cosmostheology. You're leaving the church, right? Because it doesn't sound like you're leaving the church."

"I am. But that doesn't mean I'm just going to forget or abandon my faith. I still believe in it. There are things I don't like about the church, but that's not why I'm leaving. I need to be on my own for a while. I need to figure things out. I need to mend things with you and your father," said Ethelene. She paused, then added, "Show me what you can do."

"I'm scared to use my power. It's been crazy lately."

"Oh," said Ethelene, letting go of Esme's hand. "What does that mean? Are you okay?"

Esme shrugged. "I don't know why I'm scared. I should be used to weird stuff by now. I haven't been moving things because things have been moving on their own. It's unnerving. When I was younger, up until Joseph, my powers were fun. They worked but were unreliable—like what happened on *The Morning Show*."

Ethelene gasped. "Oh! Now I understand."

"Then, I met Joseph in New York and felt on fire. When I came home, my powers fizzled..." said Esme, her voice receding.

"Keep going," Ethelene implored.

"When I came home from New York, I was useless. I could barely move a feather. Then Joseph came, and my powers changed and grew stronger again. Mom, at times, I've felt like a superhero."

Esme fell silent again, thinking about the car that flew through the sky.

"Honey, it seems like Joseph, or your love for him, empowers you. It's like he's your fuel and you're plugged into the universe when he's with you."

"It's true, I think..." said Esme, pausing mid-sentence as a box of shoes flew over the bed and rapidly tumbled to the floor.

The women's heads swiveled toward the closet. They watched slack jawed as more shoes flew over and around the bed. Soon, a pair of black, shiny heels, blue tennis shoes, and coral-beaded flip-flops scattered to the floor. Then a three-pound dumbbell and a jumping rope spiraled overhead and fell with a scatter and a thud. More shoes and flip-flops flew from the closet, followed by the contents of a plastic bin of junk. The mismatched items spun like an irregular Ferris wheel over the bed until everything tumbled to the floor. Finally, a single, dirty, white tennis shoe zipped from the closet. The shoe spun in a slow, deliberate circle as if carried by unseen hands. The shoe hovered over Esme's lap, and she reached to grab it. Instead, the shoe shot upwards and flipped, dislodging a coiled piece of string and glass. The item slipped from inside the shoe, plunking into Esme's outstretched hand.

The room quieted like an unplugged refrigerator. After a few seconds of stunned silence, Ethelene gasped, clapping her hands. Esme inspected the object in her grasp, yelping. "Mom! I thought I'd lost this! It's my necklace. It matches the one I gave dad—the one I bought in Guatemala."

"Guatemala…" Esme repeated like it meant something.

Esme picked at the brown string tied in knots. She pulled, pried the knots apart, and rubbed her finger over the large glass bead. It swirled with rainbow colors. She handed it to her mother. "Your dad still wears his," Ethelene whispered wistfully, handing the necklace back to Esme.

"I love this necklace," stated Esme, fixing it around her neck.

"It matches your nightgown," said Ethelene with a smile.

Esme touched the glass. "I think my power has something to do with Guatemala. In fact, I know it does."

Joseph

Joseph's tennis shoes squished on the sidewalk as he approached his apartment on Jamaica Avenue. After the rain, the summer humidity was stifling, and the streetlights flickered in a million little puddles. He jostled his backpack and rolled his shoulder, switching the heavy grocery bag from one hand to the other. One thing was clear: he wouldn't miss the commute from Queens to Mitzi's apartment, and he wouldn't miss all the rats. There was very little he would miss about New York. Obviously, Central Park and the food, but Mexico City had good food, too.

Approaching the double white doors, Joseph glanced up at the red brick structure before pulling out his keys, unlocking the door and entering the lobby. He figured Jared had already retrieved the mail, so he headed up the stairs to the third floor, and after fumbling with the door, Joseph entered his apartment. The room smelled like popcorn. A movie blared; he rolled his eyes.

The first thing Joseph noticed was the back of Jared's head peeking over the purple velvet sofa. Jared turned, fingers creeping over the plush cushion. "How was it with your girlfriend in Orlando?" the man asked, yawning.

Joseph laughed. "I've been back for three days. I just came from Mitzi's."

Jared muted the television and rose from the couch, wearing slouchy, blue scrubs. The man entered the kitchen with his bowl of popcorn and leaned against the island where Joseph had piled his things. "Man, that smells good. I'm going to miss your cooking. When do you leave again?"

"Soon. Next Saturday," said Joseph.

"Damn, I'll be on call at the hospital. How'd it go with Esme? You know, I told your dad you were gay. I can't believe I was wrong. Are you sure? There's this oncologist I was going to set you up with."

Joseph raised his eyebrows and sighed. "Sorry to disappoint you, but I like women. We had an interesting, fun time. Orlando is crazy. But Winter Park is nice. I miss Esme already," Joseph said, placing his leftovers in the fridge. He pulled *The Joy of Cooking* from his backpack and set the book on the counter.

Jared tugged at the book, inspected it, and flipped it to look at the back cover. "I'm happy you're training to be a chef. You're going to kill it, seriously. Does your dad know? Have you talked with him?"

"No, he's in Guatemala, on-site," Joseph said, feeling that wave of déjà vu again. It was like an invisible pull, yanking at his heart, stomach, or somewhere. When he thought of Guatemala, it made him feel so distracted and confused. Joseph turned, orienting himself towards the static, like a radio station, with shimmers of Esme's voice and other unidentifiable noises. "Dude. Are you okay?" asked Jared.

Joseph felt his cheeks grow hot. He rubbed his eyes with his knuckles. "Honestly, Jared, I don't know. It's been a weird night. I'm so excited about Le Cordon Bleu, yet I feel pulled in another direction."

Jared scooped popcorn into his mouth, speaking like a chipmunk with full cheeks, "You gotta go. Being a chef is your calling, right?" Jared paused, pointing at the refrigerator. "So, can I eat some of whatever you got there tomorrow?" he asked, pushing himself straight.

Joseph smiled. "Mole, the best you've ever tasted. Mitzi said so."

Jared made swirling motions around his stomach and winked flirtatiously, then turned. "Okay, I'm going to bed. Don't let this opportunity pass you by, man," he said, walking away.

Joseph watched Jared's back for a long beat. Then he turned, heading for the cupboard over the sink. "A drink will help me sleep," he muttered to the empty kitchen.

Joseph opened the cupboard and reached for the Tequila. *A salty, double pour of Olmeca Altos with a squirt of lime on ice,* He thought, licking his lips. Joseph retrieved the bottle and set it on the counter. He shifted to the other door—the cupboard over the toaster oven—grabbed a low ball, rummaged towards the back for a shot glass, and turned the small glass in his hand: Tikal. It was a souvenir glass from the Mayan ruin site in Guatemala. Joseph shook his head in disbelief, unscrewed the Altos, and took a big swig.

Morning light filtered through the parallel blinds in Joseph's room, and outside the window, garbage trucks beeped. It was a typical morning in Queens. Joseph couldn't wait to hear new noises, birds—probably just pigeons— and all the new morning sounds in Mexico City. The last week was a blur of preparations. Now, it was only a day away. He was leaving tomorrow morning.

Joseph stretched, tossed his sheet, and planted his feet on the floor. It had been a long, restless night. He subtly remembered having a nightmare—flying, falling—but the dream was already partially erased. Sometimes, he wished he could erase all thoughts about Esme and Guatemala. The unwanted feelings were sucking the joy from his upcoming adventure; it was starting to annoy him. Still, he couldn't shake the thoughts away. They were stuck, like burrs on the hem of his pants.

Joseph stumbled to the window, opened his blinds, and turned off the rattlebox: the old window air conditioner that barely kept the room cool. He entered the hall, visited the bathroom, and tiptoed into the living room, turning on the television. Immediately, he lowered the volume to a quiet murmuring and flipped the channel until he found the news.

As soon as he entered the kitchen, he prepared a big pot of coffee, poured his cereal, walked to the sofa, and sat down without spilling a drop of milk. He started crunching, slurping milk, and sipping coffee while watching the television. He could barely hear what the reporter was saying.

Joseph heard the coffee pot rattle around on its plate and turned towards the kitchen, surprised that Jared was up and rummaging around. There was no one there. He furrowed his brows and turned back to the television. Footage of a colonial town and a steaming volcano scrolled the screen. Joseph placed his bowl on the coffee table and inflated the volume, listening to a reporter talk about the aftermath of the eruption of the Fuego Volcano in Guatemala—Joseph couldn't believe it. Was he in an alternate reality where everything in his life kept pointing him toward Guatemala? His life was so bizarre.

He muted the television and finished his meal in silence. At least, he wasn't getting any messages from Esme, and he prayed that all was well. Joseph wandered into the kitchen and slipped his empty bowl into the sink. Then he gasped, covering his mouth.

In front of the coffee maker, he saw the word *Guatemala* smeared through overturned coffee grounds from his pot. It was like an invisible finger had left a message in the sand. "This is unbelievable," Joseph muttered, wondering for the first time if his father and Oliver were okay.

Esme

Esme read the new comment and clicked her tongue. "Asshole," she muttered.

"What? What's wrong?" asked Ethelene, returning from the bathroom with her toiletry bag and squishing it into her suitcase.

"Some jerk named Benjamin said I'm fat. He said I'd look like a young Drew Barrymore if I lost ten-to-twenty pounds," Esme said with an exaggerated sniff.

"You do look like a young Drew Barrymore. She wasn't always that thin, you know."

"Mom, it's so easy for you. You've always been skinny and beautiful. With your looks, I'd already have a famous YouTube channel."

Ethelene beamed, then pouted, fixing her hands on her hips. "Honey, you'll have to get used to comments like that. The more you put yourself out there, the more people can tear you down. Some people are mean, plain, and simple. They don't take risks; they never try anything; they sit on their computer looking for people to hurt. The good news is most of the comments are from people who are amazed by your powers!"

"You're beginning to sound like Joseph, full of wisdom and stuff."

Ethelene seemed to grow taller, straighter. "You know, even *I* need to work out. Have you tried spin classes?"

Esme bowed her head in defeat. "At least you didn't say *Pilates.*"

Ethelene rolled her eyes and continued packing. After a few minutes, she stopped in front of Esme. "You should stop reading those, seriously." Ethelene folded her arms. "I'm all packed and ready to head back to Clearwater. I'd love to take you to dinner before I leave—my treat. We could go to I-drive, somewhere touristy. Then you could perform after. What-do-you-say? I'll film you."

Esme wanted to perform. She loved to use her powers— standing in front of a crowd, feeding off their energy, and feeling like a superhero. But she was scared; scared things would go haywire, berserk. "What if I lose control, start levitating off the ground, or send somebody flying into a restaurant? What if someone gets hurt?"

"You've never hurt anyone, not even close. If things get a little crazy, people will think it is part of your act. Maybe if something big happened, you'd get noticed by another agent. Maybe it would be a good thing."

Esme closed her laptop and grinned.

"My name is Jade. What's your name?" asked Esme, squatting in front of a little girl who was wearing a green swimsuit, shorts, and sunburned cheeks. Behind the girl stood the rest of her family: an older brother, grandparents, mother, and father. Everyone wore beachy clothes, tanned arms, and relaxed, happy expressions. "Did you go to a water park?" she asked the little girl.

The girl nodded, glancing at her family for affirmation. The girl's dad smiled, giving his daughter a slight nudge. "I'm Sara," said the girl, looking over her shoulder, then swiveling her head back towards Esme.

"Sara, would you like to pick a card and hold it up, so everyone can see it?" asked Esme.

Tentatively, Sara looked around at the crowd, then reached for a card. As soon as Sara's fingertips grazed her selection, Esme collapsed the deck like a mouth snapping shut, folding the cards like an accordion. She dug into her pocket and returned with two decks of cards. Again, Esme fanned the cards in front of Sara's outstretched hand. The crowd laughed.

Sara looked across the super-sized deck, finally selected a card, and held it up—it was the eight of hearts. Esme stood tall, placing the remaining cards in her side pocket. "Perfect, you're a natural. Now, let's see if you can balance the card on your head?" said Esme, pointing at her own head.

The girl placed the card on her head and giggled, her brown eyes sparkling.

Esme reached up, pulling her magic wand from behind the feather attached to her black velvet top hat. Everyone snickered. She gave a quick, theatrical bow. Then, smiling with teeth, she swished the wand around the little girl's head. The card levitated straight up, spun around three times, and settled back on the crown of Sara's head.

Esme backed away, looking at the faces of the crowd and secretly praying the trick would work. She moved her wand again dramatically and the card flew into the air, landed on the brother's baseball cap, bounced onto the father's head, and finally settled onto the mother's wavy brown curls.

The card sat still, then jittered back and forth like a cat on the hunt, darting to the top of the grandmother's wide, straw hat. The older woman cackled with delight, then looked at her husband, anticipating the card's next move. The card fluttered and twirled, landing on the grandfather's cropped gray head and flopping around like a fish. The older man laughed and tried to grab it, but the card flew away and returned to Sara's small wet head. The crowd murmured and clapped, delighted.

Esme slipped her hand behind her back. She'd been practicing her *real* magic tricks, hoping to pull off some simple sleight of hand. She took a shallow breath and approached Sara, simultaneously moving the wand in her other hand. Esme swished back and forth with one hand and replaced the eight with a Mickey Mouse card she'd hidden inside her belt. The crowd roared when she held the new card up for everyone to see.

Esme looked at her mother, standing at the crowd's edge. Ethelene lowered her phone, shaking her head and mouthing words Esme couldn't hear. Esme beamed. She'd been so focused on her performance that she hadn't thought about Joseph—not once. But now, she wished he was here, almost desperately. He'd be so proud.

Esme bit her lip. She didn't want to ruin the fun by obsessing about Joseph. She placed her wand back into her hat and wiped away a bead of sweat that had lodged at the nape of her neck. Again, she looked at Ethelene. Across the way, her mother's head lifted, her eyes fixed on the sky. Ethelene raised her arms and her phone, filming.

Esme looked up. "Holy shit," she whispered.

The cards—all one hundred and four—had escaped her pocket. Now, they were like winged creatures, aloft on the winds.

The crowd returned, gathering around again. People pointed above their heads, muttering to one another. The cards spun, undulating, and flying on unseen wings in the sky above the parking lot of Café Cascabel. The air buzzed, and patterns started to appear, like figure eights and geometric squares, circles, letters, and outlandish designs. It was like looking through a kaleidoscope—almost like fireworks. It was mesmerizing.

Esme watched with a fluttery heart, surrounded by the crowd of onlookers. Nobody said a word. Esme's mouth felt dry. She was excited but also scared of her own power. After a few minutes, the cards slowed, forming a long, irregular line in the sky, hovering like a kite string. Esme held up her right palm, and the cards nestled together one by one as if called home to roost. All eyes settled on Esme.

At first, people simply stared at her, while silence prevailed. Then, slowly, thunderous applause ensued. Esme and Ethelene locked eyes. The aerial display exceeded what she had hoped for, and no one got hurt. Ethelene slipped her phone into her purse, clapping with the others. Esme could see her mother's glassy blue eyes. She ran, grabbed her mother, and hugged her hard as she could.

"Oh, honey," Ethelene gasped. "That was out of this world amazing."

"Mom," Esme whispered, "I don't think it was me. My powers keep getting stronger and weirder since…well, ever since Joseph."

Ethelene looked into Esme's eyes. "What could be weirder than having the power of levitation?"

Joseph

Joseph decided not to bring his copy of *The Joy of Cooking* to Mexico City. The book was too heavy, and besides, he figured he would be studying from all kinds of books, or maybe his class wouldn't crack open a book at all. Indeed, most of the training would be hands-on prep work, like dicing and slicing, sautéing, roasting, and peeling. He envisioned piles of onions and potatoes. He fantasized about daily journeys to the market to gather bunches of fragrant, fresh herbs. They'd craft their menus from whatever was in season. The kitchen would always smell like butter and garlic, bone broth, and ripe fruit. There would be cupboards with exotic spices and baskets of peppers and cactus paddles. It was all so exciting.

The knives would always be sharp at Le Cordon Bleu. Joseph rubbed his eyes, laughing to himself. He figured there would be no elves sharpening knives in the middle of the night; it would be the students and himself. Still, he was ready. He had a lot to learn, but he wasn't afraid of hard work.

Joseph realized he was so deep in thought that he hadn't turned a magazine page for ten minutes. He set it aside and looked up, appraising the gate across from his own in the international terminal of JFK. It didn't surprise him that it was a flight to Guatemala City.

But it did cause his stomach to dance. *Why is this happening?* The universe seemed to be telling him something—none too subtly—but he refused to listen. He would miss Esme, but this was important. Most of all, he didn't want to look like a flake in front of Mitzi. She had such high hopes for him and lofty expectations. Plus, she had invested so much money. He didn't want to let her down or cause her to wonder if she made the right choice—giving up a beloved caregiver. Now, she was stuck with a tattooed stranger who couldn't cook.

"Esme," Joseph whispered, sensing her thinking of him, hearing her voice inside his head.

Joseph grabbed his phone and checked his texts—nothing. There were no new emails, either. Still curious, he refreshed the page.

"I knew it," he muttered to himself.

From: Esme Wright
Subject: New Videos!
Date: June 22, 2021
To: Joseph Estrada

Joseph, I miss you so much! I was going to Facetime you, but I figured you were already in the air. You've got to play these videos (The second one is unbelievable). Mom recorded them last night. Don't be scared, okay? The second one is crazier than the hotel room, but super cool—amazing. I haven't put them on YouTube yet because I'm at work, and I know you wouldn't want me to. Let me know what you think as soon as you're able. Well, have a safe flight. I hope I can come to see you in Mexico. Don't forget about me. I love you.

Esme

Joseph checked the time and the status of his flight, then looked around his gate at the other passengers. Every seat at his gate was occupied. He sat squished between an older couple and a businessman eating a burrito. Joseph hated to give up his seat, but he didn't want anyone to see Esme's videos. He grabbed his wheel bag and stood, winding through the maze of legs and luggage, pet carriers, and strollers.

Ultimately, he leaned against a pillar across the way. Joseph returned to his phone, hitting the first link that Esme had enclosed. Even though she had told him not to worry, he still had an overwhelming feeling of dread.

Joseph watched Esme standing near Café Cascabel with a large crowd gathered around her. She looked cute in a purple silk blouse, black shorts, and the hat he had purchased. He felt his heart grow larger just watching her. She was so good with kids; her smile showed the audience how much she appreciated them. Joseph chuckled, his head bobbing as he watched her performance play out. The card jumping from one head to another was inspired. Still, it bothered him. He worried that it was all too much.

After checking the status of his flight, he surveyed the terminal. They'd be boarding soon, and he didn't want to miss his call. He listened as a garbled announcement filtered over people's heads. Now, they were boarding passengers that needed extra assistance, like mothers and babies, older folks, and people with disabilities. He figured he'd have time, so he hit the following video and held his phone at eye level.

Immediately, he gasped. As soon as the video started, it was on—for real. Esme's cards were floating in the sky, forming unique patterns. Joseph rubbed his mouth, butterflies churning in his stomach. The video was overwhelming. *Thank goodness Esme didn't put this on YouTube.* Joseph's eyes flicked to his gate, then back to the screen. He inhaled sharply. "Mother, Mary, and Joseph!" he exclaimed.

Joseph dialed the video back again, then paused it. "No way!" he hissed.

The cards hovered in the sky—briefly, magically forming a word. It was a familiar word that fought to be seen and heard. *Guatemala.* Joseph rubbed his forehead, his phone swinging in his hand. He stared at the floor, grabbed his wheel bag, and ran.

Joseph thanked the Uber driver and stepped from the car into a night as thick as clam chowder. There were no stars, only heavy clouds, and heat. Even amidst the city lights, it seemed unnaturally dark. Joseph stood, listening to the song of the cicadas, and surveying the bushes around him. He looked up at a giant oak tree covered in Spanish moss, dangling like a million tiny spiders.

After his eyes adjusted, he moved forward, his wheel bag thumping up the sidewalk as he approached the apartment building in front of him. As he neared the stairs, he heard a door swing open, then scampering feet thundering down the wooden staircase. Joseph let go of his bag and opened his arms. Esme— barefoot, wearing pajamas—thrust herself against him, kissing him harder than she'd ever kissed him before. Joseph pulled away, pecking all around her face with small, wet kisses. The feeling he always had—that Esme was like a sister—suddenly seemed farther away. It was still there, but carnal love was sweeping in and taking hold. "I knew you were coming. I woke up levitating over my bed, and when I fell, I knew you were here. Why didn't you tell me you were coming? Why didn't you go to Mexico City?"

Joseph hugged Esme again, whispering into her hair. "I need to tell you something big, something really important."

He pulled away, grabbed his bag and lead Esme to the stairs. "It's a long story. We best go inside before we get attacked by an armadillo or something."

Esme guffawed once and grabbed Joseph's hand. They climbed the stairs and entered her apartment. Joseph left his bag near the door, pulling Esme to the sofa. "Sit," he said while sitting down himself.

Esme sat down and looked around the living room. "Nothing's happening," she whispered. "This time, nothing is flying around the room."

Joseph surveyed the room, nodding solemnly. After a few seconds, he puffed his cheeks, grabbed her hand again, and squeezed it. Esme looked into his eyes. "Don't be mad. Okay?"

"I could never be mad at you. Why? Why would I be mad?"

"Because I didn't tell you something, something big. You aren't the only one with powers. I have them too, just like you. I thought Diablo possessed me for a very long time. I tried so hard not to use this thing…Whatever this thing is. But that night, that night with the car…That was me."

Esme inhaled as if sucking in a fiery sword. She looked away from Joseph. "But…" she whimpered.

Joseph used a finger to tip her face toward his. "I was wrong. I should have told you the truth. I didn't because I wanted you to feel special. You are special, you know? You want the power so much, and I don't. Now I'm scared for both of us. Esme, we need to go to Guatemala. Something is going on…"

"I know," she interrupted.

His face went blank. "Wait. Did you say you were levitating over your bed before? Is that what you said?"

Esme nodded with wild eyes. "Yeah, every night now. But Joseph, can you show me? I believe you, but can you show me what you can do?"

"I am showing you. Look around."

Esme surveyed the room. "Holy Cow," she said, grabbing the cushions.

Unbeknownst to Esme, the sofa below them floated high above the floor like a swaying magic carpet. Esme reached to touch the ceiling, her legs dangling over the cushions. Effortlessly, Joseph glided the sofa to the floor, and it landed with a cupping sound.

The room unplugged and grew ominously still. Joseph looked into Esme's eyes. He had expected her to be excited or mad, anything but grim and blank.

"What do you think? Do you believe me now?"

"Your power is so much stronger than mine, like out of this world amazing. Lately, my power has been out of control. At first, it excited me, like it always has. But now it scares me, too," said Esme, grabbing and squeezing his hands. "Guatemala feels right. But why do you think we need to go?"

"Because the signs are guiding us. I hope the signs are from God, not Diablo. At first, I tried to ignore them. I was at the airport, and I almost got on the plane for Mexico. But did you see the sign in your video? The second video?"

Esme looked confused. "You mean the patterns? They were beautiful."

"The cards. They spelled *Guatemala*. I couldn't resist any longer. I knew we had to go. I hope Mitzi will understand."

"She will. Joseph, you're going to be a great chef someday. You won't let her down," said Esme, but then she paused. "Where in Guatemala? El Mirador?"

"I think so. I see us there, running through the trees when we were children. I think we'll receive more signs. I think, once we're there, we'll know what to do."

Esme nodded. "I'm scared for my dad. Yours, too. Do you think something has happened to them? Is that why we need to go there?"

Joseph popped his eyes. "I don't know," he said, taking a deep breath.

Reaching down, he swiped a finger over the glass bead around her neck. "Do you always sleep with this? You weren't wearing it before when I was here."

Esme touched the smooth glass of her necklace, twisting the frayed edges of string around her neck. "I thought I'd lost it. I bought one just like it for my dad. It makes me feel closer to him when I wear it."

"I'm worried about my dad, too. But we'd hear something if they were hurt, right? You know, it's exciting now that I...we...have decided to go to Guatemala. I feel butterflies in my stomach, wondering what lies ahead of us," said Joseph, pulling her against his chest.

Joseph felt Esme's warm breath on his neck and heard her inhaling his scent. After she rubbed her cheek against his unshaven face, she rubbed her nose against his earlobe, her hair tickling his skin. She started nibbling and nuzzling his neck while her fingers explored his body. "I feel butterflies, too," said Esme. She pulled away, looking into Joseph's eyes. "But not because we're going to Guatemala. Can we...you know?"

After a moment's hesitation, he reached into his heart and made a choice. The choice felt right. "I'm hungry for you too,

Esme," he said. Then he kissed her, his tongue slipping into her mouth, teasing.

Joseph grabbed both sides of her face, gently pulling his lips away. "You taste like magic," he whispered. "I bet I can make your nightgown disappear."

Esme giggled and performed the trick herself.

Esme

"Joseph, if something happened to the plane, do you think we could use our powers to keep it airborne?" Esme whispered into his ear.

"I don't know. I hope we don't need to find out," Joseph whispered back.

Esme peered into the blue infinity outside her window, thinking about the whirlwind she'd experienced while preparing for the trip. Luckily, her passport hadn't expired. But other things hadn't gone as smoothly. Even so, she felt over the moon excited at the prospect of returning to Guatemala. She couldn't wait to see her dad; she would tell him everything.

Joseph gulped his drink and shoved his cooking magazine into the seat pocket before his knees. "Have you ever eaten an acocile?"

"No. What's that?"

"It's a tiny crayfish that tastes like sea salt. I've never eaten one, but I was reading the most interesting article about a Mexico City chef sprinkling chinicuiles, chapulines, and chicatanas onto his entrees. People pay *big* money to eat them. When I was a kid, my grandfather taught me how to forage for the tiny worms—or chinicuiles—hiding in the maguey plant. We would use coat hangers; it was fun. The worms are kind of earthy with a big crunch. Delicious!"

"Yuck! That's so gross. I'm almost afraid to ask what the other things are."

Joseph laughed, wiggling his fingers like creepy-crawly spider legs. "Chicatanas are ants—they taste like garlic—and chapulines are grasshoppers. You've had those, right?"

"No! Who are you?"

Joseph slapped his knee, rolling with laughter. After finally containing his glee, he leaned over Esme's shoulder, looking out the window and pointing at the island-dotted waters below. "The water is so beautiful, so green. We must be over the cays near Belize. The reef looks like an amoeba, don't you think?"

Esme smiled, nodding. "I love how the irregular coral shapes and sand fringe out from the turquoise water like will-o'-the-wisps. I feel like we're going home, don't you? I feel so happy and content. I thought I'd be scared or stressed, especially after I quit my job. But I don't. I just feel happy."

Joseph jiggled his plastic cup, nodding. "Me too. As soon as I decided to go to Guatemala, it felt right. I don't know what lies ahead, but the pull is so strong that it's a relief not to fight it anymore. The weird thing is, I feel at peace about missing my semester at Le Cordon Blue, too."

"I'm glad Mitzi was so understanding."

"I know. I was so worried. But Mitzi just laughed, saying she was old enough to know it would all work out in the end. She told me to have fun. Can you believe it? She wasn't mad. She was glad I was having an adventure. She told me to bring back some honey from Guatemala and pay her back when I'm a fancy, big-city chef. That's Mitzi," said Joseph, shaking his head.

"I wish they would have been so understanding at my job. But I didn't have any vacation days left. It was a good job," Esme said, pausing, "At least I made a lot in tips after my last show. At least I've got magic."

Joseph squeezed her hand. "You've got me, too. I'm glad you patched things up with your mom."

"Me too. Look, we're overland again. I bet we're almost there."

Joseph lodged his head near Esme's. They watched the ground transform from flat, dry lowland to hills and, finally, mountains. "Look!" Esme exclaimed as they passed over a cone-shaped volcano, spewing ash. "I feel like a kid again, traveling with my dad. I cried and cried when we left Guatemala. I didn't think I could live without you, even then."

Joseph kissed her neck, and Esme felt electricity travel to her toes. "Joseph?"

"Yes?"

"Your power is stronger than mine."

"No."

"You know it is. You lifted the car, not me. Why do you think your power is stronger, and don't say it's because you're a man."

"Esme! *Shh*...Don't talk so loudly." He squeezed her knee and whispered, "You know I wouldn't say that."

Esme's face turned serious. "I know. But your powers are stronger."

"My power is strong. So strong it terrifies me. But look at what you did with the cards. It was beautiful—utterly amazing."

Esme frowned. "It was amazing, but I don't think it was me," she said with exasperation.

"Of course, it was you. Who else could it be?" said Joseph, trying but failing not to think of the word *Diablo*. "I feel like there's going to be a reckoning."

"That sounds ominous."

"Not necessarily. I don't think anything bad is going to happen," he said, pausing to complete the sign of the cross. "At least, I hope not. That's not what I mean. Esme, don't you feel it? That we're close to something big? The pull is so strong. I was expecting a sign, but maybe we don't need one. Something is going to happen at El Mirador. I know it is."

"I hope we don't get a sign telling us to go to Belize or Nicaragua since we're bound for Flores," said Esme with a half-smile.

Joseph's face turned serious. "It's not going to be easy, hiking into El Mirador."

"You should have asked Mitzi to pay for a helicopter!"

"I didn't want to push my luck. Besides, that would cost thousands of dollars."

Esme looked into Joseph's eyes. "I guess what we need is the power of teleportation."

They both smiled cautious smiles. A few minutes later, an announcement played overhead.

Everyone, we'll arrive at the Guatemala City International Airport in approximately thirty-five minutes. We have clear skies and a temperature of seventy-one degrees. The local time is 3:30 p.m. Flight attendants, please prepare the cabin for arrival.

"One more flight," said Esme, beaming.

"One more flight, a night in Flores, a long trip in a van—with strangers—to Carmelita, hiking in the jungle for two or three days, sleeping with the jaguars. No problem!"

"Joseph, if a Jaguar slinks into our camp, feel free to send it flying to the parking lot of Café Cascabel."

"That was pretty cool," Joseph admitted.

"You're my superhero."

Esme watched Joseph sleep, admiring his messy, dark hair and thick, sexy eyelashes. She flicked her eyes to the curtains covering the window by the door. They were like insect wings, sucking in and out with the breeze, light glowing behind the thin, orange fabric. She placed her hand underneath her face and curled her legs upwards, snuggling against Joseph's warm body. She wanted to make love again but didn't want to wake him. After a few reflective minutes, she removed her hand from under her head and stroked his chest; it was as smooth and soft as a baby's bottom. Esme kissed the tip of his nose.

Joseph wiggled his nose and reached up, brushing off an invisible bug. His eyes opened partway, then all the way. "How long have you been staring?" Joseph whispered.

"All night."

Joseph laughed. Esme moved closer, kissing his neck, nibbling his ear. "Again?" he whispered.

Esme raised her eyebrows and brushed his legs with her toes. Joseph cupped Esme's breast through the sheet and kissed her mouth, pulling her to his chest. She moaned, wrapping her legs around him. He sucked in his breath, lifting his head and staring at her nightstand. "Esme, the time," he croaked.

She turned to toss an angry stare at the clock.

"It's so late. We need to find someone to take us to Carmelita. We have so much to do!" said Joseph.

Esme collapsed onto her pillow. Joseph jumped out of bed, naked, picking up his underwear, then scooping his shorts and shirt. "I'm sorry that I can't ravish you," Joseph said, kneeling and kissing her forehead. "I'm going to shower," he said, walking away. Then he peeked inside the tiny bathroom. Joseph popped his head back out. "I think there's room for both of us," he added.

Esme threw the sheet aside and sat up, tipping her legs over the mattress. She stood, her breasts bouncing, tummy jiggling. Skipping into the bathroom, she giggled all the way.

Esme sat on the edge of the bed, leaning to lace her tennis shoes. Afterward, she placed her hands on her knees and looked around the tiny, stucco room, and then out the tiny window. There was a deep blue lake framed within the open curtains. Shouts and laughter lifted from the street below, and the air smelled like someone was making breakfast, and grilling onions and peppers for an omelet. Joseph shoved the last of his toiletries into his backpack. "You put on sunscreen, right?"

"Yes, after we showered."

They exchanged smiles. Whipping the crumpled sheets and swiveling around, Esme surveyed the room for forgotten articles. "I think we're ready," she said, standing and leaning to grab the handles of her backpack, slipping the pack over her white, freckled shoulders, and fluffing out her long, red hair.

Joseph put on a red Yankee's baseball cap and smiled with his teeth. Esme grabbed a wide-brimmed, green cloth hat, placing it on her head. "You look just like your dad," said Joseph.

Esme beamed. They scampered through the exit, closing the door and descending a narrow stairway paved with blue tile. Finally, they emerged onto a bright sidewalk. A wave of heat slapped their faces with red-hot kisses. They crossed the cobbled street ahead and stood, gazing over Lake Peten Itza. Lush, green islands floated in the distance, and a curving cement wall separated water from the land below their feet. Old, wooden boats with peeling paint bounced and jingled on the lake's surface, and the men inside the vessels shouted to them, hoping for paying passengers. "No gracias," called Joseph.

They walked along the cement wall—water occasionally splashing onto their feet—for one or two blocks. Then they turned right, walking up a steep hill lined with rainbow-colored villas. Everything was old, crumbling, and cracking. Under the red-tiled roofs, vines of cable wire clung to every corner. In the street, tiny red and white golf-cart-sized cars buzzed about, and dogs and people zig-zagged. On the sidewalk, at least once on every block, they discovered someone sleeping in a doorway, prone on the dirty, hard ground. The air smelled like fresh, baked bread.

Joseph looked at his phone, then up at a red-arched doorway. "This is it. I think. They should have INGUAT licensed guides here." He peeled off his heavy pack. "Do you want to wait here with our bags while I go inside?"

Esme nodded, slipping off her pack and setting it on a purple-painted bench. She sat. After two or three minutes, she heard music floating in the breeze. Looking down the street, she watched a marching band slip around the corner. In front of the matching orange T-shirt-clad group, a mannequin on stilts spun, with a red and black striped skirt swirling at the base. When the band passed Esme, one of the revelers threw a bang snap at her feet. She yelped, pulling back her tennis shoes.

The band turned the corner and disappeared, music fading into the distance. Esme pulled at her tank top and wiped the sweat from her chest, a curious smile sweeping her face. Soon after, Joseph emerged from the red door. "What was all that?"

"A band. The performers threw a firecracker at me!"

Joseph frowned. "I have bad news," he said, sitting down. "We can't leave until tomorrow morning at five a.m. That's when the van will take us to Carmelita."

"Oh," she said, touching her stomach. "I have butterflies. That's how excited I am to get going, to get there. Now what?"

"We wait. We get something to eat. We check back into the hotel...."

Esme smiled. Joseph smiled back. "I know how you feel. Esme, I had the weirdest dream last night. I was flying, but somehow, I was different. You know how sometimes you have a dream, and you're not sure if you are the protagonist or if it's someone else?"

"I dreamt that I was flying, too!" Esme interrupted. "Tell me what you dreamt?"

Initiate Cerebral Streaming—

Recording Session Three

Studying the bizarre ocean dwellers is like looking into a microscope at atypical bacteria configurations. The Atlantic crew has a job unlike any other. Their vessel resembles a colossal blue whale, moving through the ocean, writhing with eerie sounds that echo through various chambers. I have never experienced a vessel such as this, built to fly and swim.

Dob-Dec used synthetic gills to seed and collected specimens with the Atlantic crew for three days past. I continued my examinations and attempted to stay in balance. But it is difficult in this haunting atmosphere.

Every night, after my work is complete, Dob-Dec regales me with stories of the fishes. There are rainbow-colored oddities with many legs in the shallows, but most creatures have no legs whatsoever. The eyes of the ocean dwellers are significant for their size, and their slim bodies shimmer with luminescence. My favorite creature has always been the immortal jellyfish. However, you will not find it in Atlantic waters. I have relied on the research collected from the Pacific crew. (We will leave sufficient rations for the Pacific crew to acquire independently and will not visit them on this mission.)

I do not favor the immortal jellyfish because of its beauty. It is the science behind the fish that makes it magical. The jellyfish reverts to its youthful polyp stage through transdifferentiation and begins life anew. This life cycle mimics our own. Dob-Dec said he would not leave the ocean until he saw a sperm whale. Apparently, he is captivated by the sperm whales' massive, asymmetrical brains. He loves all earthly creatures—except for cows.

Dob-Dec wants to create an ocean disc at home, although creating that much water would be problematic. We must be content to swim with them, while collecting their DNA.

Before we arrived, the Atlantic crew sampled a spiny sea urchin. The others said it resembled rambutan fruit and were simply curious. This is outrageous! Our bodies are opposed to protein. Dob-Dec also sampled a fermented juice in Antarctica. I advised all our Blue Earth researchers to refrain from testing unknown nutrition sources. I hope they will be more careful in the future.

Since my examinations are nearly complete, we will soon leave this haunting realm of peculiar beasts, sights, and sounds. Knowing that we will not recreate the ocean dwellers on Pleione is wistful. We *only* harvest the DNA for future terraforming.

I may never see the fishes in their infinite saline habitat again.

Blessed listeners, please record the following with a sacred heart, I possess a precious soul, stored in spirit stone and destined for rebirth on planet Pleione. A shadow of seriousness follows the ocean crew's movements because everyone loved and respected Antares.

I have very little knowledge of death. *Beings* live long, vibrant lives like ginkgo trees of the beautiful Blue Earth. Even after two hundred years, our immune systems are young and fresh, and our genes still defend our bodies until an outside force intervenes.

Dear listeners, death touches few.

However, *Beings* can't evade death forever. Dob-Dec understands this and has bonded with the ocean crew. Since death is uncommon, I have never touched sacred spirit stone. I feel honored to oversee the container that holds the life force of Antares. May she rest in peace until the time of her resurrection ceremony.

Resume Universal Translation Mode—
End of Session.

Commence Cerebral Streaming–

Session Ten

Our mission nears completion, and all is well inside our little ship as we sail through the restless skies of the tiny Blue Earth toward Guatemala and the ancient energy site of El Mirador. We are almost there.

We have evaded the meat-eaters so far. However, earthly weather—both exciting and dangerous—proved to be a more formidable adversary. It was a boisterous calamity of opposite but interconnected forces. We entered the eye of a hurricane as we traveled the skies over the Atlantic.

Lyra was curious. I was curious! Our ship stewards rode the winds like an albatross until we entered the eye, and all was calm. There we remained, shields up and invisible until the storm weakened over the Caribbean islands.

Earlier, we flew over the Amazon rainforest, a verdant ecosystem that rivals the largest dome on planet Pleione. Our terraformers marvel at its diversity. This time, I felt pain in my heart, for the tipping point is nigh. And yes, I have a heart.

However, I do not like to dwell on negative things. My heart swells, thinking about the time I have enjoyed with Sula. The air smells better when she is near. Together, we witnessed bristly islands sprout from turquoise waters like an artisan meat-eater's canvas. We saw whales breaching over the turbulent waters, and we watched the Earth's singular sun bleed over the ocean in a million reflections. Sometimes, I forget to breathe.

As we near our destination, I have resumed collecting and cataloging data from my tiny insect drones, like my favorite living insects: leaf-cutter ants. If I were a terraformer, I would replace meat-eaters with ants, making ants the dominant society. Ants may come in second (as the most successful animal society), but in my mind, they are the best. Leafcutter ants do not waste time chewing strange and rubbery substances. They chew the leaves they collect into a pulp, add fecal matter, and grow a fungus garden. I love gardens. I love ants; I find them fascinating. I must remain satisfied that ants win at the end when meat-eaters are dead and buried. This is humorous!

There was a glitch as I harvested my new data. I discovered one of my drones landed on a strange, white floppy-eared cow. Cattle are dirty, nasty, disgusting creatures. It doesn't surprise me that filthy creatures like meat-eaters eat them. Sula thinks that meat-eaters are cute. I'm afraid I must disagree with Sula's assessment.

Even though we disagree about meat-eaters, we have been sympatico in our thoughts. Sula has been in perfect balance. However, there is one train of thought—other than her love of meat-eaters—where we also disagree. Sula anticipates our return to Pleione with happiness. I do not. At home, Sula will reunite with her family. I will no longer enjoy her companionship nor have an excuse to hold her hand or read her beautiful surface thoughts. My heart grows heavy. My love for Sula has expanded into a feeling as vast and bright as the suns. I expect the return of my nemesis: loneliness.

Again, I must resist the temptation to dwell on the negative. Until the day I see our planet grow before us like a gigantic eye, I have nothing to fear. Sula is near.

I am excited to revisit Guatemala. El Mirador's pyramids—part of the historic power grid circling the tiny Blue Earth—are just one of the primitive sites we visited in the past. Indeed, the ancient crews had a soft spot for the meat-eaters of Guatemala. Back then, the meat-eaters revered us like Gods. In truth, we are only architects of the Deities, dutifully managing the universe. We have lost many ships—too many. The souls of the crew recycled. However, sadly, this was not the case for my parents. My Mother and Father's souls live somewhere, perhaps floating among the Deities or trapped in a portal. Maybe they were curious, like me.

Strange…

I am sensing something amiss within the ship. Listeners, do you also hear an unusual sound? There is an imbalance somewhere within the nucleus; I am sure of it. My skin crawls, and blood rushes to my core. I fear something unstoppable is underway. The ship is slowing, vibrating unevenly.

Strange…

Long pause…

Have we stopped?

Long pause. The sound of fabric rubbing against skin, metal, slipping over the glass. Breathing.

What is that sound? There is clanging and so much reverberation…

Pounding footsteps. Swift intake of air. A loud thud against the wall.

We are uncontrolled and spinning. The alarm is pulsating in such a way that I cannot think. I must go to Sula. What is happening? ……..

...........¿Qué pasa?...................

....What is happening?.............

                  ....ЧТО ПРОИСХОДИТ.....

                  ......What is happening?......................

.........Was ist los?...............

                  ....怎么了....

......What is happening?...............   ....

...What is happening?...

.... Ti symvainei?........

                  ....What is happening?.......

.چه اتفاق می افتد ....

                  ....What is happening?.........

.........Qu'est-ce qui se passe?...

......What is happening?...............

Sula!

Sula!

Sula!

Sula!

Sula!

Sula!...............................
....
....
....

Oliver

Oliver sat up and scratched his head, causing his chestnut hair to spill over his shoulders and tickle his bare back like tiny spiders traversed his spine. Just to be sure, he flicked and rubbed his back; nothing lingered except a bead of sweat.

He didn't mind the camp's hardships, and he wasn't squeamish, like some students—especially the city dwellers. But spiders were different. The golden silk orb weaver was as beautiful as a goldfinch. Even so, he didn't want to find one in his bed. He'd never get used to wondering if he might find a tarantula in his cot—or worse, a scorpion.

Across from him, Emil slept like the dead. Nothing seemed to bother his old friend. He figured it must be the Mayan in him. Even though Emil spent winters in New York and was born in New Jersey, he was just like a local. If Emil found a tarantula in his cot, the critter would probably end up on a stick roasting over the fire.

Flopping onto his side, he let his mind wander to the new frieze they'd unearthed and the protective structure they were building on the north side tomorrow. In college, he never would have guessed he'd be doing more construction than digging. Real-life archaeology wasn't like the movies, but then again, his life in Guatemala *did* turn out like a sci-fi movie. He just couldn't tell anyone.

Oliver flipped onto his back again, staring at the scratchy, pitched ceiling of the palapa. He couldn't help thinking about Ethelene: her blue eyes, blond hair, her body. A conjugal visit might be worth more now—at least to him—than a jade amulet. He wondered if she was dating and figured she was. Even though she was a handful and as annoying as hell, he knew a woman who looked like that wouldn't stay single forever. Sometimes, especially after a good roll in the hay, he felt like taking her back himself.

Outside the palapa, a howler monkey moaned somewhere beyond their camp. The beast sounded hoarse and throaty. "Monkeys are like roosters, never failing to signal the fragile beginnings of a new day," he whispered.

Oliver's mind simmered, finally settling on Esme. He wondered how she was doing with her magic. Maybe he would borrow Esteban's satellite phone and give her a call. It had been too long since he'd talked with his only daughter. Oliver knew Esme would get her career on track, eventually. She had a spark for magic ever since she was a kid. And, he figured, it would take more than one failure to extinguish it. She had skills beyond anything he could ever imagine. Still, he worried.

He rubbed his eyes, wondering if he should get up and do some reading. But reading by flashlight wasn't as easy as it used to be. Now, his eyes struggled to focus. Basically, he was getting old. "Sandman, where the heck are you?" he said, noticing a light and turning.

A muffled glow seeped across the floor of the tented palapa. Oliver knew what it was. That's why they had packed up and moved to the most out-of-the-way, obscure hovel at camp. The box—the crystal thingamajig—woke up sometimes, almost like it had a mind of its own. Oliver leaned over, dropped his head over the side of the bed, and lifted the blanket covering the glass object. "Shit!" he whispered, dropping the cloth.

The thing was going nuts. Lifting the blanket again, Oliver watched the shifting patterns of light that flashed like a kaleidoscope. Even though they had been holding onto the object for quite some time, and nothing terrible had happened yet, it still scared him.

Oliver slipped from the bed and knelt before the box, pulling it to his knees. The spinning light intensified. He felt dizzy simply staring at it. "Fuck!" Oliver yelped.

"Shit!" Emil yelped back, now shoulder to shoulder with Oliver.

"You scared the dickens out of me," Oliver scolded in return.

"The thing looks like it's going to take off like a helicopter," Emil fired back.

The men stared, mesmerized. After several minutes, the spinning light slowed, stopping abruptly. Darkness enveloped the structure. Oliver looked at Emil for some kind of confirmation, and then he reached out and touched the edge of the seductive glass object. A beam of light sprung from the top, bright and sharp, straight as an arrow. Oliver's arm constricted as if bitten by a snake. The men collapsed backward.

Seconds passed, and the beam morphed into an undulating shape. It shifted, forming a body, a face. But it wasn't a face that either man recognized. "Oliver," came a voice, sweet and robotic, as if manufactured from a computer.

Oliver opened his mouth to speak but shut it again, looking at Emil. Emil's eyes were huge, his mouth agape. "Emil," the box said in the same sweet and sexy way.

"Yes, we're here. We're listening," said Emil.

The light morphed again, shifting between earthly mammals: pixelated bears and cougars, giant elephants, zebras, and lions. The images filled the circular, tented room, and peculiar shadows danced on the walls. The light continued, manifesting into small, tiny rodents, raccoons and opossums, squirrels, cats, and dogs. It went on like this for several minutes. "What is it doing?" Emil whispered.

"I think it's putting on a show. Maybe it doesn't want to scare us," Oliver whispered back.

Suddenly, the light shifted again, morphing into Emil's dead wife. She was smiling, happy. Emil opened his mouth to speak but buttoned his lips, finally whispering, "Alma! Is that you?"

The hologram blew Emil a kiss and morphed back into the same unusual face and body. Now, they knew what it was. It was crisper, sharper. It was an extraterrestrial with an enormous head, bug-like eyes, and a long, lean body. The creature's ruler-length fingers were steepled as if in prayer, the head bowed humbly.

Pixels of light swirled and danced across the tall, undulating hologram. The image raised its head. "Greetings, human-hybrids. I have an important request. Please, climb to the top of La Danta when the beautiful, earthly moon is full, and the stars are bright in the sky. Oliver, Emil, you must bring the children."

The alien raised its long, slender fingers and arm, pointing towards the ceiling of the palapa. "We are coming from the stars on a retrieval mission, our last for many years. Do not be afraid, as no harm will come to you. You have something of great importance, far beyond the sacred box of the Deities. You possess precious lives. We must take them home."

Slowly, the image faded, the light extinguishing like an old-fashioned television set. Oliver wiped his eyes, hoping no one outside their sleeping palapa had heard the otherworldly voice. Emil's whole body shook with ugly hiccupping sobs. Oliver hugged Emil. "*Shh,* quiet down. We don't want to wake the others," he pleaded.

Emil nodded, swallowing, and swiping at his eyes with his knuckles. "I wish Joseph could have been here, you know? He misses his mother. God, I certainly haven't been much of a dad. But she doesn't blame me. I could feel her love. It was so big; I couldn't comprehend that much love."

"Shit, the moon. The moon will be full in two or three nights. What will the others think if we climb La Danta in the middle of the night?"

Emil swallowed and looked at Oliver, his face solemn, serious. "If what I think is going to happen, happens...Well, I don't think there will be anyone at El Mirador that won't see the spectacle. It will be a goddamned freak show."

"You're right. If *they* come, if there's a real interaction of the third kind, the whole fucking world might know."

Oliver shoved the box under his bed, covering it with the blanket. He contorted his face in the darkness, head swiveling towards Emil. "Wait a minute, *the children?* It said, 'Bring the children.' What children? We don't have any children at camp, do we?"

"No. Not that I'm aware of."

"Aw, hell, what do you think the aliens want from kids? And what will they do to us if we fail to bring them?" asked Oliver.

"Children, that's crazy. It's not like we can bring them, like sacrificial lambs. That would be nuts! We can't do that, can we? I mean, I don't want this to turn into another Huanchaquito sacrifice. What are we supposed to do?"

"There's only one thing we can do—climb La Danta during the full moon, alone, and hope they don't kill us," Oliver mumbled. He grabbed Emil's neck and squeezed.

The men sat as still as a Mayan ruin, staring into the darkness.

Joseph

Joseph pondered the jungle ahead, beside him, and all around. Everything was as still as a statue, quiet as a frozen lake, yet very much alive. Roberto and Alex bushwhacked easily in front of him, cutting down errant branches while watching for snakes with seasoned eyes. Behind his back, Esme plundered, and Michael, the cook—along with two large, old, and weathered mules—forged ahead with slow, methodical, mucky steps.

He'd been second-guessing the journey to El Mirador since Alex—the lead guide—laughed when he inquired about other tourists. "No loco," Alex had said with a crazy smile and head shake.

There weren't that many souls stupid enough to hike into El Mirador during the wet season. Still, he knew that almost three hundred archeologists, his father and Oliver, the students and rangers, and many other travelers *did* make the trip after much last-minute internet research.

Joseph plodded forward with legs covered in specs of mud. Even worse, his arms swatted swarms of bugs, his shoulders shifted his heavy backpack, and his brain worried about Esme. He wondered if the signs he had experienced were from Diablo all along. Maybe the Devil wanted to torment him. But in his heart, he knew they were on the right path. His certainty seemed more robust and vivid with each muddy step.

The ride to Carmelita had been full of excitement—at least for him. Esme had been quiet, watching the scenery outside the window of their van and seemingly overcome with emotion. The drive had been beautiful; as the sun rose over the forested hillside, the misty fog made everything seem magical.

They'd passed little towns selling fruit and coconuts, grassy fields, and roaming cows, but most of all, they passed lots and lots of jungle.

There were so many speed bumps and other unforeseen road obstacles—like cows—that he became impatient. They arrived in Carmelita much later than he'd expected. It had taken almost four hours, and Joseph was starving. Esme seemed increasingly nervous, too. He couldn't blame her; she had done it before. After Alex explained what to expect on their adventure—what to *really* expect—it seemed far worse than what Joseph had researched on the internet. When he translated the facts to Esme, her eyes filled with trepidation. This time, Esme wouldn't have her dad to help her.

Joseph had never actually hiked into El Mirador. He had come by helicopter. On that trip, he and his dad had watched Lake *Petén Itzá* spread out below like a reverse sky. The jungle seemed more extensive than the ocean, with sporadic volcano-like ruins scattered like chess pieces. It was easy and exciting. It was fast.

After tripping on a tree root and almost losing his balance, Joseph's arm snagged on the sharp spike of a tree. He inspected his arm and looked behind his back at Esme. She smiled weakly. "Alto!" Alex yelled ahead of them.

The group stopped. Joseph removed his cap, wiping his forehead with his arm. The mules nickered. He heard Esme's feet squishing as she pulled one foot up, then the other. Joseph rolled his eyes.

"Podemos continuar," said Alex.

The group resumed their trek. Joseph saw the tail end of a black snake slither deeper into the brush. He knew Esme wasn't afraid of the jungle. She had loved to run with him through grass and trees, laughing, when they were children. Joseph peered behind his back; Esme looked solemn. "Are you okay?" he asked over his shoulder.

"I'm not afraid of snakes," she stated.

"You're quiet."

"I'm out of shape. It was easier when I was a kid. Now, I'm worried about all the hiking. Today is short. How am I going to hike twice as far tomorrow?"

"That's why I got the extra mule. When you get tired, you can ride."

Esme smiled. Already, she had smeared mud on her chin. Joseph turned and wiped it off, giving Esme a quick kiss. Michael laughed at them. Jaco, the white-headed mule, shook his long ears.

They plodded forward, walking across rickety, hanging bridges and narrow clearings. There were occasional welcome dry patches of hard ground but primarily long stretches of mud. Alex looked to the skies every fifteen minutes, and Joseph figured he was watching for rain. The thought filled him with dread.

Again, Alex looked up into the vines of a tall stand of trees. The vines danced, shuddering, and shaking. "Mono araña," said Alex.

Joseph turned, pointing at the treetops. "Esme, spider monkeys!"

Esme looked up and smiled, her breathing audible. "I hope we see a crested guan, a red-lored parrot, or a toucan!"

"You're just like your dad," Joseph stated.

They had lunch when they came to a large clearing that was an obvious and well-used stopping place. Michael spread everything out on a long and skinny, weathered bamboo table. He prepared a small fire in a blackened fire pit, heated the rice and beans, sliced a banged-up pineapple, and took bread from a sack. After everything was ready, the crew attacked the food like flies. "We won't reach El Tintal until six or so," Joseph told Esme between bites of rice and beans.

Esme sighed. "That's four more hours," she said, tearing off a piece of grilled bread.

"You don't regret coming, do you?"

"No. Of course not. The closer we get, the stronger the pull. I feel like we're going home. I can't wait to see my dad," she said, stuffing the rest of the bread into her mouth.

Joseph looked away. "I'm glad. I was worried that you might regret coming or think I was nuts. I haven't experienced any more signs. But with every step, I feel closer to something. Something important. It feels big."

"I know. I feel it too. I have mixed feelings about it. It's like when my mom urged me to attend her Cosmostheology meetings. The church was so weird and mysterious. She thought it was important—like saving the world and brightening the planet important. But I was going for her, not me."

Joseph stared at Esme. "I get it. That's how I've always felt about my life. I've felt torn, not knowing if I should become an EMT or a nurse. My dad wanted me to become a doctor. In my heart, I wanted to be a chef. But always, I felt torn, like I was living someone else's life, making choices for them."

"I've felt that way too. I always wanted to be a magician, but I'm not very good at magic—the real kind, anyway. I've always worried that my powers would disappear or that someone would take them away somehow. They were so measly and unpredictable until you."

The duo watched Michael clean up the camp. A short distance away, Roberto repacked the mules. Alex stood, drinking water. After a beat, Alex twirled his finger, signaling them to finish their lunch.

"Here we go again," said Joseph.

Joseph opened his eyes, uncertain if he was awake or still dreaming. His stomach growled, confirming his ascent from nocturnal oblivion. Something had awakened him.

Earlier that night, after their long and grueling day, he had fallen asleep so fast it had been almost like anesthesia. Now, Joseph sat awkwardly in his hammock, listening for movement and sound. He looked to where Esme hung between two cuajilote trees. It was too dark to see her profile. He craned his neck, anyway, listening to mysterious bugs and a distant rustling in the jungle. There, amidst the blackness, he imagined a jaguar's stealthy treads encircling the camp, hungry and mean. Nervously, he settled down again and stared up at a patch of twinkling sky.

Joseph.

He turned his head towards Esme's hammock. The voice in his head sounded like her, but her hammock was as still as stone. She had to be asleep.

Joseph. Help me!

Joseph squirmed, falling from his hammock. He picked himself up and trotted barefoot to where Esme slept. She wasn't there. Looking around in the dark, Joseph blew air through his nose. *Maybe she had to pee,* he thought to himself.

Up here, Joseph!

Joseph trudged towards his flashlight, his heartbeat accelerating with each prickly step. Something was wrong; he could hear Esme's fear racing through his brain. After a tree branch snagged his hair, Joseph tripped and fell to the ground. Crawling, he scrambled for the flashlight between his water bottle and shoes. Joseph stood, aiming the beam high into a giant ceiba tree. Immediately, he covered his mouth. A scream caught in his throat like a stifled burp.

Joseph projected his thoughts into Esme's brain like her life depended on his message. *Esme, I'm coming! Hold on!*

Esme

Esme's right foot felt wet; she knew it was blood. Every time she repositioned her body, grasping the tree with her feet dangling, she scraped something new. Wedging her hip firmly against the trunk of the ceiba tree, she tried to stay calm, but she didn't know if the branch that cradled her naked butt could support her weight. It was a small branch at the top of the tree. Her nightgown clung to her body like a sausage casing; her hands were slippery from sweat and blood. She was exhausted. *How could I have levitated so high without waking up?*

Esme figured that a ceiba tree resembled an elongated manatee wearing a crown of bushy branches atop its fat head. Unfortunately for her, patches of razor-sharp thorns covered its trunk, and if her branch broke, she'd end up clinging to a porcupine.

"Ouch! Joseph!" she pleaded, looking up at the stars for help.

She wanted to scream, but how could she explain her predicament to the others? She needed Joseph.

Every movement against the tree trunk punctured her thigh, a finger, or the tender part of her under-arms. Esme wondered if she could levitate to the ground. After all, that's how she had gotten into this mess. But fear and exhaustion prohibited it. She figured she was at least two hundred feet off the ground. The statistics of her plight made her heartbeat accelerate. What if she fell? What if her power didn't work?

Joseph!

A beam of light bounced around the treetops, and she heard a new humming and buzzing sound coming from somewhere and gaining momentum. *Joseph. Joseph. Joseph.* She pleaded telepathically. Esme couldn't see him, but she knew he was coming. Air fizzled through her puckered mouth; she tasted salty tears on her lips.

Soon, a bouncing light rose towards her like the headlight of an oncoming car. Joseph appeared in front of her eyes, floating on air. "You look like an angel," she whispered.

Esme flung herself into his arms, and they descended quietly to the ground.

The predawn sky hovered over the vast, virgin jungle. Below Esme's butt, the great Catzin pyramid of El Tintal sat on a hill covered with spindly trees and years and years of topsoil. Around the pyramid and throughout the ancient city, swamps and lowland scrub covered everything with a green, feathery coat. "I can't believe eight hundred and fifty structures are scattered down there," said Esme.

"It's just trees, for miles and miles," Joseph replied, rubbing her back. He removed his cap and scratched his head.

Esme looked behind her back, searching for ants and spiders, but it was too dark to see them. She reclined until she was prone on the dusty rock. Joseph copied her. "I'm still so tired. After last night's shenanigans, I feel like a corpse. Thanks for buying the extra mule. I don't think I could have made it otherwise," said Esme.

"Yesterday was grueling. Six miles doesn't seem that far, but it felt like a marathon with the trail's condition. Thank goodness it didn't rain. Alex said in a week or two, in August, it will rain constantly."

Esme contemplated her sticky armpits and frizzled hair. She could feel every scratch, every bruise covering her arms and legs. Now, after applying endless bandages, she looked like Frankenstein. But all that couldn't keep her from seeing the sunrise on Catzin. "It feels like it could rain any minute. Oh my God, I knew this would be hard, but it's harder than I remembered. My backpack is so heavy, and the smell of bug spray gives me a headache. My cuts sting from all the salty sweat."

"You might be dehydrated," said Joseph. Sitting up, he reached for the water bottle. "Here, drink up. The mules are carrying plenty of water."

Esme turned onto her stomach, reaching for Joseph's water bottle. She gulped it dry and wiped her mouth with the back of her hand—even the back of her hand was dirty. Now, grit covered her chin and upper lip. She giggled morosely. "I think I have a dirt mustache. I want to shower, but the water in the bucket is so cold! How can it be so cold?"

"I'm taking one," said Joseph. He added, "I feel like a pig. I wish we had some pig—carnitas with cilantro and sweet onions. Annatto rice with fresh vegetables, maybe some sangria to wash it down. The rice and beans we had for dinner last night were bland and tasted like lard. I wish I had hot sauce."

Esme scrunched her face. "As I said…hard. Or should I say… lard."

Joseph snickered. Lying down again, he stretched.

Esme yawned and turned onto her back; eyes glued to the orange horizon that would soon extinguish the dark. For a few minutes, neither of them said a word. They lay silently, listening to the chorus of bugs and the burgeoning chatter of birds.

She turned to face Joseph, grabbing his hand. "You and Alex and the others are always talking in Spanish. What did you guys talk about yesterday? I felt left out sometimes."

"I will teach you Spanish," Joseph said, turning his head towards Esme. "Alex told me stories about other tourists who have journeyed to El Mirador. He could write a book. One woman drank too much tequila and threw up all over Jaco, the mule with the white face—it wasn't so white after that. Jaco smelled terrible the whole trip! There was a guy that was always smoking pot. They said it seemed to give him superhuman strength while climbing the pyramids. But the guides were so worried that he'd get hurt.

Oh yeah, and there was this other guy; he kept getting naked and wandering from camp. Alex didn't follow because he didn't want to know what the guy was doing. He sent Roberto to find out!"

Joseph started laughing, and Esme followed suit. "They probably think I'm a wimp. A fat, out-of-shape American."

"You're not fat. I love your curves," said Joseph, leaning to kiss her shoulder. "You do stink a little," he added.

"So do you, but I'd still hump you."

"Esme!" Joseph yelped.

She giggled, then turned serious. "So, today we're walking on the causeway—the sacbe—and it's easier?"

"I hope so. The causeway is fascinating. I remember my father talking about it. The manpower it must have taken to build these great cities…The causeway is like an ancient interstate highway. It's mind-boggling."

"I know. I've always been spellbound by my dad's stories too. Did you know my dad wanted to name me Jade, after the jade objects found buried with the corpses, in their teeth and genitals?"

"Yuck. Some of it was jewelry and figurines, masks." He added, "Jade is a beautiful name. I'm glad you use it for your magic persona."

"The Amazing Jade! I wonder what my dad is doing right now..." Esme thought out loud.

"My dad will be so shocked when we stumble into camp. Yours too."

"If we make it," Esme replied.

"We have to make it. Maybe we should climb down, slip into the hammocks, and sleep a little longer before breakfast. We better shake the sleeping bags to get rid of the spiders."

"Ugh! It was too hot to sleep in them anyway. But maybe being cocooned inside the bag would have kept me from levitating up into a tree."

Joseph half-smiled, but neither of them moved a muscle. The duo remained flat for several more minutes, listening to the jungle and watching the color of the sky shift like a lava lamp. Finally, Joseph reached for the flashlight. Esme intervened, summoning her final mental strength to whisk the object from Joseph's grasp. She levitated it above their eyes without moving a muscle. The flashlight spun like a drone.

Joseph watched the flashlight rotate with a smarmy grin. He folded his arms under his head. "I see your flashlight and raise you two tired, dirty souls."

Esme sucked in her breath. The air percolated with energy, and a low drumming vibration echoed amidst the chatter of birds. The flashlight Esme had been levitating fell to the surface of Catzin.

Simultaneously, their bodies lifted from the pyramid's surface, floating several feet above the structure. Esme threw out her arms. "Wee!" she shouted.

Joseph grabbed her hand, and slowly, they started spinning. Esme felt like she was floating in the ocean—free, like an undulating wave. "Joseph?" She asked. "What's gotten into you?"

"I don't know. I'm too tired to care. Maybe I should enjoy my demons."

They floated higher, the valley spreading below them like a bumpy, green quilt and above them, infinity. As if on cue, the sun peaked above the horizon. They swiveled their heads, squinting at the sun. The silhouette of a vulture flapped over them and landed in the trees below. In unison, they flipped onto their stomachs, descending and hovering at the edge of the great Catzin. They surveyed the trees below. Joseph squeezed Esme's hand.

Slowly, their bodies descended back to the dusty surface. The vulture flapped its wings below them and took flight. "Joseph, I wanted to fly! I'm not scared when I'm with you. Your power is so strong. Let's follow the vulture. I know we can do it."

"No way. That would be insane. What if something happened to you? I couldn't live with myself. Plus, if Alex saw us, he'd freak! The guys would probably think we're witches and run away and leave us here alone."

"Oh, God. That would be terrible. We'd still have the mules, though," she giggled. "I truly thought we could fly to El Mirador."

"I felt it too."

Joseph grabbed Esme's hand, pulling her to her feet. The flashlight lifted too, floated to the edge of the steep steps, and hovered in place. When they approached the crumbly edge, the flashlight hung before them like a giant wasp, lighting their descent. Joseph tossed Esme a wicked smile. "It's not me. It's Diablo."

Oliver

Antonio kicked at the sides of his short, brown mule as the beast trotted toward the dining tent. The man wore a black plastic poncho, and rain dripped from his tightly wrapped chin. Antonio approached the scene with an outstretched arm. "Señor Wright! The phone. It's for you. Emergency!"

Everyone inside the smoky food tent turned towards Antonio. Oliver swallowed, his face unreadable. He pushed away from the table and jogged toward the brown beast, splashing through puddles. His heart thumped against his chest. "Is it Esme?" he asked Antonio hopelessly.

Antonio jiggled his shoulders. Oliver grabbed the phone, placing it to his ear. "Esme?"

"No, it's me," came a soft voice from the other end.

"Ethelene?"

"Yes. Don't sound so disappointed. It's important, or I wouldn't have called the satellite phone. It's Esme…"

"Oh, God. I knew it," Oliver spat, splashing back to his seat and flicking water from the brim of his hat.

"Don't get carried away. Hopefully, she's fine. But I don't know where she is. She's disappeared and it's a complete mystery."

"Have you called the police?"

"No, it's not like that. At least, I hope not. I talked with Esme's landlord. I guess she paid rent in advance for August. She also left a cryptic text about quitting her job and taking off with Joseph. The whole thing seems fishy. I don't know anything about this man…"

Oliver emptied his lungs. "If she's with Joseph, she's fine. Joseph is a great kid. She's safe with him."

"How do you know that? He found her in New York—weird if you ask me. Saw her on television or something, I don't know. Esme wouldn't say much about it, just how in love she is—obsessed, really. Something doesn't add up with those two. It's like he has her hoodwinked or something. They hadn't seen each other since they were kids, only been together for a hot minute. What do we know about this man?"

Oliver looked towards Emil. The man was playing cards with Phillip and eating a banana, probably telling dirty jokes. He readjusted his wide-brimmed hat. "From what I hear, Joseph is a goodie-two-shoes. His father thinks he's a saint. I don't see him as a bad influence. Maybe the other way around."

"Oliver! You're not taking this seriously! Where is she, then? She's gone. I know she's always hated me, but we made up. She's not avoiding me now. She'd text me, wouldn't she? And quitting her job isn't like her. She's so focused on her career— or magic, anyway. You should have seen her street performance in Orlando; she's better than David Blaine. I'm worried, Oliver. Plus, there are wild and crazy things you don't know about. You'd never believe me."

Oliver scratched his chin. Ethelene was right about Esme being a responsible girl, never a flake. She'd never cut class in high school, watched magic videos instead of porn, and received near-perfect grades in school, and when she missed curfew, it was because she was performing on the beach in Clearwater, practicing her craft. Esme was nothing if not dependable and focused. She wouldn't just up and quit her job, run away, and disappear. It wasn't like her. "You're right, babe. It's not like her. How long has she been gone? Just tell me what the big mystery is. I promise I'll believe you."

"No, you won't believe me. Esme will tell you when she's ready. Don't distract me! Esme texted like eight or nine days ago, then nothing. It's like she dropped off the face of the Earth."

"Hmm..."

"Oliver!"

"What do you want me to do? She's a grown woman, for God's sake. I have something important to do here. You have no idea how big this thing is."

"More important than your daughter? I can't believe it's *you* who's saying this. And you thought I was the irresponsible one," said Ethelene, vinegar bubbling inside her vocal cords.

"Let me think! I haven't been mulling this over for a week like you. I need time to process, okay?" said Oliver, pinching between his eyes.

"You need to come home; put us first for once. El Mirador isn't going anywhere, and you need to find your daughter. I have a bad feeling...There's something weird going on."

"Things are even weirder here. Trust me. I'll call you back with my decision. Don't worry, we'll find her."

"Wait! Don't go yet. Oliver, I left the church."

"Really? You left Cosmostheology? I didn't think you could do that."

"Funny."

"Babe, I'll call you later."

"Okay. Bye, Ollie."

"Bye," said Oliver, hanging up.

Oliver emitted a disgruntled, Tarzan-like yell, collecting a look of surprise from all onlookers. Emil tossed his banana peel outside the tent and walked over.

"What the fuck, man? What's going on?" asked Emil.

"Ugh! The timing. It couldn't be worse. It's my daughter. I guess she's disappeared, and even her flaky-ass mother is worried."

"Shit."

"Yeah, shit."

Oliver lowered his voice and leaned toward his friend. "Do you think the aliens will wait on my kid? No, I don't think so. *Arrgghh!*" Oliver exclaimed. "Oh yeah, get this; she disappeared with your son."

Emil scrunched his face, swinging both arms up in the air. "What? No way!"

The men stared at each other, hands at their hips. "Well, she's okay then. You know Joseph wouldn't hurt a fly. Remember, in the old days, our little jungle rescue animal hospital? I always told him he should be a doctor or vet," said Emil. "He's so damn smart."

Oliver took off his hat and threw it on the table, tussling his hair.

"You're not thinking of actually leaving, are you?" asked Emil.

"Listen, I know Joseph is a great kid. I'm not accusing him of anything. But think about what's been happening to us. No one would believe it. If something like this can happen to us, then who's to say that something truly out of this world isn't happening to them? What if the aliens abducted them?"

"I didn't think of that. Although, I don't know what the aliens would want with my Joseph. I can see God needing some new recruits, but little green men? All I know is that I'm not missing this. Oliver, it's tonight. Why not wait one more day? Maybe the aliens will give them back."

"Funny. You're an asshole. You know that, right?" growled Oliver.

Hearing a shuffling outside his palapa, Oliver looked up but returned to his task. He shoved the new beef jerky a student had brought for him into his backpack and grabbed the extra rain gear he had confiscated earlier. Carefully, he rolled the plastic jackets like a cigar, wrapped them with a rubber band, and placed them into his pack.

Emil burst through the plastic enclosure, placing his boots on a rug. "This rain is turning camp into one hell of a mess," Emil grunted and shook his head like a wet dog.

Oliver looked back and forth. "Do we have any Pepto Bismol around here? Or anything like that?"

"You got the shits?"

"No, I need to take it with me. I need mules, too. How many do we have available?"

"Hell, if I know. Ask Antonio. Why do you need so many mules? Oliver, you sound crazy. Leaving in this rain when tonight might be straight out of a science fiction movie? It's nuts!"

"I need towels or sweatshirts, something warm, sleeping bags…" said Oliver, looking around again. Sitting down on his cot, he counted imaginary things with his fingers.

Emil sat across from his friend. "You're not making any sense. Oliver, take a helicopter. If you think this is a big emergency, have Esteban call for a chopper. I mean, don't be so goddamn cheap."

Oliver looked at Emil. "Being a tightwad has nothing to do with this. I have a feeling, and I know it will sound nuts, but I think I need to schlep it because there's something out there, something I need to find. It's what I have to do..."

"Since when? I thought you needed to find Esme," Emil interrupted.

"I do. But something is compelling me. It's like somebody is whispering in my ear. I need to listen."

"I wish you'd listen to me. Stay and meet *E.T.* You will regret this for the rest of your life."

Oliver sighed. "Yeah, I know."

He felt his pockets, reached inside his pants, and handed his iPhone to Emil.

"What am I supposed to do with this? We can't call anyone— no internet."

"No, but Esteban charged it for me. You can use it to film tonight. Seriously, take Antonio if you need to. I want to see them. I can't miss it, not entirely, anyway. This way, at least, I can watch what happens."

"Well, if they allow it. Maybe the aliens will zap the thing out of my hand; maybe they don't want to be filmed."

Together, the men looked at the floor. It was dark underneath Oliver's cot. "You'll need to take that thing, the glass box. I don't know what they'll do when you show up without '*the children*,' said Oliver, making air quotes. "You know, I got the feeling from the hologram that they are peaceful creatures. But requesting children is creepy. Menacing."

Emil rubbed his knees. "To tell you the truth, I'm scared. But, if you tell anyone that, I'll kill you. Oliver, don't make me do this on my own—face those creatures. You saw them. They look fucked up. Scary, like monsters. Bug eyes and fingers like spider legs. Come on, man, don't make me face them alone."

Oliver twisted his mouth. He took a deep breath. "You're not at *all* concerned about Joseph? I can't believe you're scared. Nothing scares you."

"They do! And I *do* care about Joseph. But I don't think the kids are in trouble like you do. They're—and I'm sorry to have to tell you this—but they're probably screwing each other's brains out, somewhere, maybe in Cancun or the Bahamas."

Oliver growled and rolled his eyes. The men stared at each other. "If you're scared, take Phillip. Take the whole camp if it will make you feel better."

"Come on. There's only room for a few people on top of La Danta. I'll take Antonio. He already knows about this clown show anyway." Emil shook his head and stood, heading for the door flap. "I'll go see about the mules and that pink crap. I've got your back if you're determined to do this."

The men locked eyes. Emil completed the sign of the cross and stepped into his boots. Oliver stood and walked towards Emil, grabbing his friend's shoulders. "Good luck. You don't know how much I want to be there. It's just…I have this feeling inside that I can't ignore. Maybe I'll catch a glimpse of the ship on my way tonight. What do you think it will look like?"

Emil turned with a grim expression. "Armageddon," he replied.

Oliver left camp around five p.m., riding a giant mule and dragging two others behind. The other mules carried all the supplies he thought were needed; they looked like *Princess Leia*, with two black plastic bundles on each side of their bellies and some supplies that probably weren't necessary at all. Frankly, he felt foolish, crazy, but he couldn't ignore the calling.

The rain came down in waves, like the currents of an ocean. The mud sucked at the hooves of the mules, and sometimes, the beasts stopped defiantly and nickered. Oliver just kicked and prayed—hoped—that he'd find something, anything. And, more importantly, after this wild goose chase came to an end, he hoped he'd find Esme, too.

Already, he felt cold. Water was pouring over the sides of his wide-brimmed hat like a waterfall. The sky above was gray and foreboding. The jungle below was wilting under the weight of a water-world. Everything was adding up to be the worst night of his life. But he was in it for the long hall. Whatever happened, he wasn't turning back. He felt like crying when he thought about the aliens. Still, he kept moving forward toward La Muerta.

Joseph

Joseph appraised his mud-encrusted Crocs, wincing as water cascaded over his nose like a leaky faucet. Acid sloshed in his stomach, and he knew it was only a matter of time until he lost his lunch, and they were nowhere near La Muerta, the closest suburb of El Mirador. Joseph turned to assess Esme.

She looked green-faced, bouncing on Jefe, the black mule with a white nose. Jaco was trailing behind her, loaded with their water and supplies. Behind the mules, Roberto and Michael plodded forward with dire expressions.

Joseph turned to face Alex. The day before, Alex had seemed like an unstoppable dynamo, whacking at the jungle like a deranged chef. Now, the man's gait had withered to a snail's pace, and his arms tepidly moved branches, his machete hanging limp on his hips. Still, he had more energy than the rest of them. Joseph wiped his face and sighed.

For almost an hour now, the only sounds Joseph had heard were rain, the repetitive mucky muck of their footsteps, and his growling stomach. He was growing so weary that he kept forgetting to blink. Joseph expelled a groan of air, and his arms flailed about him.

He had stepped into a rut, twisting his ankle. Joseph lost his balance and fell onto the slippery mud. As he lay crumpled on the ground, he retched. Alex stopped and turned. Esme tumbled off her mule and lurched to Joseph's side. As soon as she smelled the contents of Joseph's stomach, she bent and puked herself.

They continued down the trail.

The closer the group got to La Muerta, the sicker Joseph felt. Roberto and Alex shook their heads. Michael mumbled in Spanish. Esme could no longer ride on Jefe because she needed to puke every few minutes while Joseph prayed for relief.

Relief didn't come.

Thirty minutes later, Jefe, the black mule, nickered and whined. Joseph heard a loud thump; the group turned toward the sound. Esme screamed, and the others swore in Spanish. Jefe appeared to be dead.

Roberto ran, his legs plucking through the mud. The man dumped his body between the beast's splayed legs, tossing dirt in every direction, feeling the beast's neck. Roberto started crying.

Alex threw his walking stick onto the ground and shouted inexplicable words. Esme plodded forward, kneeling by the mule's head, and rubbing his bristly coat. Joseph stood over the creature, rain dripping off his baseball cap. He rubbed his eyes, wondering how they could survive this ordeal—sick, wet, cold, and worst of all, mourning a dead mule. The timing was unimaginable.

After a few solemn minutes, the group rallied. Joseph talked with Alex for several minutes, huddled under a tarp, until another wave pummeled his stomach. He jogged a few feet, placed his hands on his knees, and retched again. Then he fell to his knees in the mud. Esme wiped her mouth and slumped beside him. She started crying. "Joseph, we're so sick. What are we going to do?"

They hugged each other and locked eyes. "We need to get there tonight, don't we?" whimpered Esme.

"Yes, I feel it too."

Joseph looked at Jaco. "Alex and I talked. He says we're close enough to leave our supplies. Just take water and some food. But Esme, we must get there. Alex said he could pack the hammocks in his backpack, but we'd be sleeping in the rain—no shelter if we don't make it to the outskirts of El Mirador. If we leave the supplies, you can ride Jaco. How is your stomach?"

Esme sighed. "There's nothing left. It's a little better now, maybe. Is your ankle, okay? It looks swollen."

As soon as Joseph thought about his ankle, he could feel the pain. He removed his right Croc and then his muddy sock. Esme gasped. "Oh no, Joseph. It looks terrible! You've sprained it. How will you walk the rest of the way to El Mirador? You'll need to ride Jaco. I'll walk," she said, chewing her lip.

Joseph could see doubt written across her face. They grabbed each other's hands, and Joseph prayed.

Esme

Esme felt like a house cat locked out in the rain. Her clothes stuck to her body like a soggy tortilla, and her tennis shoes vomited mud with each step. They were approximately fifteen minutes down the trail from where they had left Roberto, most of the supplies, and Jefe, the dead mule. Now, Esme followed Alex and Michael on foot, and Joseph rode Jaco. Somewhere along the line, Alex had given her his headlamp and walking stick; the latter she squeezed between pruned fingers like an exoskeleton.

Above the brim of her dripping hat, the sky was an eerie shade of green. Esme squinted, trying to distinguish shapes between the trees. It was growing dark. Turning to glance at Joseph, she illuminated her headlamp. He appeared to be watching the jiggling of Jaco's mane. She knew he felt embarrassed; she'd been listening to his thoughts.

Joseph covered his mouth and narrowed his eyes as if suppressing the need to puke. Esme's heart sank for him, but she couldn't help him. She was using every crumb of strength—even her power—to stay upright on the trail, to abstain from heaving. Now and again, her feet would levitate off the ground, then slip back into the muck. She no longer cared if the guides saw her; she needed to use everything at her disposal to keep moving. Esme wished that Joseph could use his power to fly them to El Mirador. Unfortunately for them, he didn't seem to have anything left in the tank—neither did she.

They weren't walking fast enough to stay warm. They *couldn't* walk fast. Esme was starting to shiver. She thought about the night she had spent with Joseph in Flores—the sultry air and their sticky bodies clamped together after making love. It seemed like a lifetime ago that they were warm and dry. Yesterday was hot and humid. Now, her teeth were chattering.

Esme wanted to turn around again, to check on Joseph, but she didn't want him to see her shivering. He was already worried and racked with guilt. She kept moving forward.

After another grueling hour, they finally arrived at La Muerta. The rain had slowed to a drizzle, and the sky shimmered with moonlight. Esme could hear an owl hooting in the distance; the sound startled her. It had been so long since she'd heard jungle noises. Even the howler monkeys were quiet in the rain. Esme figured it must be at least eight or nine at night. But really, she had no idea.

Before she turned to check on Joseph, she wiped her face and took a deep breath. Esme swallowed her pain and torment and tried to sound cheerful. She turned. "How are you doing?" she asked, plucking through the mud to the side of Joseph's mule.

He slipped off Jaco and hugged her. "I'm so sorry to put you through this. At least we're almost there."

They stayed clenched for several seconds until Esme's resolve cracked. She convulsed into sobs. Joseph kissed her forehead.

All at once, the group turned towards a sound, a nickering, and the clomp of hooves through the mud. Esme gulped her sobs, wiping her eyes. Alex raised his flashlight, shining it in front of them. Esme's headlamp illuminated a dark, shrouded trail.

"Extraño," said Alex. In English, he added, "Nobody hikes from El Mirador at night."

The sound grew closer while Esme stared into the night. Joseph gripped her hand in his own, squeezing. "I'm too tired to be scared," she said, half-smiling and looking at Joseph.

Michael laughed morbidly while Alex swished his flashlight from left to right. A mule and rider approached with two mules behind. The man jumped off and pushed his hat higher up his forehead. Esme took a step forward. "Dad? Is that you?"

The man started jogging through the mud, splashing. Finally, he scooped Esme into his arms. Esme cried all over again, her hat slipping down her back. "Sweetheart, my baby. What are you doing here?" asked Oliver, pushing her away so he could look at her face.

"We had to come…"

Oliver interrupted Esme's sentence. "I had a feeling that I might find you on the trail. But it seemed so crazy, I just couldn't believe…"

Oliver stopped mid-sentence, gasping. "The children," he uttered dumbstruck, looking behind Esme's head at Joseph. "You. It's *you*. You're the children. Now, I understand. *Our* children—but why?" Oliver asked the night.

Oliver motioned for Joseph, opening his arms. Joseph hobbled over, crumpling against Oliver's side. Esme hugged both men like a runaway reunited after a night in hell.

The skies still wept gentle tears. Alex and Michael held a green tarp as high as possible while Esme and Joseph changed into the dry clothes and shoes Oliver had brought for them. Esme smoothed her new sweatshirt and yanked up the too-tight black leggings. She pranced like her feet were standing on hot coals. "Are you decent?" asked Oliver.

"Yes," said Esme, looking at Joseph's matching Guatemala sweatshirt.

"Dad, where'd you get these clothes?"

"The college students. I felt like an absolute fool, asking for their clothes."

Oliver looked at Joseph. "They looked at me like your dad did when I asked him if he had any Pepto Bismol."

Joseph jiggled the pink bottle like it was fifty-year-old scotch, taking another pull. "This is a lifesaver. How did you know? How did you know about everything?"

Oliver shook his head. "The same way that you knew to come. There's something big going on—you'll never believe it. Hurry up; we need to go." He jogged back to his mules.

Oliver led the fresh mules to Esme and Joseph. "Are you guys ready for the adventure of a lifetime?"

"Why are you so cryptic? Just tell us what's going on. We wish the adventures were over at this point," said Esme.

"You wouldn't believe me if I did. No, I think this will be something you'll need to see to believe," said Oliver with a strange expression.

Esme huffed, lifting her tired frame onto the white mule. Sighing, she closed her eyes in slow motion. "I don't think I could have walked one more step."

"Me either," said Joseph, trotting over on the back of a large, brown mule. "Oliver, I tried to care for Esme the best I could. I would have never let anything bad happen to her."

Oliver smiled, his eyes far away as if he were calculating something important. He looked at Esme, raising his eyebrows. She smiled back with a blush spreading over her cheeks. "I'm happy for you two," said Oliver. At that, he yanked on the reins of his jittery, black mule and looked up through an opening in the jungle ceiling. Now, the full moon glowed overhead like a beacon of hope. Suddenly, as if God had waved a magic wand, the rain stopped, and the clouds parted. The only sounds were the trees dripping and the snorting and stomping of three anxious mules. Esme looked up, opening her arms with unbridled joy. "Thank God! Dad, I'm scared. I feel weird, nervous, excited, or..."

"You feel like you're splitting apart," said Joseph.

"Yes, that's it. You're reading my mind."

"No. I don't need to. I feel it too."

Esme reached behind her back into the side pocket of her backpack and threw a handful of rubble onto the jungle floor.

"What was that?" asked Oliver.

"I collected some rocks. I'm throwing them for good luck."

"We'll need all the luck we can get," said Oliver. He adjusted his wide-brimmed hat and kicked his black mule. "We need to hurry. We don't have much time."

The group disappeared into the jungle.

Oliver

Oliver urged his mule forward, the tension in his heart percolating as they narrowed in on El Mirador. Now and again, he'd look up at the sky, anticipating a fireball or a bright swirling disc. But he only saw distant stars and the full moon resembling a ticking clock.

Periodically, he'd look back at Esme and Joseph. They appeared even more nervous than he was, but they didn't know what Oliver knew. That was a relief, especially since they were the sacrificial lambs. Not that he'd let anything happen to them; he would sacrifice himself before he'd let anything happen to Esme.

Oliver inhaled the humid night air, imagining what was about to happen. Would they be green? He knew they weren't the little people the world expected. They were tall and thin, all eyes. He wondered if they would be gracious and kind or menacing. And what would their spaceship resemble? Oliver pictured the *Millennium Falcon* or *Star Ship Enterprise*. His pulse raced; they were getting close.

They passed familiar trail markings, like tall ceiba trees and dark, outlying lumps. The closer they got, the more Oliver's mind bubbled and stewed. What if the aliens sent holograms or robots? What if they sucked Esme up within a beam of light before he could intervene? Maybe they wouldn't get there in time to see the aliens at all?

He gulped and scratched the stubble under his chin. Taking his daughter to slaughter was crazy. He shook his head. *No.* It wasn't like that; he would take the aliens at their word, and they'd said they meant no harm.

Still, he worried.

Oliver wondered if Emil was on top of La Danta with the crystal object. A part of him hated to give them the box of light. It was the most exciting thing he'd ever found in his life—or ever would find—he was sure of it. Heck, it was probably the most exciting thing that any archaeologist had ever seen in the history of the world. But the other part of him was glad to be rid of it. It scared him. For all he knew, it was a weapon of mass destruction. Oliver repositioned his ass in the saddle and took a cleansing breath.

His mule sensed the familiar; the beast snorted and trotted faster. Oliver turned and said, "Kids, we're getting close."

Esme and Joseph looked at each other with invisible words, then looked at Oliver with wide eyes. "Do we have to climb a pyramid? If we do, I don't think I can. Dad, you have no idea how tired I am."

Oliver's heart sank. He heard Joseph whisper to Esme, "We'll fly. We'll fly if we need to."

Oliver sat straighter. He didn't know what Joseph meant, but it wasn't any weirder than what awaited them. They kept moving.

After a time, Oliver swallowed, clearing his throat. "You know, El Mirador was discovered by rubber harvesters and wasn't excavated at all until 2003."

Joseph nodded.

"Yes," Esme said. "I remember that."

Oliver probed his noggin, reaching for anything to cut the tension, to calm his nerves, but his mind was blank. "Dad, what's happening? Why won't you tell us anything?" Esme pleaded.

Again, Oliver adjusted in the saddle. His balls were killing him; he'd never been much of a horseman. He turned towards Esme. "Well, we do have a climb ahead of us. When we get there, we must climb La Danta...and then, wait."

He looked at Joseph. "Your dad will be up there with the most exciting find since Tutankhamun. Heck, we might be able to see it from here if there weren't so many trees."

Oliver turned, facing forward. He didn't want them to see the fear in his eyes. Esme, however, pulled up beside him and turned off her headlamp. "La Danta is the largest pyramid in the world."

"Not as big as the pyramids of Giza," Oliver countered. "We must climb it. We're meeting someone."

Esme stared at her father for several seconds. "I'll try. I don't know what's happening exactly. But I know something big, something unknown, is ahead of us. And you know my magic tricks—the levitation? It's not a trick. I can move things with my mind. So can Joseph."

Oliver bowed his head and left it there, bouncing along on his mule like he'd fallen asleep.

"Dad, are you okay? Are you praying or something?"

Oliver lifted his head and laughed like he'd lost his marbles. "No," he said, reaching for Esme's hand. "Honey, given everything that's happened lately, that doesn't surprise me. You've always been special. I love you, sweetheart."

Oliver felt overcome with emotion. Out of nowhere, he hooted into the night, howling like a coyote. The sound reverberated through the jungle, and then all was quiet. Esme looked at him like he was crazy, then she turned towards Joseph. Joseph smiled, his white teeth collecting moonlight. Everyone burst into laughter at that exact moment.

They continued in silence, plucking their way through a maze of hidden structures, each one seemingly larger than the one before. There were open patches where they could see the sky and other areas devoid of light. In those places, they were in the shadow of pyramids—volcano-sized structures covered with jungle flora and fauna. Occasionally, they would smell smoke wafting from the cooking fires that fed the students and crew. Sporadic mummering and tents zipping, along with laughter, and shuffling could be heard as they passed the encampment.

Oliver sat straighter in his saddle. The three mules and riders plodded forward, whispering to each other in the night.

After fifteen more minutes, the sky fell away. All was dark. Esme illuminated her headlamp, looking around. She shut it off when she found there was nothing to see. "We're here," said Oliver.

Esme adjusted her spine and dismounted. Joseph slipped off his mule, swearing under his breath when he landed on his ankle. Oliver slid off Loco, and together they stood, looking up at a soft glow hovering over the ruin. They heard the purr of bugs and the din of distant voices. The air was warm now. Oliver looked up again. "The voices, that would be your dad and Antonio. Do you see the light up there? Well, it's not from a flashlight."

"Oliver?" asked Joseph.

Oliver turned toward Joseph. In the distance, lightning crackled, and he wondered if it was mother nature or something else. Joseph grabbed Esme's hand, then Oliver's. They stood in a circle enshrouded in darkness, with their feet encased in quicksand-like mud. Oliver looked back and forth between them. "Would it be okay if I said a prayer?" asked Joseph.

"Of course," Oliver replied.

Seconds ticked by. Then Joseph whispered, "Father, Mother Mary, watch over us. Protect my Esme and Oliver, my dad, and guide Roberto, Michael, and Alex on the return journey to Carmelita. Watch over Jaco, too. Please, heavenly father, whatever happens, whatever the future brings, be with us always, in our hearts and minds. Amen."

Joseph squeezed each hand and looked up. "Oliver, Esme, hang on tight. We're going to fly."

Oliver gasped when his feet left the ground.

Joseph

Joseph squeezed his eyes and corralled all errant thoughts, humming like a mosquito trapped inside an ear. Typically, his power shifted into gear without effort, but not now. He was depleted and exhausted, but he had to help Esme.

Opening his eyes, he looked between Oliver and Esme. The group ascended like an elevator, legs flailing, past scrubby trees and debris that clung to La Danta like fragile tentacles. He saw a rickety stairway leading to the top of the pyramid, attached to the ruin like a loose pair of eyeglasses. Joseph held his breath as they neared the top, sneaking a peek at Oliver's horrified face. The man looked as if he might emit another terrified howl.

Esme, on the other hand, was beaming. As they crested the top, night faded away. There was a bright light somewhere on the surface. Joseph stuck his good foot out, gingerly setting both feet firmly on the pinnacle of La Danta. Oliver and Esme landed, too.

The top of La Danta resembled the slab of an old house after the structure had burned to the ground. It was the size of a small swimming pool. His father was standing on the platform's edge, entirely engrossed by the night sky. Emil didn't see the newcomers at all. However, the man standing beside Emil witnessed the whole thing. The younger man stared at Joseph, his mouth resembling a wilting tulip; the man pulled on Emil's sleeve. Emil turned and almost stumbled off the narrow ledge. "Dad! Watch out!" Joseph screamed, hobbling over to where his father stood.

Emil slowly put one foot in front of the other as if afraid to approach a ghost. "Joseph?" he grunted.

The two men stumbled into each other's arms. "I don't understand. How'd you get here? What are you doing here?"

Emil pulled away, looking into Joseph's smiling face. He grabbed his son by the ears, and a tear escaped the older man's cheeks. "I saw your mother. I *saw* her! Your mother was full of love. Oh, Joseph. I wish you could have seen her," said Emil with wild eyes.

Joseph shook his head in disbelief. Emil looked over Joseph's shoulder at Oliver and Esme and bent over with laughter. The man grabbed his knees. "You old dog, you made it back! And you brought the kids. I told you they'd be fine. I told you…"

Emil's face went blank. Joseph watched his father narrow his eyes and rub around his mouth, then he moved his hands to his hips in contemplation. Meanwhile, Joseph shuffled his feet nervously, his eyes darting between his father, Oliver, and Esme. Emil looked at Oliver. "The children," he stated.

"Yup," Oliver returned.

"My God!" Emil exclaimed. "They knew. Somehow, they knew it would happen."

All at once, the glass box started throbbing, swirling, and refracting light like a disco ball gone berserk. Emil looked to where he'd placed the box in the middle of La Danta's debris-filled roof. Esme and the group of men circled it, staring. "Dad, what is it?" asked Joseph.

"We don't know," he replied.

"All we know is that it's pretty damn important to someone, and they are coming for it tonight."

All eyes stared at the glass box while waves of light pulsed from one face to another—blue, purple, red, orange, yellow, green. "It's like we're standing at the end of a rainbow!" Esme gasped.

Antonio pulled Oliver's phone from his pocket and started filming.

The pulsing light continued. Around the glass, dirt vibrated and puffed from La Danta's ancient crown. In the distance, lightning crackled. The group looked up. Joseph squeezed Esme's hand.

Oliver and Emil scanned the sky, breaking apart from the circle. The two men walked to the ledge, staring into the night, and pointing. "Do you see a disturbance?" asked Emil. "You know, an area where we can't see stars?"

Oliver stared. "We're expecting a spectacle. But really, we don't know what to expect."

While the men looked elsewhere, Joseph grabbed Esme and embraced her. Joseph peeled Esme's headlamp and hat from her head, dropping the items onto the rooftop. He ran his fingers through her red hair and softly kissed her lips. "We made it. Esme, we made it. We're here."

Joseph felt a strange sensation. He looked down at his hands, where a soft glow radiated from his skin. "Do you feel as weird as I do?"

Esme

Esme looked at Joseph's hands, then her own. The duo slid apart as if they were suddenly contagious. "What is that?" Esme said, flipping her hands over and over.

"I don't know," Joseph whispered.

"I feel so weird."

"Me too."

Antonio turned away from the strobing glass box, pointing Oliver's phone at Esme and Joseph instead. The man started whispering in Spanish.

Esme felt light-headed and strange. She held up her hands, waving her fingers like glow sticks on the Fourth of July. Her skin radiated bioluminescence. The light seemed to come from somewhere inside her body, shooting out her fingertips like a laser pointer. Joseph started spinning, pushing up his sleeves and staring at his arms. Esme looked at her dad and Emil. They only had eyes for the sky.

"What was that?" Oliver shouted into the night.

Everyone raced to the edge, looking beyond Oliver's outstretched arm. All was dark. There were only bats swooping below their feet and the buzz of cicadas. "I thought I saw a shaft of light," said Oliver.

"It must have been lightning," Emil returned.

Esme's eyes returned to her glowing fingers. She felt like a pot of boiling water, her emotions ready to bubble over. She grabbed Joseph's hand, reading his thoughts. Joseph was praying silently. Esme already knew she loved him. But, hearing him pray for her, for all of them, caused her heart to swell. "I love you so much, Joseph," she said.

Joseph pulled her hand to his lips, kissing her glowing fingers.

"There!" Emil shouted.

Antonio held the phone high, but only a dark sky was before them. They kept watching.

"What are we waiting for?" asked Esme.

"A spaceship," said Oliver.

Joseph and Esme locked eyes; a spark of recognition flashed between them. Esme felt her heart swell even more as she thought about when she and Joseph ran through the jungle as kids. Why had they been running? Because they had heard something— something loud, something out-of-place.

"Again!" Oliver shouted, pointing.

This time, there was no denying what was going on. Emil grunted, holding onto his baseball cap as if it might blow away. Esme held her breath, squeezing Joseph's fingers so hard that he yelped.

In the distance, shards of light penetrated the jungle floor like a beam from a helicopter. The light shafts hit in an irregular succession, one after the other. They could hear a sucking sound. "Dear God," said Emil. "The lights are getting closer."

"But there's no spaceship," Oliver whispered.

The sky went dark. Esme blew air from her lungs. As soon as she relaxed her shoulders, the sky exploded with a pattern of strobe lights all over again—one after the other, each closer than the last. The group stepped back from the ledge. "Emil, look! I can see something. I can see something inside the shafts of light. I know what's going on! It's the wreckage. They're pulling it up! They're taking it home with them," exclaimed Oliver.

"God damn," Emil whispered.

"Shit!" Oliver shouted, racing to Esme's side.

He swiveled Esme, grabbing her shoulders, then her hands. "You're glowing," said Oliver, gulping. He held Esme's hands in a steely grip.

"Ouch. Dad, you're hurting me."

Oliver eased his grip, looking her over from head to toe with horrified resignation. "Honey, I need you to listen to me. Whatever happens, don't let go of my hand, okay? I'm serious. Hold on as if your life depended on it," said Oliver, looking deep into her green eyes. He kept staring while sweat trickled into his own eyes. "Whatever happens, we're in this together."

"I will. I mean, I won't let go," said Esme, grabbing Joseph's hand again, too.

Cautiously, the group investigated the night sky. "They're getting closer," said Emil.

Oliver started humming. *She'll be coming around the mountain when she comes...*

And he kept humming.

Esme could feel her heartbeat throbbing in her neck as she watched the sky. Her hands were sticky, clasped inside the fingers of the two men on either side. She loved them both. The spectacle was so profound her throat went dry from forgetting to swallow. She peeked at Joseph, then her dad, matching their nervous excitement, mano a mano. Esme looked back at the sky.

Now, they could hear shouts and screaming below their feet, somewhere in the distance. The camp had awakened. It sounded like confusion and chaos on the jungle floor. In the sky, the shafts of light grew closer, penetrating the earth like an invisible backhoe, lifting, and digging up every piece of...Esme sucked in her breath. Again, she thought about running with Joseph, plucking through the jungle. She remembered hearing strange sounds and seeing something shiny. They had watched something extraordinary flashing through the sky like a falling star.

"Oliver! I think I saw it. The ship. Now, nothing," said Emil, his voice receding.

All at once, the group floundered. The light blinded Esme— red, swirling, bright like the sun. Everyone stumbled, falling backward hard on La Danta's dusty crown.

The seal of safety slipped away. Esme's hands flailed as she repositioned, sitting up and shielding her eyes against the blinding orb. Oliver squinted, scrambling towards her. "Honey, your hand!" he screamed.

Joseph crawled toward Esme, rubbing dirt from his lips. Emil and Antonio squirmed and stood. Cautiously, they looked toward the heavens, shielding their eyes as best as possible. No one said a word. A bug flew into Esme's mouth, and she spit it out, unfazed. The light dimmed, and a cigar-shaped spaceship came into focus. The air felt like an inferno.

Everyone gasped at that exact moment, whispering obscenities. Esme's fingers were growing numb, but she held on tightly with both hands. She squeezed the men harder—no one noticed.

In front of her blinking eyes, moving parts whirled like an inside-out kaleidoscope. There was no sound. The ship hovered before them like a wingless bird, long like a double-bus and twice as wide. In the center, a circle of light pulsed like an artery of blood. Tears streamed down Esme's cheeks, even though she didn't know why she was crying.

The circle of blood pulsed and then stopped. Slowly, a portal opened, and Esme could see inside the ship where strange crystal hardware and mechanical systems shifted with rainbow colors, just like the glass box. "My God!" Emil cried out. "I may have just shit myself."

A tongue of light flowed from the portal, seeping towards them like water in motion.

"They're coming," Oliver hissed, tightening his grip like a vise.

Esme felt lost in time, like plankton floating in a warm ocean. She looked at Joseph; he was glowing like an X-ray. Her chest started shaking. Upon further reflection, she was shining like an X-ray, too.

Joseph and Emil began reciting the Rosary, their voices mumbling in and out of unison. Esme looked at her dad's ashen face, then looked back to the doorway. Several *Beings* floated out. They were tall and thin with olive-colored skin and enormous black eyes. Instead of a spacesuit, they wore flowing, white silky sheaths. "Beautiful. So beautiful," Esme whispered reverently.

One of the *Beings* floated closer on the tongue of light, turning its head towards Esme and staring. The *Being's* eyes shimmered with undulating colors. Esme sucked in her breath, holding onto it like a lifeline. Oliver protectively moved slightly ahead of her. "Dad, I want to see!" Esme pleaded, pushing her way to the front.

The *Being* cocked its head, eyes flashing a radiant green like the northern lights, then turning black again. In slow motion, the creature turned its bulbous head—almost like it had two brains—and looked from one end of the group to the other. Antonio's arm was outstretched, shaking his phone, filming everything.

While the *Being* stared at them, the ship disappeared as if sucked through a black hole. The sky darkened—the air cooled.

The *Being* lifted its hand and threw a handful of light into the sky. The light dispersed like fireflies released from a bell jar. All around them came a hypnotic voice, "My name is Rigel. Behind me are my friends. We mean no harm. We have come on a sacred mission."

Rigel turned her long, slender fingers, palms up. Behind Esme, the glass box lifted from La Danta, floating through the sky and hovering over Rigel's outstretched hands. Suddenly, Rigel splayed her arms like she was welcoming the group home. The crystal box hovered in place with rainbows splashing over their white faces like a police siren. Rigel appeared to smile despite her small, lipless mouth remaining closed. Still, Esme perceived a slight uplift of the *Being's* cheeks, and again, Rigel's eyes turned a luminous neon yellow green. Esme licked her lips; her whole body shook.

"Do not worry, human hybrids. You have nothing to fear. We are indebted to you."

Again, Rigel waved her outstretched hands like Jesus addressing his apostles, moving her eyes toward Joseph. "Sula, it is time to go home," Rigel implored.

Joseph looked down over his body; he exhaled. Simultaneously, the glow of his skin intensified, creating a foggy aura that swirled with energy and sparkles of light. The fog accelerated away from Joseph and connected to the lightbox. But it was still tethered to him.

The seal broke.

Esme screamed. Emil grunted. Joseph stared in shock, letting go of Esme's hand. In front of their eyes, a hologram materialized. It was a beautiful alien form, wearing a flowing, white dress. She looked like Rigel, with enormous eyes, except she had a smaller head. The new form seemed to radiate happiness. Esme felt a sudden calm. Peace. A feeling of joy swept over her. The hologram stared at Joseph. "My name is Sula," said the *Being*, gesturing towards her chest. "Joseph, thank you for holding my life force, my spirit energy, for all these years. My beloved family will always be indebted to you. You represent the pinnacle of human potential, a sacred vessel. I will miss you."

Sula's ghost looked towards the heavens and whispered something unknown and unheard. Then she bowed gracefully, dissolving into the glass box. Joseph rubbed his eyes and looked at Esme.

She let go of her dad's hand because she was no longer afraid. Esme stared at Rigel. The *Being* stretched a long, lean arm toward Esme. Another subtle smile appeared. "Dob-Dec, we are waiting for you," said Rigel, her words floating in the air like a melody.

Esme gulped and winced but felt no pain. A cloud of mist erupted around her, swirling into the spirit box, then back out again, forming another ghostly image. The new *light-being* appeared to have a peculiar face with eyes like eggplants. The *Being* wore white drapery, like a Greek God in a play. The ghostly image bowed its head towards Esme, and she covered her mouth in anticipation. The *Being* appeared to smile.

"I have a name, and it is Dob-Dec. I am also indebted to my exceptional meat-eater, my Esme. Thank you for allowing me to live within you for safekeeping. I no longer dislike meat-eaters like you. Truly, meat-eaters are more than glorified apes! I have decided that I like you better than ants," said Dob, placing his hand over his chest for emphasis. "I will miss playing the levitation game with you. My heartfelt wish is that you will always enjoy a magic-filled life." Dob-Dec giggled. "And yes, we have a heart. Goodbye, Esme."

The hologram turned, fizzling into an airstream, and disappearing into the glass box. The box dimmed. Everyone looked toward Rigel, blinking with their mouths open. Rigel clasped her hands, a look of serenity and happiness gracing her unusual features. Her eyes flashed red, then turned black again. "My new friends, I bear gifts," she said with the same hypnotic voice.

Rigel raised her arms, cupped her hands above her head like *Bird Girl*, then placed them back at her side. Rigel's gesture launched another *Being* into action, who brought forth an arrangement of peculiar glass flowers. The flowers looked like delicate gardenias with long, fragile stems. "Joseph and Esme, will you step onto the light? I wish to honor you," said Rigel.

Oliver grabbed Esme's arm, but she assured him, "It's fine. They're our friends; can't you feel it?"

Oliver bit his lip and nodded, letting go. Esme waited for Joseph to complete the sign of the cross. Then the duo stepped off the rim of La Danta into the night air. The light below Esme's feet felt like a million creepy-crawly ants; it was pure fizzling energy. She giggled with excitement. Joseph chuckled, too.

Rigel moved closer. Esme stretched her hand to Rigel, and the alien accepted it. "You're cold," said Esme, then added, "Your voice is beautiful, Rigel."

"Thank you, Esme. We have a syrinx here," Rigel said, pointing at her throat. "It vibrates like a singing bird. And yes, we are cold-blooded. We are descendants of creatures akin to the iguanas of the beautiful Blue Earth. At home, we feel warm to the touch. But here, on Blue Earth, we turn cool. Even so, you will find that our hearts are always warm. You are like us, human hybrids. We, too, breathe oxygen. Our planet is much like the tiny Blue Earth. Although, it is older, dryer, and hotter!" said Rigel. She laughed, paused, and craned her neck towards Esme and Joseph. "We feel love like human hybrids, too," she said, pointing at her heart. "We appreciate the beauty of the Blue Earth and all its inhabitants."

Rigel turned towards Joseph, selecting a crystal flower, and slowly placing her long, slender hand in front of him. As soon as Joseph accepted the glass stem, the flower morphed into an opaque ball, swirling with life. The ball was like a snow globe, except the particles floating inside were like dark flecks of pepper. "They are genetically modified mason bees," said Rigel.

"How do I open it?" asked Joseph, holding the globe closer to his face.

Rigel appeared to smile, her eyes dancing with bursts of white light. "Just say *release,* and it will happen. The bees are special pollinators modified to withstand the many disturbances that plague the beautiful Blue Earth. We have released bees in many strategic places. But this globe is yours to disperse in a place of your choosing. The bees will hibernate until spring, so release them before winter's frosty bite."

Rigel turned and nodded her head towards the *Being* on her right. She selected another artificial flower and handed it to Joseph. He accepted it with wide eyes. The flower morphed into a bubble, then a tiny, earthly jar. It was the color of amber. "This jar contains honey from our home planet. You will be the first human-hybrid to taste our otherworldly dessert."

Joseph giggled like a kid on Christmas morning. "Thank you, Rigel. My heart is bursting. I love these gifts so much. It's like you read my mind," said Joseph, his head bobbing.

Rigel nodded. "We did."

Rigel turned towards Esme and selected another flower. This time, Rigel manipulated it between her hands, balancing it in her slender palm and hovering her other hand like a magician. Esme laughed. "Are you doing a magic trick?"

Rigel's eyes flashed with white light. "We always use magic. But for us, it is not magic at all."

She pointed a long, slender finger at the center of her large forehead. "We use our brains. I can see into your heart, Esme. You will miss the magic Dob-Dec performed for you with tonal technology. This gift will give you some of his power. But use it wisely. Carefully."

Esme plucked the flower from Rigel's hand, studying it closely as if it held all the knowledge of the universe. After a few seconds, the flower morphed into a flat piece of glass. Then it morphed again, forming glass tubes that slowly converted into a thin, transparent, and malleable glove. Esme studied the glove, running a finger over a small matrix on the palm like a tattoo. "What is it?" she asked with a trembling voice.

"When you wear the glove, you can move objects with your mind. A slight prick will occur as the power core enters your central nervous system. But don't be afraid."

"Is it safe?" Oliver queried in the background.

Rigel looked at Oliver for the first time. She placed a hand over her chest. "The glove is safe, Oliver. We live with love, honor, and integrity. We would never harm other creatures, especially our honored hosts, Joseph, and Esme," said Rigel, turning her head back to Esme.

She looked into Esme's eyes. "However, the glove will stimulate the hidden code in your DNA. Eventually, your brain will learn to levitate objects on its own."

Esme smiled, riding a wave of adrenaline and happiness. She looked at Joseph, wondering if he would miss his power. She tried to read his mind but couldn't.

"I'm glad you got your power back, Esme. I don't want to be a superhero. You always made a better one than me. I only want to taste this honey and be a great chef," said Joseph, flashing his teeth and holding up his jar.

Esme sensed movement and turned to face Rigel. The alien and her friends were already floating away from them, the beam of light dissolving into thin air. "No! Don't go!" Esme shouted.

Rigel bowed and waved, gesturing towards the heavens. Involuntarily, Esme and Joseph moved backward through the air to the surface of La Danta. Above El Mirador's trees, the *Beings* floated farther and farther away until their massive spaceship exploded into view behind them. The portal opened, and the *Beings* slipped inside, the ship whirling and pulsing with unnatural light, as silent as a dust mote. As soon as the red portal closed, the vessel disappeared. Esme knew it would be forever. She turned towards Joseph with glassy eyes.

Joseph lowered his head. "My heart just shredded, and the good part is gone."

"Just a minute ago, I felt on top of the world. Now, I feel sad, empty."

"How can I miss someone so much; someone I never knew?" Joseph asked the night.

"I feel so alone," sniffed Esme.

Joseph half smiled. "You'll never be alone, not as long as my lungs breathe air."

Joseph hugged Esme, and they turned towards their fathers and Antonio in unison. The group stood frozen.

Esme and Joseph looked up into the starry sky.

Esme

Esme selected a bench and sat, brushing leaves off the open space beside her. Joseph scrunched in, too, crossing his legs and stretching his arm above her shoulders. She placed her shopping bag at her feet and looked up into the gnarled branches of the oak tree above their heads. A black crow stared back at her, emitting a raucous caw.

"I think my gift spooks the crow," said Joseph.

They both stared at the sparkly glass ball cupped in his hand. "The bees *really* are the greatest magic trick so far. But what if the bees are dead? How can they live without air or food? I don't understand how it works."

"Me neither," said Joseph, holding the ball up into a shaft of light filtering through the treetop. "I'm pretty sure they're alive," he added, almost whispering.

Esme watched the black flecks float inside the gel-like liquid. Sometimes, the specks floated randomly like inanimate objects, snowflakes. Other times, they appeared to wake up, roaming around, searching, and emitting strange, wave-like energy. It was the weirdest, most mesmerizing thing she'd ever seen, and she didn't want to let it go.

"Joseph, I wish we could keep the ball as a souvenir, but I know we can't. At least the bees are going out with a bang. I'm so nervous about the show. What if no one shows up?" she asked, touching the glass ball with a fingertip.

Above their heads, the crow bounced on a branch and took flight. Esme swiveled, watching the bird's trajectory across the Conservatory Gardens of Central Park. She saw skinny benches lining the sidewalk and wise, old-growth trees growing majestically around them. People crisscrossed everywhere, and gangs of pigeons pecked the sidewalk near their feet. Busy squirrels bounced around like rubber balls, dutifully caching nuts, and sporadic yellow flowers glowed in the afternoon sun. It was a beautiful September day in New York, warm with a slight breeze. Joseph followed her gaze.

"They'll come," he said.

Esme appraised herself, raising her feet and inspecting her new, shiny black heels. Then she peeked inside her bag and nervously rummaged around, ensuring she had everything she needed. "I feel like I forgot something," she said.

Joseph handed Esme the glass ball. Carefully, she placed it in her sack, cushioned it inside her magic hat, and positioned the feather like a cat's tail, making sure it didn't get squished. Esme looked at Joseph with a peculiar expression. "Do you think we'll wake up one day and realize this was all a dream?" she asked.

"No, not after the radiation burns from the spaceship—Diablo's kisses. The ship was only in the sky for a minute, and that's all it took," said Joseph, trickling a finger down Esme's cheek. Catching wayward hairs caught on the breeze, he curled them behind her ear.

Esme examined her hands and touched her cheek. "It was painful, the worst sunburn I've ever had. Now, I know why the ship left so abruptly. I miss Dob-Dec. I don't think I'll ever get used to being alone. It's like losing a twin sister or brother. Is that weird?"

Joseph nodded. "Same here. I feel like a different person. But at least I don't have to feel guilty about eating meat anymore."

Esme rubbed Joseph's stomach; happy she'd lost weight while he gained.

He looked at his abdomen.

"I know, I've gained a few pounds. I've been doing so much cooking. Even though we have each other, I still feel sad, lonely, and off kilter. I guess I've been drowning my feelings with food. I'm proud of you, Esme, for throwing yourself into your new online magic classes."

"I'm determined to become a better magician. Now that I know my power won't disappear, you'd think I wouldn't care about learning more magic. But I do. I want to prove that I could do it independently if I had to."

Joseph grabbed her hand.

"You haven't even told me how much you're going to miss me!" he exclaimed.

Esme started laughing. "I *am* going to miss you. But I thought you'd be happy I'm over my obsession."

"A little obsessed is okay," he whispered into her ear, tilting her head towards his and gently kissing her red lips. He pulled away. "I don't want to mess up your makeup. You look so pretty."

Esme beamed.

"Just don't forget about me when you're a famous magician, and I work in a cramped kitchen in Queens."

"You'll be toiling in Manhattan. Joseph, as I said, I *am* going to miss you terribly. So, when can I come to Mexico City?"

"Anytime but watch out. I may put you to work as my new sous-chef."

Esme rolled her eyes and heard a familiar bark. She looked down the sidewalk. "Doug!" she exclaimed, opening her arms.

A shaggy sheepdog pulled to escape his leash and loped to a halt by Esme's feet, whimpering. She jostled the dog's ears, parted his bangs, and kissed his nose. Behind the dog stood Oliver.

Her dad wore a green collared shirt, dark indigo jeans, and a new, short haircut. Esme grabbed the leash from his fist, and Doug settled near her feet. "Dad, I almost didn't recognize you without your birding gear and ponytail."

"It's me unless the aliens replaced me with a younger model," said Oliver with a devilish smile.

Esme and Joseph moved down the bench, and Oliver scrunched in beside them. Esme had never felt happier. She was sandwiched between the two men she loved most in the world—*her* world, anyway—and a jolt of complacency filtered through her soul, her one and *only* soul.

"You still sound corny, like my real dad."

Oliver smiled. "We had a nice walk, Doug, and me. He's a chick magnet, that's for sure," he said with a wink.

"Dad! That's gross."

"I guess this means you're staying in New York since you got a dog."

"Well, this is where Joseph will work when he finishes training at Le Cordon Bleu."

"There's a lot of restaurants in Orlando, too. You love Florida," stated Oliver.

"Mitzi's son owns several restaurants here, and Maximilian said he'd hire me after my training. It's a great opportunity. I haven't pressured Esme to stay in New York, honest," said Joseph.

"Dad, I want to stay in New York. I like it here. It's new and exciting."

Oliver smiled and patted Esme's hand. "Just checking."

"Did you see the stage?"

"Sure did. It's all set up. I can't wait to see your performance. Although, I wish you'd get rid of that glove. It scares me."

"Now you sound like Joseph. You're such a hypocrite."

"Who, me?" asked Oliver, placing a palm over his chest.

"Yes, you. As if you'd ever give up one of your discoveries, like a jade mask or beads, chert tools, or whatever."

"Unfortunately, I don't get to keep my whatevers."

Esme looked at her dad. His face was unreadable.

"Dad, I'm sorry you had to give up the crystal box of souls."

Oliver chuckled. "Is that what it's called?"

They all laughed somewhat nervously and for a short time, silence prevailed. Sparrows chattered in the bushes behind them, and cars zoomed in the distance. Esme watched people for a few minutes, including Joseph picking dog hairs from his pants. Oliver sat contentedly, his chest rising and falling.

Finally, Joseph cleared his throat. "I'm sorry, Oliver. My dad told me about everything you guys went through. Giving away the most exciting thing you've ever discovered must have been hard. My dad's heartbroken."

"He won't be for long."

"What do you mean?"

Oliver whistled a long, looping note and looked down at Doug's head resting on his knee.

"I think Doug is looking at me, but I can't tell," said Oliver, scratching the dog around his ears.

"Dad, tell us!"

Oliver investigated his lap, sat up straighter, stretched his arms, and cracked his knuckles. "Well, there's something I haven't told you. That night when Rigel was handing out gifts, well, she gave me one too." Oliver paused, looking at them and raising his eyebrows seductively.

Esme punched her dad's arm. "Keep going."

"She told me something... something big."

"But she didn't even talk to you," Esme interrupted.

"No, she didn't say anything to me—at least not with her invisible lips. Still, it was loud and clear. It's funny you mentioned a jade mask because she gave me a mental map of where I can find one, and it's even bigger than the Kinich Ahau jade head—all in the blink of an eye. It was when she looked at me. It felt like she zapped a text or sent an email straight into my brain."

Oliver rubbed his hands together. "The mask is still buried deep, in a jungle even more remote than El Mirador. Honduras. That's why Emil couldn't make it today. He's down there trying to get permission for us to get in there. Ciudad Blanca was only a rumor for decades. Now, it's real. It's somewhere we've wanted to go since 2012 when a rickety old plane flew over the site with a million dollars' worth of Lidar and found a whole undiscovered civilization. I wanted to go there even before Rigel whispered in my ear. Now, I'm spitting chiclets. I know where to look, and I just need to get there first, before someone else accidentally digs it up, or before it gets looted."

"Are you finished at El Mirador?" asked Joseph.

"El Mirador!" Oliver exclaimed, his arm swiping the air for emphasis. Doug barked while Oliver slapped his other knee. "I can't stop thinking about La Danta. Unbelievable. The aftermath was pure insanity. After you two left on that chopper and things calmed down...The students, heck, no one knew what to think. Some kids thought it was just a storm. Others saw the strange, penetrating lights and thought it was Armageddon. Some thought meteor showers. Oddly enough, most people didn't see a spaceship at all. I'm sure everyone involved will be speculating for quite some time." Oliver paused, shaking his head in reverie, before continuing, "Heck, if they knew what happened on top of La Danta, it would have been a runaway train. Anyway, El Mirador is in the rearview mirror. The season's over when the students go back to school. El Mirador can't be beat. *Ever.* But now, all I want to think about is the *Lost City of the Monkey God.* It's more than one city; it's a whole undiscovered civilization. The jade mask is the cherry on a massive cake. It's not like I can keep the mask, but I want to find it first."

"Dad, I'm so excited for you."

"I'm excited for you, too. How did you pull all this together? Did you need a permit?"

"Yes. It came through a couple of weeks ago. As soon as we got to New York, we started wracking our brains, trying to come up with something big worthy of Rigel's bees. It was Brooklyn Struthers—her assistant, anyway. I met Joy—she's Brooklyn's assistant—on the set when I was on *The Morning Show.* Joy follows my Instagram. When Joy saw I was back in New York she told Brooklyn that I was planning a magic show, and as soon as my permit came through, Brooklyn announced it on air," said Esme, swinging her arms.

She looked at her dad and Joseph. "So here we are. Dad, I'm glad you came. Mom's coming, too. At least, she said she was."

Oliver rolled his eyes. Joseph looked at his phone and said, "I think it's time to head over. Get ready for the show."

Esme pulled her phone out, too. "Oh, my God. Why am I so nervous?"

Esme peeked through the billowy curtains, watching Mitzi roll to a stop just below the small stage platform. She giggled when Mitzi's hair caught on the breeze, flying around, and sticking up like tufts on a lemon meringue pie. Behind Mitzi's wheelchair stood a medium-sized group of onlookers and a long expanse of grass with a circular fountain that sprinkled the air with a natural melody. Closer to home, Esme made a mental check around the stage. She saw the pedestal, cards, and velvet pillow, then turned her focus back to the crowd, scanning faces. "Who's that big guy with Mitzi, the guy with the tattoos? Is that her son Max?"

Joseph stuck his head through the curtains, waved at Mitzi, and ducked behind again. "No, that's her new personal care attendant," he said with a frown.

Esme took another peek at the crowd gathered to watch, smiling at her dad and Doug standing near the small stage like groupies. "My mom isn't here yet. I'll never forgive her if she flakes. I'm so nervous! I've never been on an official stage before. It feels like a real show."

"It *is* a real show! Don't think of it as a stage. It's just a raised platform so that people can see you. Just pretend you're still on I-drive, doing your card tricks. You got this," said Joseph. Grabbing her hands, he swung them from side to side and squeezed.

Esme squeezed back, and then she let go, blowing a torrent of air through her teeth. First, she pulled the glass ball from her sack and handed it to Joseph for safekeeping. Next, Esme donned her black magic hat, slipping her wand into the velvet band beside the fluffy white feather. Finally, she pulled a black cape from the sack, snapped it like a towel, clipped it to the applets of her green velvet shirt, fluffed her hair, and swirled around, her cape flying about like she was Superman. Esme tugged at her short, black skirt, wishing she had a mirror. "How do I look?"

"Perfect. Except for one thing."

She raised an eyebrow, reached into her shopping bag, and pulled out a black velvet box. After prying it open, she peered inside and pulled out a clear glove. The glove felt spongy, and a strange fluid seeped inside the skin like blood through an artery. Slowly, she slipped her right hand inside it. A small metallic tattoo shifted like the mechanics of a clock. Esme yelped when the power core entered her flesh.

"It scares me every time," she said, goosebumps erupting over her arm.

"What does it feel like?"

Esme held her hand before her face, waiting for the glowing energy pathways to stop pulsing. "Drugs, maybe?" she said with a smirk. "Well, I suppose it feels like being hooked up to an I.V. It doesn't hurt, but it feels unexplainably weird, like being plugged into the universe."

Joseph held up the glass ball. "Look, the bees are going nuts! I think the ball is growing and getting bigger. Isn't it?"

Esme bent, looking through the ball. From the other side, her eyes looked distorted like a funhouse mirror. Now, the ball was swirling with starbursts of energy. "We better start the show before it explodes! What if it bursts before we're ready?" she said with wild eyes.

Joseph lowered the ball. "I'll pray it doesn't."

Esme inhaled and stepped through the curtain.

Esme felt giddy listening to the applause, and even Joseph was clapping. She blew Joseph a theatrical kiss and he grabbed it, moving to the side of the stage with his arms akimbo.

After shuffling her cards, she fanned them, and reshuffled. Without hesitation, she thrust the whole deck of cards as high as she could muster, concentrating and trying to visualize each one. Simultaneously, her mother eased into the crowd. Esme shook her head; she couldn't lose her concentration. At least her mother came and late was better than never. At least Ethelene would see the grand finale.

Esme refocused, intent on the cards scattered in the sky. Every card was defying gravity, floating, hovering as if God had pushed the pause button on the scene. Esme twirled her wand and thought about that first night in the hotel room with Joseph—objects swirling, spinning, moving like ants swarming an anthill. Esme closed her eyes; she had to stay focused. Esme imagined all fifty-two cards (which took much mental fortitude now that Dob-Dec wasn't doing all the work). She squeezed her eyes and stuck out her tongue. After a few seconds, she opened her eyes.

The cards floated like cottonwood seeds on a swirly breeze, settling into formation and hovering in place. Now, Esme could see the word: EDAJ—*Jade* spelled backwards. Again, she reversed her wayward thoughts while concentrating on the cards and holding steady.

Towards the back of the crowd, people clapped. Her mother

was cheering and waving her arms. Others—the ones underneath the cards—stepped backward, their heads craned towards the sky. After a few seconds, recognition registered on their faces.

Esme bowed and held her breath with her hands curled into fists at her side. She wasn't finished yet. She stuck her wand into her hat and raised her right hand, holding her palm flat. Slowly, one by one, the cards tumbled home to roost. Esme remembered to breathe.

Joseph raced to her side, raising his hand. Esme smacked a high five, handed him the cards, and streaked to the pedestal. She hovered her hands over the velvet pillow, casting an invisible spell. Esme flicked her eyes toward Ethelene; her mother was filming now. She looked at her dad; he was filming too.

Esme looked at Joseph and nodded her head.

He jumped from the stage, threading his way to the back of the crowd. Esme winked at her dad, feeling a mixture of excitement and loss, rolled up with worry that the bees just couldn't or wouldn't wait.

Sitting on the velvet pillow in front of her chest was the glowing ball sparkling as if filled with miniature stars. Esme scooped it up, holding it high for all to see. The ball fizzled in her hand, burning a dazzling amber hue. She heard laughter, sounds of wonder, and elation. Now, the ball was dancing with bursts of black and gold and growing larger by the second.

Esme plucked the wand from her hat and twirled it around the ball. The ball burst forward, then slowed, floating high over the crowd. All heads swiveled.

Esme wanted to take her time. She wanted to fly the ball in fancy circles over treetops and around the crowd, but she wasn't in control because the ball could burst at any moment. Esme directed it to Joseph. The crowd turned, all eyes on him.

Now Joseph is the magician. She stepped from the stage and almost ran towards Joseph until she stood beside him. She heard Joseph whisper, "Release. Fly free. Go!"

He grabbed the ball and threw it into the air. The ball expanded into a wiggling, diaphanous bubble. Esme chewed her lip. Joseph steepled his hands. *Pssst! Poof! Pop!* The ball exploded.

A cyclone of tiny bees formed a wispy, amber-colored cloud. They were gone in seconds. Esme and Joseph scanned the sky, but all that remained was a gentle buzzing in the distance, and after a few seconds, clapping and cheering overpowered everything. Joseph grabbed Esme, swinging her off her feet. Esme found his mouth and kissed him as hard as she could.

Esme felt a pawing on the back of her legs. She turned. Oliver, Doug, and Ethelene were waiting. Immediately Esme and Joseph broke apart, reforming a four-person hug. Doug barked several times while everyone jiggled in a big, awkward clump.

Amid the jostling reverie, Esme closed her eyes. "Thank you, Rigel. I'll never forget you," she whispered.

Rigel

Thousands of zoological glass domes spread over the sand like sparkles on an endless lake. The domes were hollow and tall like an earthly skyscraper, creating a perfect cycle of cooling clouds and rain. Rigel hovered over the sands of the Canidae dome, one of the most extensive domes on planet Pleione.

Outside the domes, olivine-colored sand blustered over the dunes, swirling with an unstoppable velocity. One thousand feet above Rigel's giant head, faceted glass triangles formed a conical web, reflecting every rainbow color. Below Rigel's waist and all around, irregular beasts with thick follicles and droopy ears frolicked, each specimen created from earthly DNA files.

Why are these beasts of such merit, such value? Rigel knew the hybrids adored them above all others. Watching the beasts dance like idiots amused her as they rolled and flopped, biting and drooling. The beasts' tongues dripped from dirty mouths, long like runga fruit and just as sticky.

Rigel's eyes flashed blue with disgust, but her opinion was irrelevant. One of these creatures would be the perfect gift. She must decide.

Lifting her hand, she sliced the air before her bulbous forehead and adjusted her position. She maneuvered mentally, lifting a foot sheathed in leathery fachen leaves and curling her slim legs beneath her. A dress of white robotic muslin hung from her hips like flower petals. With her balance restored, she steepled her long fingers, looking from one creature to another.

Rigel chose a small and fuzzy creature with short legs that plucked through the green sand like baby akwops. The animal appraised Rigel with glossy brown eyes, instigating an unusual tug at her heart. The canines, she realized, were intuitive. It was almost as if they possessed some of her power—the ability to communicate without moving a muscle.

Rigel practiced her telepathy more than most females. Ever studious, she strived to become the most potent female in all aspects of education: godliness, universal knowledge and star-mapping, mechanical engineering, cultivation, terraforming, social interaction, body chemistry and molecular science, levitation, and an endless list of other neural acumen.

Balance proved hardest of all. Her thoughts often drifted to uneven, jealous places—Sula, the small-headed healer whose brain cells seemingly traversed a perfect figure eight. Rigel was wiser than Sula, but content? Seldom. She wanted a mate.

Rigel tilted her head and placed her slender fingers at the nape of her long, slim neck, her eyes undulating a yellowish ochre. "No, not you, poor little canine," she told the earthly dog with black and white fur and a mouth stained from the juices of bovine meat.

The canine ran back to his dugout made of brown craca vines, turned around twice, and flopped down. Rigel summoned a larger beast with shiny golden follicles. This time, her eyes glowed a luminous neon green, and her long fingers massaged and manipulated the air.

The canine blinked at Rigel, using the tiny muscles near its eyes to communicate an important question. As the beast's brown eyes twitched, Rigel tilted her head. *We are simpatico*, she thought.

She suspected there was little difference between the neurons of human hybrids and canine beasts. "At least canines are so ugly; they're cute. Nothing can make a human hybrid look cute. They have swollen muscles and minuscule heads with bulbous noses, and puffy lips. Their genitals hang loosely like shriveled fruit on a vine!" said Rigel with audible laughter.

Time hung in the air until Rigel clicked her tongue, addressing the dogs again as if they were listening. "The hybrids have shaggy follicles under their armpits and loins," said Rigel, gesturing broadly. "They reek of dying cells—disgusting. Hybrids have weird, greasy ears resembling seashells and eyes as tiny as shunt seeds. And worst of all, none are green!" She pointed at the blond canine. "You. I choose you," said Rigel, her chest vibrating with laughter.

The beast waved his tail and panted loudly. Rigel folded her arms and after watching the canine with a look akin to admiration, she summoned the beast handler telepathically. A male *Being* arrived on foot.

Rigel greeted the male with a tilt of her head, appraising him and smiling internally at his head size and shape that resembled an unripe pumpkin. The male *Being* was short and full of playful emotions. The duo continued their silent negotiations until the transaction was complete.

Minutes later, Rigel exited the small animal dome alone and erect, immediately sheathing her eyes from the suns with her cat-like inner eyelids. Below, her long feet traversed the hot sand like earthly skis through the snow.

She looked to the heavens and stopped short of the transportation tube. Sand swirled around her legs, and her white sheath billowed about her. Rigel pressed the tip of her finger to the metallic tattoo adhered to her wrist. A tiny maze whirled, as intricate as a spider's web, and a hologram materialized like a fuzzy, pixelated ghost. A warning of solar flares streamed along with imagery from her living dome. She watched the massive golden cover of her dome close over the glass arc like a metal cap.

Straightaway and all around, the zoo domes that spread over the olivine dunes like shimmering glass islands closed their lids, preparing for the storm. Now, the Canidae dome sported a canopy of gold, sparkling in the afternoon suns and reflecting Rigel's image like a mirror.

Rigel noticed she wasn't alone.

Behind her back, furry akwops peeked from their sand tunnels, inspecting Rigel with small, beady eyes. She knew that akwops— like avians— had a unique molecule inside their eyes, enabling them to see and hear low frequency infrasound, even from thousands of miles adrift. The storm was gaining momentum.

Rigel crossed her arms and dropped into the transportation tube. The glass walls of the tunnel flashed with rainbow colors, lulling her into a deep state of meditation. For Rigel, traveling between domes was her time to refocus, rebalance, and create peace.

As the tube slowed, Rigel regained consciousness. Slowly, her eyes opened, briefly flashing purple, then green. Already, she could feel the dome's humidity.

The chatter of birds floated in the air, along with the heady smell of sage and rose petals. Rigel had been back from her mission for months, but the garden's atmosphere still felt replenishing. She wanted to absorb every sensation like an earthly sea sponge because her next mission would be the longest yet, and this time, she would have a mate.

Rigel levitated to the surface, her eyes adjusting to the darkness, tiny nostrils dilated, and inner ears perked. She spread her arms wide, expanding her diaphragm. Inside her dome, gentle breezes snagged against the fabric of her dress and a cacophony of bird sounds assailed her senses. At her feet, turkeys and chickens darted, pecking an irregular path through the jungle. A great curassow ran for cover under the large, purple-veined leaves of coppa plants and stinky tomato vines. Above the flora, lightning bugs whirled, circling Rigel, and lighting her way forward.

After finding herself nestled in a magical display of light, she deemed her ship's artificial light harsh and unforgiving. Until now, she hadn't fully realized how much she'd missed all the natural wonders of Pleione. She filled her lungs and her feet lifted off the jungle floor. Soon, she was dancing and floating with the firebugs, initiating an invitation, a message to the others.

They came.

The other *Beings* exited their classrooms with bright, glowing eyes and swayed in unison, briskly levitating above the exotic palmetto, papaya, and banana trees of Earth. Rigel's living dome held a cornucopia of nutrition sources, like long pods of delicious runga fruit dripping like snakes from spindly branches, with a tiny flower attached to the end of each pod like the eye of a cyclops. Earthly varieties like pear, apple, and oily nuts sat dormant while guava, soursop, and rambutan dripped with fruit. Coka and meera plants hung from soilless pots, and earthly vegetable varieties littered the garden floor, creeping over the pathways like weeds. The wings of butterflies were like heartbeats attached to all things green. This abundance went on for three square miles.

Above the garden, one hundred and fifty females, their mates, and countless children took flight. The firebugs swirled higher, surrounding the *Beings* like flies' around ripe fruit. Everyone swayed. Below, night birds cooed. A barred owl hooted in a faraway tree, instigating a dissonance of rustling as all matter of birds bounced and took flight. A few *Beings* picked fruit from the treetops and ate while they danced and swayed. Others spread their arms and floated horizontally as if in sleep. Rigel spun in happy circles.

The females hummed, filling the air with melody, an eerie droning—the harmonic code. The males hummed an alternate, higher-pitched version. The night dance continued until a shaft of sunlight sliced the thick air. Quietly, the golden cap receded, flooding the dome with blinding light. The threat was over.

All souls descended to the garden floor, plucking fruit, and picking vegetables and leaves like locusts on a binge. They returned to their classrooms and the *living* rooms surrounding the dome's perimeter, like a ring on an earthly finger.

On her way home, Rigel plucked a mango from a low-hanging branch. She nibbled, her tiny mouth stretching to eat the large, soft fruit. Juice dripped down her little chin. She caught the drop on the tip of a finger and licked it. The taste was divine.

Soon, she would enter her favorite period: physical chores to balance her muscles. But first, she hurried to her classroom to finish the day's assignments. Later, after her labor duties were complete, she could see her future mate. Rigel blushed, her eyes turning a fiery red.

Rigel swiped her calculations aside like virtual garbage. Learning a new ship's controls and the math required to map the stars was difficult. There was also the endless search for twenty-six flexible crew members to sail by her side. She needed the best minds for the new mission.

A chickadee in autumn buried food in one hundred places and grew its hippocampus by thirty percent to remember them all. That is how she felt before each delicate mission. Even so, after thousands of calculations, after organizing her neurons into perfect alignment, things still went wrong—like losing Lyra and her crew—Dob-Dec and Sula. But what was lost had now been found.

Rigel stood, collapsing her study zone into the floor with the swipe of a finger. Today, she would travel on the supersonic tube and join the physical laborers, building a new city of domes in the far corner of the Pladoon plains: a flat desert surrounded by olivine mountains made of layers and layers of crusty silica. Physical work was much more complex than neural tasks. That's why she loved it. It was a challenge, and afterward, she always slept for two solar cycles like a child of twenty—deep sleep, as if she inhabited a dark sky world.

Darkness. Rigel missed darkness. It was a luxury, something she enjoyed on her missions through space. There was only dimness here as their planet swirled around two distant suns.

Rigel left her study zone, her feet intermittently levitating. She entered her sleeping pod, a room unlike homes visited by the insect drones scouring the beautiful Blue Earth. Human hybrids required possessions, their homes resembling a pharaoh's undiscovered tomb. On planet Pleione, all *Beings* lived the same way, simply possessing what was needed and collapsing what wasn't in use.

Even so, there were special events that required something new. "Room. Show me my new dress," said Rigel with a sing song voice.

The room answered.

The sand-colored tile below Rigel's feet opened like a mouth, a glass cylinder popping up like an akwop from its tunnel. Rigel reached into her wardrobe and pulled a dress from within, admiring the dove-like softness.

Now was not the time for robotic silk sheaths. However, it *was* time to walk through the recalibration unit, a weekly ritual of electromagnetic energy that would rejuvenate Rigel's cells, making her feel as fresh as spring buds on a lilac bush. She walked to the middle of the room, her long feet whispering over an electric grid embedded in the floor—her whole body tingled. Around her, a golden circle spun, rising like a coil of rope, and inside the ring, Rigel walked, hands steepled in meditation, her feet traversing a small serenity maze in slow motion.

When Rigel reached the last step, the purring ended, and the golden wheel stopped. She opened her eyes, repeating a silent prayer.

Refreshed, she floated to her wardrobe, selected protective solar garments, and rubbed her fingers over the beaded fabric. The fabric tickled her fingers; it felt like tiny grains of sand. As soon as she draped the garment over her shoulders, the material morphed, shapeshifting and snuggly hugging her olive skin.

Rigel exited the room, glancing back at the sleeve of her brand-new dress, still visible within her *open* wardrobe. Suddenly, the garment flew into the air and danced on unseen wings like an ethereal spirit. Rigel had no intention of closing her closet—not today. She smiled internally and exited the rear portal into the sunlight, bright and hot.

Rigel stepped into her spa, washing away every grain of sand with a strong mist of rose water. She luxuriated for several minutes and then initiated the drying vent, relishing the seductive smell of honeysuckle and orris. Rigel spun in circles through the perfume, her feet levitating.

Now, she felt as clean as a sparkling Pleiadian, as happy as the Gods. It was time to visit her future mate and prepare him for the ritual. She slipped into her new dress, exited her living dome, entered the garden, and made a beeline for the rose bushes. This time, she picked a hybrid blue, arranging the delicate petals carefully in the hidden sash of her cloak. Rigel walked, passing a group of male *Beings* harvesting burra-cherries and preening branches inside the dormant olive grove. She paused to watch a cluster of peahens, marveling at their beauty. Rigel craned her long neck, searching for the male partially hidden behind a bushy orange tree. She waited, catching the sweep of bright tail feathers as they weaved between tree trunks.

It was mating season.

Rigel thought about the physical act of love. For *Beings*, mating was quick, like earthly dolphins coming together mid-jump. But the aftermath of pleasure lasted for hours.

She thought about the males of planet Pleione. They reminded Rigel of peacocks, even though they possessed none of a male bird's beauty. Still, they were fairer than females. Their skin was softer, a lovely light green and their eggplant eyes were full of emotion. Their bellies were fuller, and their minds were more straightforward, not as complex, but full of curiosity.

Rigel laughed—she was thinking about him. The rose bush shook as she plucked one last petal and rubbed the velvety flower between her fingers, slipping it into her cloak.

She floated away.

When she reached the tube connected to the healing dome, she entered, alert. This time, the ride was short, and there was no time for meditation. "Sula would be calm, balanced," she chastised out loud. Balance was futile, for her thoughts were a jumble of disorder.

The reunion was nigh.

After Rigel reached her destination, she levitated from the tube. The healing dome possessed no garden. It was bright and sterile, all glass—clear glass that reflected a deep blue, cloudless sky— and polished gold, with only a few healing plants, like aloe, scattered around the perimeter. Rigel disembarked at the heart of the healing dome. She nodded to other healers and visiting *Beings* as she progressed, sending them wordless greetings filled with energy and exuberance. The chamber she sought was rarely ever used. Still, it was the most sacred room of all.

Rigel weaved around glass partitions, floating around circular corridors—sometimes levitating, sometimes walking. Her mind played music, inventing a life not yet lived. When she reached the center unit, calm prevailed. She could sense him. His body smelled like chemicals, saltwater, and pine—the smell of embryonic plasma lingered. Rigel touched her sash, waiting for the healer to finish preparing the body for the ceremony. Golden cabinets lined the walls. Sunlight warmed the body lying in the center of the room.

"He is perfect," Rigel told the other female.

"Perfectly imperfect," the healer replied.

The females giggled.

"He is ready for the ceremony. I accelerated his maturity to the peak of fertility: seventy-five years. Everything is balanced. When you have washed him, I will remove the vital tubes. The ceremony will begin," said the healer, bowing her enormous head. She exited the room.

Rigel blushed at the word: *Fertility*. The term perfumed her soul. She went to work, preparing the sacred water and adding the rose of Jericho, rosemary, lavender, orange peel and the velvety blue petals. After closing her eyes, she blessed the mixture, feeling the energy cells hovering around her.

Rigel grabbed a sea sponge from the beautiful Blue Earth and started cleansing the rigid new body. She stared at his child-like face, caressed his new cheek, touching the tip of his tiny nose with her middle finger. Her heart smiled. The fresh *Being* looked as innocent lying here as he had in life. She couldn't wait to peel away the life tubes and watch what would happen next.

The beast handler sent a mental message. Before Rigel could respond, the blond beast absconded through the nearest portal, smashing into her legs and landing on her long, green toes. Rigel tilted her head in admonishment, and the dog settled, looking up with sweet, brown eyes. The dog was fresh and clean, brushed perfectly, and smelled of eucalyptus. Rigel nodded her approval, and the handler tilted his head, exiting the room.

Again, Rigel closed her eyes, gently exhaling through her nostrils and initiating a message to the other chamber. The healer returned, carrying a luminous crystal box in outstretched arms. Rigel removed the life tubes, watching as the box pulsed with electricity—rainbows swirling and refracting.

As the healer neared the body, her eyes bulged, and she snapped her hands from beneath the glass, shaking her head. "I should have known better," the healer whispered.

The box hung in the air, with a precious soul waiting inside, full of muscle memories, neural pathways, likes and dislikes, and the spark of life.

The crystal object floated to the other end of the table, hovering over the sleeping face below. Underneath, the patient's sleeping eyelids moved ever so slightly. Above, the box pulsed a screaming white, almost blinding. The healer lowered her inner eyelids and grabbed one of Rigel's hands.

"You've been waiting a long time."

Rigel lowered her arm, squeezing her inner eyelids against the glow. It was finally happening; her dreams were coming true. She repeatedly nodded, a feeling of helpless anticipation sweeping over her. She couldn't calm her mind, nor could she control her pulse. "I've been ready for over fifteen years," Rigel said, filling the room with an echoing, audible sound.

The blond dog barked, feet prancing and tail flapping against the porcelain floor. Rigel smoothed her dress and grabbed the lifeless hand in front of her.

"I'm ready for my future to begin," Rigel whispered, her voice as haunting as an earthly loon.

Commence Cerebral Streaming—

Session Eleven

Dear listeners: Session Ten did not end well. If you are eavesdropping on my neural data for the first time, I died in the jungles of Guatemala and roamed the Blue Earth for what felt like a millennium. In truth, it was a blip—approximately fifteen years, stuck on my earthly host like a bloody tick. I felt disjointed and adrift, but even so, I learned more about the meat-eaters than the data from a trillion insect drones.

The intel was invaluable. Still, I missed Sula and my friends. I discovered that I missed life on my home planet. During my imprisonment, I realized that I wasn't lonely before. If I had opened my mind's inner eyelids, I would have known my extended family included the crew, Sula, and my new mate. I had no idea what direction my future would take when I was with my host, Esme. I thought my life as I knew it was over.

Now, years later, I have never been so happy. I feel the kind of silly glee that one encounters at zoo discs, watching muscular horses of the Blue Earth kicking their long, slender legs towards the heavens and rolling in the olivine sand, their abdomens exposed with complete, addle-brained joy. That is the feeling exploding within my heart.

Rigel chose me! She could have mated with the wisest *Being* on planet Pleione. Instead, she chose me. Somehow, simple Dob-Dec—a *Being* as dim as Orion's stars—became a sparkle in her warm, undulating eyes. When my ship crashed in the jungles of Guatemala, she grew a youthful, new body from my DNA files, and after the resurrection, Rigel proposed. The rebirth was a night of complete and utter euphoria. To feel new and fresh, connected to a pristine body, defies description. I felt filled with helium when my spirit connected with my new form. I soared over the golden table, in both mind and spirit. I was alive again.

I awoke from my slumber, bursting with all my previous memories while looking into the face of an angel. How could I have overlooked my everything?

After Rigel's proposal, I levitated into a sky-dance like an earthly woodcock—a bird with an upside-down brain, huge black eyes, and the most spectacular courting ritual. My version of this *sky dance* was the gift I gave my Rigel. I rocketed, hands held high, while bowing and weaving most irregular. My everything felt profound joy during my display. I know because I was listening.

Months later, Rigel and I connected our central nervous systems during a traditional marriage ceremony. Now, I can't imagine inhabiting a singular mind. How peculiar that would seem.

I've been levitating—literally— ever since.

Rigel laughs internally at my boyish enthusiasm. She has never felt displeasure with me. Our comingled minds feel complete peace and satisfaction during our endless voyage to the faraway planet Naia.

Listeners, I wish you could see the precious life nestled inside our incubation unit. Two perfect eggs gestate warm and secure under the rays of our solar panels. I can't take my eyes off our children. I know they will be as intelligent as their mother. Maybe, they will be curious like me. I finally understand the supreme attachment to parenthood and sympathize with Sula and what she endured on the tiny Blue Earth.

After her resurrection ceremony, Sula felt tethered to Pleione. I will always love Sula. But my obsession has been replaced with fraternal love.

My new obsession is with Rigel and our perfect eggs. Soon, we will be educating our family on a new planet. I may never see Sula again.

But I am not disheartened as space travel is expanding my cortex. I look forward to arriving on planet Naia. The large planet is like Pleione in chemical makeup, size, and density. Except, it is much, much younger. The mountains are verdant, the atmosphere ripe. We will not live in domes; there is water in abundance. The soil already teems with organisms. Most importantly, primitive life is ready for experimentation and advancement.

My everything has promoted me. I will oversee our ever-expanding animal DNA files. In addition to the residing single-cell organisms, we will grow a diverse variety of all matter of beasts and birds, flora, and fauna. It is a delicate balance. The new species must be in order—to fail would be to suffer the same consequences as the meat-eaters.

Our crew will be part of an extensive network of terraformers on planet Naia. I hope I will rise to the task, quite literally. This is humorous!

Now and again, my thoughts meander to my earthly host, to Esme. I wonder about the magic she performs and if she misses my influence. We played countless games together. But now I have my beloved canine beast and Dulfim; both bring joy to me. There is no loneliness in my life anymore.

While my everything rules the ship, Dulfim, Deneb (my canine beast), and I play. Dulfim is the new collector of specimens and lead researcher. But since we have not yet arrived on planet Naia, neither Dulfim nor I have anything to do but learn and play. We have achieved such wisdom in our efforts: spinning elaborate fantasies about terraforming planet Naia, playing complicated knowledge wars, and playing the levitation game with Deneb. My beast loves to jump and grab dried bovine with his juicy mouth. It is disgusting, but physical exercise is essential for a canine. I am happy playing games. My brain is growing, and my heart is ready to burst like overripe Runga fruit.

There is a long pause and a succession of barks.

My communications with Rigel leave me tingling, floating on air—again, literally.

Deneb is a brilliant beast. He always knows when Rigel and I are conversing. I think he feels the pangs of earthly jealousy. I fail to read Deneb's thoughts. However, my everything tells me he watches all with a loyal heart, protecting and loving with never a beastly thought entering his primitive brain. My everything thinks I am much like Deneb. She cannot hide this.

I feel Rigel laughing with me. I see her standing erect at her station, watching infinity, stargazing, and planning. She is forging our path, keeping the ship balanced, and always mindful of each precious soul. She juggles all aspects adeptly. Listeners, she is as beautiful as a million pieces of compressed carbon.

My pulse quickens as her neurons mingle with mine. It feels like bees buzzing in a hive; it sounds like birds greeting the suns. I feel so alive! I must go, for it is time to feast. Listeners, my communications will be few going forward. I no longer feel the need to record them. I am too busy being happy.

End of Session—Continue Universal Translation Mode.

Joseph

Joseph looped the long ties of a clean, white apron around his back, tying the loose ends in a tight knot over his belly button. He rolled up the sleeves of his purple, tailored shirt and appraised the giant kitchen before him. There were no other chefs; he was alone tonight. All was eerily quiet except for ubiquitous street noise, sporadic firetrucks, and the hum of the enormous walk-in refrigerator.

Even though no one had told a joke, he couldn't help snickering. Lately, he felt like erupting into boisterous fits of laughter just because he could. He was happy. The kind of gladness that makes you feel as light as marshmallow fluff or as energetic as baby birds vying for food.

The scent of cardamom-laced churros lurked somewhere in the kitchen. There were other smells, too: bunches of cilantro that needed mincing; the ripe musk melon he'd scooped into perfect balls earlier that afternoon; a tray of spicy Spanish chorizo, drying on a paper towel; sweet corn, charred into an earthly blackness; and garlic, lots of garlic. Every smell made his mouth water. However, only one smell reminded him of the most exciting time of his life: Guatemala.

After his adventures with Esme, he bought two pounds of cardamom before their flight home and stuffed it into his backpack. Now, the smell was like an olfactory passport. Knowing that it was grown on the Guatemalan mountains near Coban—a part of Guatemala he didn't get to explore...He must go back! Guatemala, nothing would ever top it.

Joseph returned to his work: whisking the honey vinaigrette until his arm felt like noodles; crisping several trays of Prosciutto de Parma; sampling, savoring, assembling, and tasting the sticky, delicious chocolate appetizers; chopping bunches of herbs and dicing bowls of vegetables; kneading the pizza dough; stretching, rolling, and par-baking the crusts; preparing the guacamole; selecting the wine pairings. And on it went.

After all this, Joseph wiped his hands on his apron and calculated his handiwork. Only one task remained: poaching the shrimp. Earlier, he had rinsed and deveined an enormous bowl of plump, jumbo shrimp. Now, he turned to the stove, filling a colossal saucepan with vinegar, salt, sugar, lemon juice, spicy red pepper flakes, coriander, and a single bay leaf. He brought the contents to a rolling boil, stirring until the last crystal of sugar dissolved. Then he turned off the heat and patiently hovered for five minutes until he finally added the shrimp.

Joseph gently stirred, watching, and waiting. Approximately four minutes later— as soon as the shrimp turned from gray to pink—he poured the shrimp into a colander.

"Perfect," he whispered.

He turned to the chef's table inside *Diablo Cocina's* expansive kitchen, placing his fingertips along the edge and inspecting his handiwork. Joseph narrowed his eyes and took immediate action. He smoothed the white linen tablecloth between place settings, walked the perimeter of the tripped-out table, and straightened each knife, fork, and spoon. Effortlessly, Joseph refolded one of the beet-red linen napkins into a perfect triangle. Looking closer at the place setting below his belly, he picked up a spoon, whipped a dishtowel from the pocket of his apron, and polished the silverware until he could see his distorted face over the conical surface. Joseph repositioned the spoon into faultless alignment. Then he circled the table again, moving off-kilter wine and short highball glasses into alignment.

The fussing and fidgeting continued.

Finally, Joseph paused near the center of the table and leaned to push the silver ice bucket ever so slightly to the left. Short-stemmed red roses overflowed from the bucket, adding even more fragrance to the room. He plucked a rose from the arrangement and held it to his nose, inhaling. Joseph circled, hovering over two snug white place settings. He placed the rose into a singular vase beside the place card. The card read: *My Esme.*

Again, Joseph surveyed the table. Rubbing his hands together, he smiled with sparkling teeth. Soon, he could return to his final preparations. There was only one thing missing. He left but returned a few seconds later to place a large white card on each plate. The menu read:

TONIGHT AT
DIABLO COCINA

el Apertivo
MEXICAN CHOCOLATE AND SPICY CHORIZO DATES

For the sweet tooth: Medjool dates stuffed with an irresistible mixture of Mayan chocolate, Vietnamese cinnamon, and cayenne. Wrapped with crispy ribbons of Prosciutto de Parma, drizzled with honey.

For the savory palate: Medjool dates stuffed with a spicy mixture of Spanish chorizo and soft queso fresco, wrapped with crispy ribbons of Prosciutto de Parma, drizzled with honey.

Ensalada
CANTALOUPE AND PROSCIUTTO SALAD
WITH HONEY-TEQUILA-LIME VINAIGRETTE

Included: Cantaloupe and red onion, minced jalapeño, cilantro, and pepitas. Garnished with flakes of crispy prosciutto ribbons, sitting on a bed of microgreens.

Plato Principal
SHRIMP AND GUACAMOLE PIZZA

A crisp, cornmeal-laced crust, brushed with a lively cilantro and garlic pesto, topped with mozzarella and cotija cheese, charred sweet corn, and pepper medley. Drizzled with honey and topped with generous dollops of guacamole and poached coriander shrimp.

Postre
CHURROS WITH SUGARED CARDAMOM AND SEA SALT

Heart shaped churros dusted with sugar, cardamom, and sea salt, accompanied with a Mayan chocolate honey crème.

Joseph puffed his chest and folded his arms akimbo, nodding. "Perfect," he whispered.

"Esme, will you help me serve the appetizers?" Joseph whispered in her ear.

She followed him to the center of the kitchen. Other eyes followed them. There was Oliver, wearing black jeans and a crisp, green linen shirt, and Ethelene, who looked dazzling in a slim white dress with tropical flowers and hummingbirds. Mitzi sported a bedazzled, sequined blue dress. Next to her sat Maximilian and his wife, Greta—who was dressed conservatively, just like her husband. Then there was Joseph's dad and his new girlfriend, Doris. (She was much younger than Emil, wearing a sexy, black lace dress and a jean jacket.) Lastly, there was Saul, Joseph's favorite sous chef. Saul wore a black sports jacket over a red Metallica T-shirt and jeans. "No hanky-panky now!" shouted Emil from the middle of the group.

Joseph turned from the stove, appraising his dad's black leather jacket and a crisp white T-shirt. Emil was holding up his empty highball, waving the glass impatiently. "When does the tequila start flowing?" asked Emil, turning his glass upside-down for effect.

Joseph shook his head. Esme chewed her lip. "I'm sorry I was so late," she said, looking sheepish.

"Don't be. Flying is nuts. How are things going with your mother?" Joseph continued his work, carefully arranging the sticky dates onto a white ceramic platter, wiping his hands, and grabbing the wine.

Esme followed him across the kitchen. "Good. Great, even. She loves being my manager. She got me on *The Late Show with Guillermo*

Galan in New York. That's on Tuesday. Then I fly back to LA for some big Hollywood executive's birthday party. Oh, and I'm in the finals of *Universal Talent Quest*, so I need to fly back to London and film the finale in two weeks. Things are happening. I mean, who knew my mom would be so good at this? Having an inquisitive and beautiful mother isn't so bad after all. Instead of searching for meaning, she's funneling her energy into searching for me!"

Joseph nodded, popping the cork. "I know, right? I'm glad, Esme. I'm so proud of you. I can't believe I have a famous girlfriend!" He planted a quick, wet kiss on her lips.

Esme blushed. *"Famous!* I wish. " Do you think I'm famous now?" she asked, her voice squeaking.

"You've been famous for months!"

"Hey, we're hungry. No, kissing until we get the appetizers," said Emil.

"He's earned a few kisses. Joseph, come here and let me kiss you too," cackled Mitzi.

Joseph handed the platter to Esme, then hopped over to Mitzi with his wine bottle, offering her his cheek. Mitzi grabbed his shoulders and planted an audible smack. "There!" she said, laughing.

Everyone else laughed, too. Joseph circled the table, pouring wine into out-stretched wine glasses. Meanwhile, Esme offered the platter of dates. By the time she had circled the table, the dates were gone.

"!Amigos! You just got served by a famous magician!" Joseph exclaimed.

Everyone clapped and hooted.

Joseph pulled Esme back into the heart of the kitchen. They stood hip to hip at the steel table, across from an intimidating line of stoves. Joseph refilled the platter, sneaking mischievous glances at Esme. "Doug missed you. I missed you," he said with a sideways glance.

Esme whispered something into Joseph's ear. He blushed.

After Joseph updated the platter, he shoved a chocolate-filled date into his mouth and grabbed another, offering it to Esme. She bit half, chocolate oozing out the end and honey sticking to her lips. "Amazing," she mumbled with an eye roll. "Joseph, the honey. Is it *the* honey?"

He nodded, smiling from ear to ear. Esme popped her eyes and chewed slower, seemingly contemplating each bite. They returned to the table. Everyone was talking and laughing, wiping their hands, and sipping wine. "Well, did you like the dates? How about the Pinot Noir?" asked Joseph, blinking expectantly and slapping his hands together.

Maximilian loosened his tie and flashed the okay symbol with his hand. Emil waved his hand in circles, beckoning for the refilled platter. Oliver made swirling motions around his stomach. This time, Joseph sat, passing the platter to Esme. She took two dates and handed the platter to Oliver, letting it circle the table, hand over fist. The platter was empty when it was returned to him. Esme placed one of her dates on Joseph's plate. "I was eating dates all afternoon. I'm almost sick of them," he said, returning the prosciutto-wrapped date to Esme's plate. "Besides, you look even more delicious," he teased, trickling a finger down her bare arm.

Esme wore a crazy-short green sheath dress with black butterflies flying about the fabric. At her throat, a jade circle pendant hung on a gold chain. They had purchased the necklace in Guatemala City before their flight home. Esme's red hair was redder than ever, dyed a deep auburn, and hanging loose in sexy curls. He couldn't resist slipping a hand into her hair, and letting it trickle down her back.

Joseph's gaze returned to the table. Plates were empty, and glasses drained. He emitted a contented sigh. "*¡Amigos!* Are you ready for the salad? I'm serving it with a dry *rosé*."

Everyone smiled and nodded. "Yes, please," said Ethelene, refolding her napkin over her skirt.

Emil bonked his highball with his knife. Oliver held his glass, clinking it against Emil's.

"Okay, you win. I was going to serve the tequila as a final course!" said Joseph, pushing away from the table.

Saul pushed away, too. "Chef, sit. I'm taking over."

Joseph raised a hand in protest, but Saul silenced him with a wave. The tall, lanky man strolled into the kitchen, grabbed the rosé, and popped the cork. He walked back to the table, filling all extended glasses. Saul returned to the kitchen, retrieved the Siete Leguas Blanco and a bucket of ice, circled the table, and placed two cubes into each expectant glass, then a stream of clear spirit.

Emil sprinkled salt into his glass from a tiny bowl beside his plate, lifting his highball to his nose and inhaling. Oliver squeezed lime over his glass and sipped, raising his eyebrows. Mitzi took a big gulp and snorted. "Mom!" Maximilian exclaimed, dropping his fork.

Before Saul sat, he filled his glass and raised it above his head. "To Chef Joseph, Diablo Cocina's very own James Beard Award Nominee!" he shouted.

The table exploded with hoots and hollers, prompting Joseph to blush profusely. Esme hugged him, kissed his cheek, and wiped off the salty smear with her fingers. Joseph felt like a warm butter pat, melting at room temperature. Everyone except Mitzi stood, leaning onto the table and clinking glasses in a cumulative high-five. Mitzi raised hers, too, and took another big drink. "To Joseph!" everyone crowed.

Joseph took a massive bite of pizza and wiped the guacamole from his chin. He chewed, his eyes wandering the table, feeling the same joy as watching cute kitten videos—his family and friends loved his food.

He felt Esme squeeze his leg; he winked at her. Across the table, Mitzi burped, dropping a piece of shrimp into her lap. "Ack!" she cried, picking it up and slipping it into her mouth.

Everyone laughed and chewed, emitting sounds of pleasure and fullness. Emil's voice grew louder, his cheeks redder. His laughter caused a ripple effect around the table—more giggling, snorting, and laughing from everyone. Somehow, while gesticulating, Ethelene tipped her glass of sparkling wine and stood in a flourish. Oliver dabbed the table with his napkin and stole the last piece of pizza from Ethelene's plate.

Beside Joseph, Maximilian and Greta ate quietly, alternately giving Joseph vertical thumbs and happy smiles. In the middle of the table, Saul reigned supreme, baking and serving the pizzas, filling wine glasses, replacing dropped silverware, and monitoring Oliver and Emil's highballs. No one went hungry or thirsty.

After a time, Joseph slumped in his seat, feeling full and drunk. Beside him, Esme whispered something into her dad's ear. Oliver smiled back and pulled a folded magazine page from his back pocket. The man smoothed the page over the table's edge, revealing an intricate jade mask that resembled a scary vulture snarling up from the wrinkled page. The headline read: *Priceless Jade Mask Recovered from the Lost City of the Monkey God.* As Oliver discussed his time in Honduras, he smiled the smile of angels.

The night continued.

Eventually, Saul served the cardamom churros and chocolate honey crème. Everyone moaned with delight, sugar spilling onto dresses and shirts, gooey mouths smiling.

At some point, Emil got up, dropped his napkin onto the table, and knelt beside his son. "Joseph, the meal was exceptional. You've made your mother proud tonight. Me too, kid. My money's on you to win best new chef." He squeezed Joseph's shoulder, completed the sign of the cross, and returned to his seat.

Mitzi pointed her churro at Joseph, sprinkling cardamom in her wake. "I was right, wasn't I, Max?" she bellowed, elbowing her son in the ribs.

Maximilian finished his churro and nodded. "Best investment I've made so far," he said with a wink.

Joseph wiped his mouth and stood, raising his glass. "To Rigel!" he yelled as loudly as he could. Afterward, he looked at every face. Oliver and Emil took a big swig of tequila, shaking their heads in affirmation. Esme raised her glass, and Joseph clinked it. "To Rigel, Dob-Dec, and Sula," Esme repeated, enunciating each name.

Mitzi and Maximilian threw sideways glances, searching for an explanation, but no one offered one. Joseph knew he couldn't explain it, so he didn't try. The room grew quiet when Joseph didn't sit down. Napkins lay discarded, glasses sat watered and drained, utensils crisscrossed dessert plates, and all eyes stared at Joseph.

He left, rummaged loudly in the kitchen, and returned to the table, opening his palm. A glass jar floated from his hand, hovering, and pulsing an eerie neon light. The glass pot morphed into a ball, exploding with white light, then refracting rainbow colors like the spirit box. After a beat, the ball dimmed but stayed suspended. Finally, it returned to Joseph's outstretched hand and flickered out.

There were whispers and applause. Everyone shook their heads, looking at Esme with wonder and delight. She didn't take a bow. Instead, she gazed around the table with a coy expression, extending her hands to Joseph. He cleared his throat. "Everyone, I want you to know you just sampled an out-of-this-world honey in every dish tonight," he said, expanding his arms. "You might think I'm nuts, but it's from the planet Pleione, far, far away." Joseph pointed at the kitchen ceiling, took a nervous breath, and giggled like a schoolboy after a prank.

The room fell silent, eyes blinking, fingers fumbling. Mitzi looked around the table, emitting a shrill laugh. "Poppycock!" she cried.

Q&A with Sharon Wagner

What mystery in your own life could be a plot for a book?

My dad's battle with Parkinson's disease inspired my first unpublished novel, Chorus of Crows. A brain with Parkinson's can inhabit a world of hallucinations worse than a horror movie. Real life really is stranger than fiction, and I lived it alongside my dad. Eventually, I purged my feelings and wrote my first novel. In Chorus of Crows, a retired farmer and his difficult daughter confront mysterious and malevolent visitors that may or may not be real.

What books are on your summer reading list this year?

I must read every Isabel Allende and Silvia Moreno Garcia book. Starting now…

If you could travel to any fictional book world, where would you go, and what would you do there?

I would travel to Westeros and become a dark-haired Daenerys

Targaryen from Game of Thrones. I'd ride my dragon to the cerulean sea, burning bad book reviewers and instilling fear among internet trolls.

What theme or message do you hope readers will take away from your work?

The essential theme in my novel is the power of sound. Since I suffer from misophonia, sound affects my daily life in beautiful, bitter, and malevolent ways. The sense of hearing can be as pleasurable as a trilling mockingbird or as undesirable as someone chewing a wad of gum—my kryptonite. Why do people eat with their mouths closed around the dining table, then chew with an open mouth when they chomp gum? Ugh!

Plus, kindness and conservation mingle between the lines of prose.

What are the secret revelations behind The Levitation Game?

Spoiler alert!

After a catastrophic crash in Guatemala, Dob-Dec's spirit stuck to Esme, and Sula's energy adhered to Joseph.

Joseph bounced between the healing arts and culinary pursuits because of Sula's nurturing influence. I tried to season (Do you see what I did there?) Joseph's storyline with culinary references, like clouds that resemble marshmallows. The centrifuge was fun for both characters. They were conflicted about eating meat because Beings from Pleione are vegetarians.

Dob-Dec's passion for gameplay sent Esme spiraling around treetops and other gravity malfunctions. She, too, collected rocks and seashells. My favorite writing sections were the scenes when Esme and Joseph reunited, and chaos ensued because Dob-Dec and Sula were so excited to see each other. I painted my cover with an energy vortex of sundries from Esme's hotel room to reflect my favorite scene.

Of course, Dob was hopelessly in love with Sula, but sometimes, life has other plans. It was fun to write a happy ending!

Can you tell us a two-sentence horror story?

Sharon sat alone in a dusty corner of Bleeding Heart Bookstore with her pile of unwanted, unsigned books and a leaky pen. Silence prevailed until a woman approached in a plastic, sing-song tracksuit, chomping an enormous wad of pink gum...

What's your advice for aspiring writers?

Read and persevere! Be kind and collect writing friends. That's all you can do.

To get in the right frame of mind, I read from my literary stack resembling the mattresses from The Princess and the Pea. Reading is the best inspiration. I've never found real peas in my books, but chocolate would be nice. Motivation can be as shy as a skittish spider or as available as the nearest Subway restaurant. But you can't count on it, so you must plant your butt firmly in a chair and write.

What are you currently working on?

While researching modern-day witchcraft for my upcoming supernatural novel, I found a Wiccan rede (a moral code) that stuck with me, "Eight words the Wiccan Rede fulfill: An ye harm none, do what you will."

I wish the world could coexist like this.

My novel follows a coven of earth-focused green witches. Green witches are nature lovers that are in tune with the universe. They heal with herbs and embrace the energy of nature and animals. I tried to create real-life witches, not movie cliches. Even so, I swept up plenty of magic!

Readers meet Owletta, the coven's serious-minded supreme in The Savannah Book of Spells. She has large owl-like eyes that see paranormal visions. Her power of clairvoyance influences the coven in peculiar and impractical ways.

Nettle, the coven's dark and prickly member, has the power of clairgustance. The ability of supernatural taste ensures that Nettle is a talented herbalist, concocting spells that may or may not align with the coven's moral code.

Wren, the coven's youngest member and merry sweet waif, has clairaudience. She hears a relentless supernatural soundtrack that might guide the coven into the light or lead them into danger.

Sensual and seductive, Willow has the power of clear touching or clairtangency, a power that can be an inspiration or a mighty curse.

The book begins with a terrifying incident that will cause an intergenerational curse. After an untimely death, the coven relocates to Savannah, Georgia, settling into Owletta's ancestral home. Soon, they expand their online store Global Witchery, opening a brick-and-mortar location on Bull Street. Things simmer like sweet herbal tea until an uninvited guest stirs up a cauldron of irregularities, forcing the coven to fight for more than their lives, possibly their mortal souls.

Where did you get the idea for *The Levitation Game?*

I love my origin story. I was touring Sedona, Arizona, researching my first unpublished manuscript, Chorus of Crows. One night, I dreamt of levitating over my bed with increasing fear and dread. As my fear intensified, I levitated higher until an enormous pop erupted around me. Sedona's power grid failed in my dream, sending the town into near blackness. At the same time, I fell into my sheets. Bad dream, right?

I traveled home. But I kept dreaming about levitation until I listened to the universe and started writing The Levitation Game. I never dreamt of levitation again.

About the Author

Sharon Wagner is a warm-weather nomad, beach bum, and travel junkie. Roaming to exotic beaches and jungle ruins is grueling work, but the perfect winter temperature needs investigating, and she's willing to make the sacrifice. Costa Rica has the best January temperatures ths side of the equator and beaches ideally suited for wandering feet—or tails; she's a Pisces.

What else? She's an inexhaustible travel blogger, spirit investigator (liquid, not ethereal), cat wrangler, amateur photographer, baker of sweets, and freelance illustrator of children's books, including *Maya Monkey.*

A creative from birth, she never stops dreaming of supernatural worlds to unravel with words. Sharon has loved a good ghost story since her high school English teacher, Mrs. Laverty, praised her book report on Charles Dickens' classic, *A Christmas Carol.* But real-life tales of her aunt's psychic dreams and childlike curiosity about extraterrestrial abductions ignited a spooky flame. Television shows like *The Planet of the Apes* and all the hoopla surrounding the Bermuda Triangle fueled the fire.

Her mother's antique typewriter was the catalyst that triggered her shift from illustrating children's books to painting with words. The old typewriter was the sole survivor of the auction that preceded the sale of her family farm. After the auctioneer rattled his final call, the typewriter remained, and she took it as a sign. Three manuscripts and much literary drama ensued until Sharon's debut novel, *The Levitation Game*, was given the green light by Ten16 Press.

Sharon lives in Minneapolis with her nice husband and two naughty cats.

Discover more at https://sharonwagnerbooks.com/.

Acknowledgments:

Kudos to Shannon Ishizaki at Ten16 Press for giving *The Levitation Game* the alien-colored green light. Glory be, grammar is my kryptonite, and Jenna Zerbel is my Superwoman. Kaeley Dunteman used her creative powers to shape my illustration (Yes, I painted the toilet paper and underpants!) into a book cover. Thanks to Josh, Ashton, Veronica, Lauren, and the whole team at Ten16 Press.

Literary props go to my husband, Dean, for supporting my dreams from the first word.

Credit goes to my ongoing literary comrades at Aloha Writers, my intrepid critique team. They always have feedback with an aloha spirit. Thank you to Amanda, Vera, Wendy, Joy, and our newest member, Rodney.

Thanks to Kate Arrington and Neddy Games for your out-of-this-world partnership.

Cachet to my cats, Hana and Akua, for investigating my lap whenever I reach for my laptop. I mean, who needs to work, anyway?

Thank you to all my blurb authors, book reviewers, and early readers!

Coming soon!

Don't miss Sharon Wagner's next book...

The Savannah
Book of Spells

Read on for a preview...

Owletta

Owletta led the coven down a long avenue of live-oak trees, ethereal strands of moss dripping from twisted branches, old age, and wisdom embedded in the bark like wrinkles on a crone. The dead remained quiet, but the cemetery was alive with signs of Beltane: green grass sprouting amidst the tombs, mausoleums, and gated plots; mid-season azalea bushes lush with pink flowers, and a mixed tape of calling birds.

A mockingbird sat on an iron gate to the coven's left, serenading the parade of witches with its singular playlist. Owletta wondered if the bird was a fairy in disguise because fairies were active in spring, and on Beltane, there was a special connection between the world of mortals and the fairy realm. Most likely, though, the bird was simply a messenger from her long-dead great-grandfather, Phineas. He was buried here in 1908, shortly after Savannah purchased the property and turned it into Bonaventure cemetery.

The burial ground was famous for being the final resting spot for Johnny Mercer and Conrad Aiken, synonymous with the Bird Girl Statue and the novel Midnight in the Garden of Good and Evil. For Owletta, Bonaventure inhabited a thin astral plane. It was a haven for birds and wandering spirits and the home of her favorite elder tree. She always left an offering under the tree when she returned to Savannah. Now, Savannah would be her forever home.

Threading her long black hair over a shoulder and behind an ear, she reached into the felty pocket of her wool shawl to retrieve a handful of dried cherries, then left an offering for the magickal bird.

The coven continued down Mullyrn Avenue in silence. Owletta rubbed the vessel wedged in the crook of her arm. "What was will be again," she whispered.

Her mother, Orietta, resided in the Summerlands now. Death was a positive passage for a witch, so why was sadness wrapped so tightly around her heart? Over the previous year, her mother's senior coven had withered like a tomato vine in November. The coven's supreme had died of cancer the year before, and not long after, her mother suffered a fatal stroke. The remaining two witches—grief stricken—decided they needed a change and moved north to Lilydale.

Owletta wanted a change, too. Her bones ached for Savannah. Now, she wanted to leave New York and return to her childhood home on Gaston Street, and as the supreme, the rest of the coven must follow.

She wiped a tear from her eyelashes, turning toward the others: Wren, radiant daughter of the North—full of sunshine, ethereal white hair, effervescence, and waves of turbulent emotion, ran to her side. The women hugged.

"We should perform the ceremony somewhere private. Bare skin is a witches' Sunday best," said Nettle, walking at the back of the group with loud, lumbering footsteps, impatience peppering her words.

Owletta heard Willow giggle and turned her head. The skinny witch unfastened her belt buckle and opened her puffy coat, exposing ripe, naked flesh. Willow held her coat open and spun, her brown curly hair tumbling over boney shoulders and large round breasts bouncing as she turned. Willow closed her jacket with a smirk.

Three of the women laughed. After a beat, Owletta eyeballed Nettle. Unexpectedly, the last witch looked to the sky and opened her coat, exposing rolls of flesh and flat breasts resembling spindly gourds. Nettle wiggled, sending all parts in motion. A devilish cackle escaped her lips, and she closed her lengthy, black jacket. The coven burst into fits of laughter.

"Stop it!" scolded Owletta. "You'll get me laughing so hard, I'll drop mother," she added.

"Laughter will protect us from dark forces," countered Wren.

The coven nodded in agreement and continued, turning left onto Wiltberger Way. Merging into a tight-knit group, they wandered down the street, past monoliths, intricate sculptures, weeping trees, and lichen-covered stones. A crisp Spring breeze jostled the Spanish moss above their heads, and goosebumps traveled down the coven's bare legs. Savannah was rarely this cold in May, Owletta thought with a shiver.

"Is this it?" asked Willow.

Owletta inhaled and nodded before stopping before the Wainwright plot. A rusted iron gate—only as tall as Owletta's knees—surrounded the gravesite. The interior was overgrown and neglected, with bald areas of soil amidst sporadic grassy patches. One of the gravestones had tumbled to the ground; another stood cracked, leaves filling the rectangular stone bowl at its base. Only the intricate granite stone erected for her grandfather Phineas stood pristine: a large carved book, a witches' grimoire, with a beautiful stone owl sitting on the top, protecting with outstretched wings. "The owl looks just like you," said Willow, grabbing Owletta's free hand in a swinging motion.

Indeed, Owletta's enormous, owl-like, clear-seeing eyes were her namesake. Her mother knew her daughter would have the power of clairvoyance as soon as she kissed Owletta's red, blotchy cheeks for the first time. Now, Owletta's skin was the color of bronze, her eyes as black as coal.

Owletta stared at the inscription across Phineas' stone grimoire. There was no mention of her grandmother, no birthdate, death date, or anything. It was as if her ancestor had never existed. The family assumed the woman had died in childbirth or ran away. The family mystery had proliferated for generations. Owletta possessed the power of clairvoyance but couldn't uncover the truth of her past. It was almost as if Gaia was hiding it. The trees must know. She thought wistfully, looking up to survey the treetop.

A sigh escaped her lips, and she slipped free from Willow's grasp to enter the plot, leaning to place the ern near her grandfather's gravestone. The coven followed, with each member carrying an offering for Owletta's mother.

Nettle approached first, buckling her heavy frame and placing her bundle amidst the stone bowl of leaves. "Mugwort for safe travels," she said, rising and expelling air in a gush.

Willow reached into the pocket of her red jacket and placed a tiny stone atop Phineas' granite grimoire. "A moonstone to protect you during your journey to the Summerlands," she stated, backing away.

Wren wiped a tear from her cheek and pulled something white from her purse. She walked to the corner of the plot where an oak tree grew just beyond the gate. "Birch bark for new beginnings," she stated, placing the bark against the iron gate.

Finally, Owletta withdrew an object from her pocket. She stepped before her grandfather's grimoire and placed a small stone on top. "Bloodstone to connect our hearts forever," she whispered.

Bending, she lifted the ern, opened it, and cupped a handful of her mother's ashes, a fresh tear dripping into the mix. She sprinkled the handful over the plot like she was seasoning a stew. Traditional burial was terrible for the environment—this a good witch knew. Still, it was her mother's wish to disperse to the ground of her ancestors. Owletta replaced the lid, retaining the remainder of the ashes for Botany Bay, her mother's favorite place in the world: a South Carolina beach covered in driftwood sentinels and oyster shells.

Owletta cleared her throat; the others stopped whispering and fumbling, listening. "All hail and blessed be. The cycle is complete. Mother Earth, embrace Orietta back into your loving arms. My mother's work is complete. You, Mother Earth, are the origin of our life and power. Be Orietta's new home and protector."

Cold air drifted across Owletta's face, and she tightened her coat. Just then, the granite owl atop the grimoire shifted in and out of focus. Owletta inhaled sharply, watching the wings flap as if taking flight. Seconds passed, and all was still. "Did you see that?" asked Owletta, turning to the group.

"See what?" asked Nettle.

"I only saw a squirrel jump from the oak tree," said Wren.

"I think I saw someone down by the river—a man," said Willow.

"You're always seeing a man!" admonished Nettle.

Willow stamped her foot and crossed her arms, leering at Nettle. Owletta realized she must have seen something from another dimension—or something else. A shiver trickled down her spine, but it wasn't from the cold.

Nettle

Nettle paused outside the iron gate, repositioning the small barrel cactus wedged under her arm, letting go of her suitcase with the other. The Gaston house was different than she expected: four stories of dark, slate-colored brick, with a circular turret in the middle and an off-kilter double balcony that clung to the left side of the house like false teeth. Nettle tilted her head and pushed her tongue against the roof of her mouth. Indeed, the place was prettier than the coven's New York City walk-up—a skinny, treeless apartment smushed between old buildings. Nettle always disliked the low light and bad energy in New York. Still, this house was foreboding and irregular, unbalanced.

A rabbit jumped from a bush by the gate, startling her. Nettle smiled and opened the gate, pulling her suitcase up the sidewalk. She clumped up the cement steps, letting go of her bag and awkwardly digging into her purse for the key. Across the double wooden doors was a small plaque with the date: 1868. Old—maybe too old.

Old houses store secrets.

A feeling of dread settled around Nettle's heart as she rattled the skeleton key inside the old lock. She wished, suddenly, that the rest of the coven was here instead of back in New York, settling the coven's affairs and preparing for the move South.

Nettle opened the door, peeking inside the entry. The house smelled like patchouli and dirty socks. Entering a grand foyer, she swiveled, glancing right, into a dark living room, opposite, into a dining room, and straight ahead, up an imposing stairway. Above her head, an ornate chandelier dangled like a metal octopus. Swiftly, her gaze fell on a gnarly, handmade broom wedged near the front door. Nettle grunted.

She discarded her suitcase, grabbed the broom, veered into the dining room, and placed her cactus on a long wooden table. Nettle continued into the kitchen, her eyes circling the room and stopping on a side door. Nettle carried the broom across the room, unlocked the door with a twist of her fingers, and threw the broom into the garden. "There," she said, standing in the doorway, smacking her hands together as if shaking off crumbs. "Cliché," she muttered under her breath.

She took a moment to appraise her new yard. It was vast and sprawling. The coven could grow enough vegetables and plants, herbs, and flowers to supplement the new store that Nettle would rent on Bull Street while the rest of the coven traveled from New York. Nettle looked around wistfully, feeling a pang of jealousy that caused her to burp. She tasted garlic, and she hadn't eaten any.

With a shoulder shrug, she turned to appraise her new kitchen. A copper kettle sat on the gas stove, ready to make tea. There was an enormous double refrigerator, a new dishwasher, and a deep white porcelain sink with a few dirty dishes left over from the prefuneral gathering of Owletta's extended family and Orietta's witchy friends. Nettle hadn't attended the life celebration. As always, she was the odd witch out—who stayed behind, fulfilling online orders for their business: Global Witchery.

Nettle stood straighter, thinking about the brand she had started independently, all on her own. Owletta might be the supreme, for now, but Nettle kept the coven in the black—literally. Nettle gave her shirt a firm tug, turning her attention to the cupboards; they looked original, caked with layers of grey paint, old and bubbly. Nettle moved closer to the sink, looking out the window to the backyard. She stared at a giant fountain, sitting silent, leaves filling the basin. Hearing water, Nettle leaned in, looking closer; the spray was dry. Nettle turned; it wasn't water she was hearing; it was a rattle, like a snake, somewhere inside the house.

Nettle returned to the dining room but stopped, listening, with her eyes plumbing the baseboards. She heard cars on Gaston Street and voices somewhere outside, but no snakes. Grabbing her suitcase, she ascended the stairs, stopping on the second-floor landing to listen again—nothing.

She left her suitcase on the landing and went from room to room, searching high and low. There was no hissing or rattling or snakes. However, she discovered a bedroom with a large attached, black and white tiled bathroom that suited her tastes. It faced north, overlooking Gaston Street and a row of picture-perfect mansions with wise old trees.

Nettle retrieved her suitcase and unpacked, pushing foreign clothes aside and hanging her dresses in the tiny closet. After a few minutes, she placed her lingerie in an antique dresser with an oval mirror. There were another woman's socks and sundries inside several drawers. Nettle pulled those items out and put them on the bed for later disposal. She breathed deep, tasting lavender and yarrow—boundaries. This space was hers now; she looked around and smiled. Yes, this was the right room; her power of clairgustance—clear tasting—had never let her down. Again,

Nettle smacked her lips and entered the bathroom, kneeling with a grunt over the massive clawfoot bathtub. She opened the tap and returned to the bedroom. There, she gathered the appropriate herbal sachet from her suitcase: cedar to block unwelcome energy, lavender for peace, sage for clearing and protecting, and the mother of them all, mugwort, for everything else.

Returning to the bathroom, she dimmed the lights, lit the well-used candles that surrounded the tub, undressed, and settled into the tub with a gentle splash. Nettle closed her eyes and sighed.

Nettle lifted her head from the pillow; she heard it again, an ominous rattle, a crescendo that trailed into a few ticking beats. The sound was coming from downstairs; she was sure of it. Blinking the sleep away, she arose from her nap, clumsily slipping from the high bed and wrapping her naked body in a fuzzy green robe. Her feet whispered down the hall and descended the stairs. At the bottom, she investigated the living room. Night had fallen, and someone had drawn the curtains; it was dark, but clearly, a human silhouette was sitting in a chair by the fireplace. Her heart thumped—a relative, perhaps? Nettle fumbled along the wall, flipping the light switch and gasping. She tightened the belt of her robe.

"Who are you? How did you get in here?" asked Nettle, alarm polishing her words.

The man recrossed his legs and flashed a seductive smile. "I'm a friend of Orietta's, and I have a key," he purred, holding up a tarnished silver key and fidgeting with a ring on his pinky finger.

Nettle couldn't conjure the right words. She stared at his mouth, almost certain she'd seen a forked tongue while he talked. Nettle pinched the robe tighter over her breasts, contemplating her next move. The stranger shouldn't be here, but she wasn't sure what to do, and something about him intrigued her. Her eyes darted; she crossed her arms, appraising his purple suit and boldly striped socks. The weird man also wore a paisley tie and a black bowler hat, complete with a large purple feather. He looked rather odd and comical, like a circus barker. A half smile passed her lips.

"The life celebration was three days ago," Nettle finally muttered.

"I'm not here for that. I'm here to talk to you," said the man with a grin.

Nettle laughed morbidly; she couldn't help herself. The situation was so bizarre. She shook her head. "You don't even know me," she said.

"I like your dimples. I'm partial to blonds, especially meaty blonds," the man said, flicking a tongue across thin lips.

Nettle inhaled, her nervous smile vanishing. "What's your name? You really shouldn't be here...." Her voice stopped when she heard a sound behind her back, like swishing, brushing, or something else. She turned, discovering the broom she had thrown into the garden. Now, the thing was animated, sweeping the dining room all on its own. The broom zigged into corners, zagged back and forth, twirling up a pile of dust until it stopped. Then it stood like a statue as if waiting for further instructions. Nettle swiveled with a racing heart. "What's your name?" she asked in a firm, hushed voice.

"Azrael," he stated, standing, moving towards her, and offering her his hand.

Nettle stepped back but shook the man's hand anyway, regretting it immediately. Was this man a witch? Even if he was, no witch was capable of anything like the spell she'd just seen—it was on a different level entirely. It was magic, pure magic. Nettle opened her mouth to speak, but the man hushed her with his fingertips pushed gently against her lips.

Azrael arched an eyebrow, doffed his cap, and headed toward the front door, but then he stopped and turned. "I'll be seeing you. Oh, be sure to look for Phineas' grimoire. It's hidden in Sparrow's room, in the floorboards. You'll find it; they're loose—the boards. Good day Nettle," said Azrael with a nod and a swish of his seemingly forked tongue.

Nettle's feet felt cold and glued to the floor. She watched the front door in a trance, sure that Azrael had vanished instead of actually opening the door and departing. She rushed to peer out the front window, pulling the curtains aside. But she couldn't see the man anywhere. She ran barefoot out the front door, up the sidewalk, to the gate. Azrael was gone. Nettle stood at the front entrance, gripping the pointy metal with sweaty hands, looking up and down the dark sidewalk.

She tasted garlic. "Yuck," she spat.

Phineas Wainwright: Savannah, Georgia, 1879

Phineas circled the dining table nine times, stopping to check his pulse; it ran fast. The room was eerily quiet, the only sound a sporadic crackle emanating from the fireplace. He could almost hear the rush of blood flowing through his veins.

Silence suffocated him while his fingers traced the filagree atop a chair at his hip. The streetlamps lining Gaston Street flickered and blurred before his eyes; he rubbed his temple as if removing a stubborn stain from his skin. "There is no light bright enough to illuminate my dark, dank soul," he whispered.

Phineas hurried to the circular windows before him, snapping the draperies shut while still holding the fabric taut between his fingers. He leaned forward, burrowing his face into the plush velvet, weeping, his shoulders shaking in fits and starts.

Then he straightened as if electrocuted, listening to the swish of skirts behind his back. He turned to find Ottilie standing in the doorway, holding a silver candlestick, the flame guttering and sending shadows across her face. She wore a dress of peach blossom silk, her plump bosom tipping over the tight bodice, dusky skin glowing in the firelight.

The woman surveyed the dining table, clutching her skirt with white knuckles and shaking her head in denial. Phineas stumbled towards her, sobbing openly now. Ottilie grasped his cheeks and kissed his tears away, rubbing a hand over his mouth. With both hands, she opened the tiny oyster buttons lining his shirt, ripping the shirt from his chest and throwing it to the floor.

Phineas twisted her towards the wall and carefully needled the silk fabric buttons lining her back. He unpeeled each button until the peach dress fell to the floor in a heap of flounces and trim. Gently, he rubbed her bare shoulders and kissed her right and left before grabbing them with firm hands. "Tell me, Ottilie. Have I redeemed myself for the day I purchased you on Butler Island?"

Ottilie's shoulders stiffened, and she emitted a hiccupping gasp but didn't say a word. Slowly, she removed her skeleton petticoat, set it aside like a baby oak tree, and stripped from her chemise and undergarments until she was skyclad, glistening in the candlelight. Ottilie lingered with her back to Phineas, staring at her portrait on the wall, painted just six months ago by the best artist in Georgia. Slowly, she shifted her feet, facing her lover.

Phineas stepped from his trousers and removed his undergarments, throwing them aside. The duo stared at each other in the flickering light, and time seemed to stop. After a few pregnant seconds, he moved to the buffet, grabbing the fluffy capelets he'd fashioned from two ethereal barn owls: the bird's heart-shaped, curious faces perfectly matched Ottilie's own.

Phineas fastened a small capelet to her shoulders, then tied an oversized, prickly cape of feathers around his neck. He picked up a narrow crown crafted from soft, downy pinfeathers and placed it on Ottilie's head. They held hands, stepping over the pile of salt, circling the dining table, and sitting side by side, naked except for their feathery adornments.

Spread across the table were dozens of flickering white candles and tiny piles of herbs, bowls of water and oil, pumice, dried datura blossoms, and other, more unseemly curiosities. In the center of the table, Phineas' handwritten grimoire sat splayed like a shrine.

Phineas grabbed a dainty silver spoon and scooped up a miniature owl heart from a tiny bowl, swallowing it whole. Ottilie stared at her bowl in horror, swallowing nothing but air. "It will be the gallows if you don't eat it, Ottilie," he urged.

Ottilie plopped the tiny heart on her tongue and covered her mouth, chewing with her eyes squeezed tight. She grabbed his hand for support.

Above the dining room, the gurgling sounds of an infant beckoned. Ottilie rose from her seat; Phineas held her hand firm.

"It's too late, Ottilie. We've said our goodbyes. I've arranged for Mrs. McAvoy to enter through the kitchen before the morning is nigh. All will be well with our little Sparrow."

Ottilie stared stoically at the brick fireplace against the far wall, tears welling under her lids. Phineas knew each cry was like a knife to her heart.

"Sparrow, my dear, sweet girl," Ottilie murmured.

They drank the blood from their crystal goblets.

"Proteus, hear our prayer!" Phineas boomed, gulping his glass and slamming it to the table. Phineas closed his eyes, speaking to the room:

> *Feathers, feathers, light as air*
> *Grant us wings; lift us there*
> *Feathers, feathers, strong like bone*
> *We want the sky to be our home*
> *Feathers, feathers, never break*

We leave our flesh and feathers make
Earth at rest
Air our support
Beak in song

Wings, wings, we wish to fly
Our souls will only belong to sky
Proteus, Proteus, hear our prayer
Shift us higher this night
Let us take to the air
Silent as an owl
Strong as an eagle
Efficient as a condor
Endurance of an albatross
The agility of a hummingbird
Speed of a falcon
Wings, wings, come to me
So mote it be

Ottilie joined the chant.

The duo repeated the mantra in the dark room, over and over, dark shadows dancing on the walls. Across the room, the fireplace roared into an open flame, unbidden. Phineas could feel the heat on his bare skin. "The devil is talking," Phineas whispered, his voice quivering.

Above their heads, Sparrow cried, unchecked. The fireplace sparked and spat until a disturbance of warm air drifted around the table. The duo chanted louder, pleading with Proteus for wings and flight. The warm air suddenly turned frigid, stiffening Ottilie's nipples. Phineas heard unholy whispers; their ears popped.

"Proteus, we call to thee!" Phineas exclaimed, breaking the chant.

Something circled the table, forming a cyclone around them. The duo chanted faster. Ottilie's voice wavered, speeding up, slowing down. Above them, Sparrow's tiny wails punctuated the night. Someone pounded on the front door. "Doctor Wainwright! We've come for the witch! Open the door!"

The unholy duo chanted louder, with guttural, inhuman sounds escaping their mouths. "Doctor! Open the door!"

Phineas and Ottilie sat like cold stones while the front door slammed against the foyer, and feet pummeled the hall; revolvers pointing into the dining room. Phineas and Ottilie raised their clasped hands to the ungodly winds. The faceless men stood in the portal of the dining room, shouting at them over the din. Phineas ignored them. He felt a pulsating, fizzling sensation journey down his spine. "It's working, Ottilie!" he cried.

Behind their backs, the men watched with unseen looks of fright. Phineas let go of Ottilie's hand, reaching under the table, scrabbling for his own revolver. The men mobbed the room, grabbing and dragging Ottilie from her chair. Phineas grabbed his revolver and pointed it. "You're too late!" He spat at the strangers.

"Don't do anything stupid, Doctor Wainwright. She's not worth the gallows."

Phineas cocked his revolver.

"No, Phineas! Think of Sparrow!" Ottilie screamed.

The men dragged Ottilie down the hall and out the front door; she kicked and screamed. Phineas ran after them, his penis and revolver flailing. One of the men fired at Phineas, hitting the wall clock in the hallway. Phineas laughed, almost tripping over the displaced rug lining the hall.

He felt a hollow steel circle against the back of his skull and unseen hands pushing him toward the door. Phineas saw Ottilie on the grass, a fat white arm clenched around her breasts, a revolver against her head.

Phineas spat sideways. "Proteus! Help us!" he screamed at the top of his lungs.

Ottilie shrank on the lawn, slipping free of the fat arm encompassing her; the man behind her jumped away as if he'd just been stung by a bee. All eyes watched Ottilie as she shifted and changed. One of the men fell to the ground and retched into the grass. The others walked backward, revolvers shaking.

Now Ottilie resembled a pufferfish, a plucked chicken. She was condensing, growing feathers. Her eyes morphed from black to gold; the skin covering her arms and legs melted. Phineas blinked, and Ottilie looked like a supernova, flapping away into the night. The men ran away from the scene as fast as their legs could travel.

Phineas looked over his unchanged body and cursed the air. He was still human, and Ottilie was gone. An eerie howl escaped his lips.

Phineas heard Sparrow's wailing and returned to the house; grabbing his grimoire from the dining room, he ripped a handful of pages from their binding and ran up the stairs to Sparrow's bedroom, where two sets of unholy wails assaulted the night.

I hope this book entertained you. Please consider
leaving a review on your favorite social media platform.
Dob-Dec thanks you, and so do I!

© illustration by Sharon Wagner

Printed in the USA
CPSIA information can be obtained
at www.ICGtesting.com
JSHW030905181023
50148JS00011B/24